ADVANCE READER COPY | NOT FOR RESALE

This is an uncorrected proof and text may change before final publication. Please verify with the author or publisher before quoting directly from this text.

PRAISE FOR AMANDA LAMB

No Wake Zone is an intriguing read with the salty tang of realism that could only come from someone who can walk the walk and talk the talk.

DOUGLAS SKELTON, AUTHOR OF THE REBECCA CONNELLY CRIME SERIES

Like an Agatha Christie mystery, *No Wake Zone* weaves together an intriguing tapestry of authentic, multi-dimensional characters and fast-paced action.

STEVEN B. EPSTEIN, AUTHOR OF *MURDER ON BIRCHLEAF DRIVE*

Amanda Lamb's brilliant writing keeps you on the edge of your seat right to the very end!

HOLLY RICHARD, AUTHOR OF *ONE HUNDRED AND TWENTY-SIX DAYS: THE UNTHINKABLE JOURNEY*

Dead Last will captivate you from the start.

LIZA WEIDLE, FRS COMMUNICATIONS

Dead Last entertains. [It] proves original and intriguing.

BEN STEELMAN, STAR NEWS ONLINE

WHISPERS ON THE MOUNTAIN

ALSO BY AMANDA LAMB

Dead Last

Lies That Bind

No Wake Zone

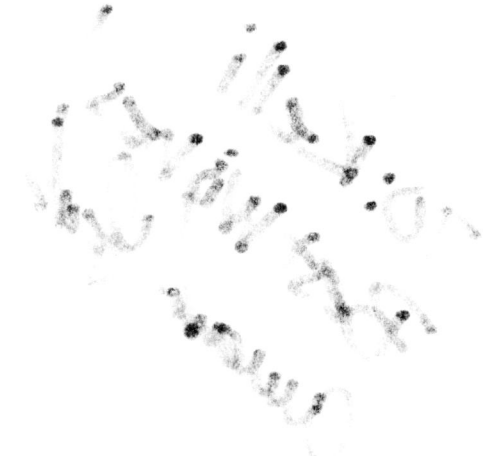

WHISPERS ON THE MOUNTAIN

AMANDA LAMB

Torchflame Books
Vista, CA

Copyright © 2025 by Amanda Lamb

All rights reserved. Torchflame Books supports copyright. Copyright fuels creativity, encourages diverse voices, promotes free speech, and creates a vibrant culture. Thank you for buying an authorized edition of this book and for complying with copyright laws by not reproducing, scanning, or distributing any part of it in any form without permission, except by a reviewer who wishes to quote brief passages in connection with a review written for insertion in a magazine, newspaper, broadcast, website, blog or other outlet. You are supporting independent publishing and allowing Torchflame Books to publish books for all readers.

NO AI TRAINING: Without in any way limiting the author's [and publisher's] exclusive rights under copyright, any use of this publication to "train" generative artificial intelligence (AI) technologies to generate text is expressly prohibited. The author reserves all rights to license uses of this work for generative AI training and development of machine learning language models.

ISBN: 978-1-61153-607-2 (paperback)

ISBN: 978-1-61153-608-9 (ebook)

ISBN: 978-1-61153-609-6 (large print)

Library of Congress Control Number: 2025903831

Whispers on the Mountain is published by: Torchflame Books, an imprint of Top Reads Publishing, LLC, 1035 E. Vista Way, Suite 205, Vista, CA 92084, USA

Cover design and interior layout: Jori Hanna

The publisher is not responsible for websites or social media accounts (or their content) that are not owned by the publisher.

This is a work of fiction. Names, characters, places, and incidents are either the product of the author's imagination or used fictitiously, and any resemblance to actual persons, living or dead, business establishments, events, or locales is entirely coincidental.

For my daughters, Mallory and Chloe.
Thank you for giving me the time and space to write
and the inspiration to make you proud.

PROLOGUE

You can't change the name of something that's been called one thing for over a century and expect everyone else to follow suit. To the locals in Annandale County, the trail will always be called "Deadman's Pass," even though the fancy resort renamed it the much less threatening "Overlook Trail." This was to appease the tourists, to make them feel more comfortable hiking the craggy, overgrown trail where one stumble could lead to death. But anyone who has hiked this trail knows that the foreboding rise and fall of the path through a twisted maze of brambles and foliage feels at once thrilling and terrifying.

Locals used to throw carcasses of animals they killed over the steep edge into the gorge below after they were scraped clean of edible meat. At that time, they shared a superstition that burning or burying the remains of the animals was a sin. For some reason, flinging them into a free fall over the gorge became an acceptable alternative practice.

This practice usually occurred after many hours of hunting, sitting by a campfire, and consuming large amounts of moonshine. It wasn't unusual for a man who had a little too much to drink to take a walk alone and lose his footing and slip off the edge of the trail into the dark abyss below. His friends might look for him when daylight came, only to assume that he had fallen to a certain death. As the legend goes, if you went to the bottom of the gorge and searched long enough, you would find a mountain of bones—both animal bones and human bones. Sometimes, it was hard to tell the difference because there were so many bones piled on top of one another that had decomposed over the years.

This was how the trail came to be known as Deadman's Pass. Today, it is considered a technically difficult path, popular with extreme athletes, both men and women, who like to hike or jog the steep, twisting terrain full of roots and rocks. These pitfalls can easily trip even the most experienced hikers and send them over the edge, just like the unlucky, inebriated hunters. The ruggedness and danger of the trail only add to the desire of many people who want to conquer it—to be able to say that they did it, to brag about it.

Pamela Stevens was on Deadman's Pass when she disappeared. An accomplished athlete and trail runner, Pamela was a formidable match for Deadman's Pass if there ever was one, but she never returned from her hike.

If a woman falls off a mountain ledge and no one is around to hear her scream, does she make a sound?

1

CELIA FINCH

I ALMOST DIDN'T HEAR WHAT SHE SAID. SHE INSERTED the words so quietly between the pool hours and the dress requirements for the formal dining room that they almost got lost. Almost.

Missing hiker.

It was louder than a whisper, but not loud enough for anyone else but me to hear. My husband and my two boys stood behind me, oblivious to what she was saying. Her face twisted when she said it, as if it might be physically painful to say the words any louder than a whisper.

"We're just sick about it. We've done everything we can. Our staff has searched every inch of the property. Now, the local sheriff's office and the state police are involved. You might see them out on the trails. I just wanted to give you a heads-up. We don't want to alarm the guests."

I turned around to see the boys arm wrestling and my husband scrolling through something on his phone. I looked at the beautifully appointed lobby with its rustic accents—large furniture fashioned from logs, containing pillowy, oversized cushions, massive vases of fresh wildflowers, overflowing fruit bowls on wooden pedestals, a fireplace you could literally walk into, and floor-to-ceiling windows that provided a perfect view of the lush, rolling mountainside. Nothing about this pristine setting screamed "missing hiker." But it was so over-the-top, as if the décor was compensating for something I didn't yet understand.

"So, here's your key to the cottage and an itinerary of the activities you signed up for. Let us know if you need anything, anything at all. We look forward to seeing you for dinner tonight in the main dining room at seven."

The check-in woman smiled broadly at us and handed me the keys like we didn't just have a conversation about the missing hiker. Her silver nameplate on the lapel of her tan linen blazer read "Simone." It was like she and I had shared a secret that I was now supposed to forget. She fulfilled her obligation to tell the incoming guests enough about the unfolding tragedy to keep us from getting too alarmed. But now, I was more alarmed than ever. Knowing too little was a teaser of grand proportions for someone like me with a galaxy brain that spun stories out of minor details into epic narratives. Unchecked, my mind could easily go to the darkest places. Had the hiker been attacked by a bear? Was he hurt and bleeding somewhere? Was he disoriented and dehydrated, walking in the thick forest in circles, praying for someone to rescue him? I needed to know more.

I pulled my husband, Matt, closer to me as the boys raced ahead to the waiting shuttle van that would take us and our luggage from the main lodge to our cottage down the road. He turned and looked at me with an annoyed face as I tugged at his sleeve again. I was pretty sure I was pulling him away from his Instagram addiction. He could spend hours lost in the social media vortex, mindlessly scrolling through the many posts of people he probably didn't even know. I was beginning to think he needed an intervention, but then I thought about how hard he worked and decided this vice was a minor one compared to how other people dealt with stress.

"What?" he said curtly, scowling in my direction.

"There's a missing hiker," I said just above a whisper, not unlike Simone.

"What do you mean? How do you know?" His voice softened a little. We both looked in the direction of the shuttle and watched the boys fighting with each other to be the first one to get in the door. They were both elbowing one another out of the way and screeching with joy each time one of them succeeded in keeping the other one from getting through the door.

"The lady, the check-in woman, Simone. She told me." I put my head close to his so as not to be overheard. I wondered if the hiker's family was still here at the resort. They might even be in the lobby. I couldn't risk them hearing us talking about their tragic situation. I certainly didn't want to add to the pain they were experiencing.

"That's creepy. What's the deal?" Matt asked.

"I don't know, but I'm gonna find out."

The boys were both now in the van, yelling for us to hurry up and come on. We hustled toward the vehicle and hopped in. I got in the backseat with the kids. Matt got in the front seat with the driver. My mind was spinning with questions about the missing hiker. I knew I had to set it aside and try to keep the boys calm until we were at the cottage. They had boundless energy that could not be contained by the backseat of a van.

"So, what's this we hear about a missing hiker?" Matt said to the driver just as the van pulled away from the curb, wasting no time. He was like that, unfiltered. Telling him a secret was akin to shouting it from a mountaintop. I slunk into the seat behind me, embarrassed by his directness and worried that the boys might overhear their conversation. As it turned out, the boys were not at all interested in the adults talking in the front of the van. They were now flicking each other in the forehead with their index fingers and squealing at an annoying pitch akin to a smoke alarm with a failing battery.

I stared out the window as we traversed down the winding road lined by massive trees and dense forest. It was still sunny outside, but the tall trees blocked much of the sunlight as we hugged the hairpin curves. *No one could survive getting lost in this place. No one*, I thought. It was beautiful, all right, but there was also something beneath the surface that I couldn't put my finger on. It was as if the forest was a living, breathing wild animal that might turn on you if you got too close.

"Yep, huge search going on here," the young man with a red beard and a work shirt that read "Morris" said with no affectation in his voice. "If they don't find her soon, they won't find her until winter when the leaves are gone, and the brush thins out. Just too hard to see anything right now. It's a needle in a great big green haystack, if you know what I mean."

Her. The pronoun floated above me in the air in Morris' monotone delivery and hung there. He sounded so disinterested, like he might as well have been reciting his lunch order at a drive-through. Until this moment, I hadn't considered that the missing hiker might be a woman. Of course, I hadn't had time to consider much of anything. Why was she by herself hiking this rugged terrain? As if he had read my mind, Morris answered my question before I could ask it.

"She was a long-distance trail runner. Training for some extreme race out west in Wyoming. Must have fallen. That's what we think, at least. Lots of places to fall around these parts. It's a pretty treacherous trail if you don't know the footing. And it changes with each storm. A new rock or root gets exposed and pops up where there used to be just soil. You've got to pay close attention. It's really not suited for people who aren't from around here."

Matt reached behind the seat and squeezed my hand. He knew exactly what I was thinking. I wasn't going to be able to let this one go. Once I was hooked on a case, I had to follow the story through to the end. This was the curse of being a journalist. This was the curse of being me.

Despite the intensity of the landscape leading up to the cottage, it was even prettier than it had looked in the photographs online. It had a massive front porch with rocking chairs and a hammock, a large, two-story den with oversized leather couches, a gas log fireplace, and a huge flatscreen television on the wall. The kitchen was well-appointed with updated appliances but decorated to look rustic. Still, the marble countertops and stainless-steel appliances gave it a modern vibe. There was a long, screened-in porch running the length of the back of the house with a breathtaking view of the mountains, which was exactly what we came for. There were three bedrooms. Matt and I took the peaked roof room on the third floor with the king-sized bed. The boys chose the large bedroom in the finished basement with two double beds and a tile floor that they could easily slide across in their socks, which was one of their favorite pastimes.

While the boys busied themselves downstairs, Matt and I headed to the screened-in porch. He opened two cold beers that we had brought with us in a cooler and handed me one as I sank into a long chaise lounge with a big, fluffy yellow cushion on it. He sat in a wicker chair next to me and raised the neck of his bottle, clinking it delicately with mine.

"Here's to a family vacation, finally," Matt said, tipping the neck of the bottle back and taking a big swig. I stared up at the ceiling fan whirring above us and remained silent.

"Seriously, Celia. You're not going to get obsessed with this, are you? You've got to learn to turn it off. You're on vacation.

We're on vacation as a family. You're not a reporter right now. You're a wife and a mom. It's not your problem to fix or solve."

He shook his head in disapproval. I had heard these words so many times before over the years when my job as a newspaper reporter bled into my personal life, creating fuzzy boundaries. I waited to speak, choosing my words very carefully.

"Matt, you know how hard it is for me to just 'let things go.' It's not in my DNA. You of all people should know that. Once I know about something that's going on, I can't just un-know it. I have to pursue it. It's just how I'm wired."

He put a hand gently on my knee and rubbed it a little too hard, like he was trying to erase an indelible Sharpie mark from my skin. I knew his passive aggression in this instance came from a place of good intentions. He was frustrated because he wanted everything to be perfect on this trip, a trip we had been planning for months.

"I get it, babe. I do. I really do. But this is bigger than us. We need to focus on the boys for the next few days and not get all wrapped up in someone else's drama. We've been down this road before. We talked about this with the therapist. Promise me you will at least try to put this aside and focus on our family this week."

I looked into his pleading eyes and considered how important it seemed to him that I say the words he wanted to hear. This was how marriage worked. At least, this was how our marriage worked. It was a script we replayed over and over throughout the years. We knew the lines by heart. We didn't always do the right things, but we said the right things, the things we learned in therapy, in the hopes that our actual words might manifest themselves into real actions.

"Okay, I'll try to forget about it," I said half-heartedly. He squeezed my knee tightly and smiled. We both knew I was lying.

"So, because they're under eighteen, you'll have to fill out these liability waivers for them. They know how to ride, right?"

Nelly was a hardcore, no-nonsense mountain woman. She wore heavy work boots, khaki pants, and a short-sleeved button-down shirt with her name embroidered on the right breast pocket. Her tanned face was creased with lines from too much sun and maybe some hard living. But her pleasant smile and calm demeanor softened her overall appearance. She had a twinkle in her green eyes that seemed to say, *I've walked over a million hot coals and come out on the other side without getting burned.*

"Yes, they ride horses at home in Pennsylvania, where we're from. It's horse country, you know," I said overexplaining as usual. I knew this woman didn't care where we were from, or whether my boys were proficient riders, just that I was absolving the resort of any liability if they got hurt. She stared at me, obviously unimpressed with my mention of "horse country."

"Okay, then sign here to show that you know the risks of horseback riding and are willing to accept them on their behalf," Nelly said, handing me a pen and pointing at the signature portion of the long form with tiny writing that was attached to a clipboard.

Matt had signed up for a fly-fishing class on the river a few miles away from the lodge. He was picked up early that morning by Morris in a van full of strangers that I assumed he would be having beers with by the end of the day. I had promised I would take the boys horseback riding. While I didn't enjoy riding myself, they had a guide who would take them on a mountain path while I sat on a bench in the shade at the barn and happily read my book. This was my idea of a vacation—uninterrupted reading time.

I was honestly afraid of horses after a few bad experiences at a dude ranch when I was a teenager. I always got the horse that the trainer said was "the sweetest one in the barn." Unfortunately, the sweetest horse in the barn always seemed to sense my anxiety. One time a "sweet horse" bucked me off, causing me to roll around furiously on the ground, avoiding his angry hooves. That was the end of my riding days. I was determined not to pass my fear of riding horses along to my kids, so they had started lessons at a very early age.

"Bye guys! Have fun." I waved a little too enthusiastically as they raced one another to the stables in the distance, where they would meet their guide. I always felt a little guilty about the sense of relief I got when they were gone, but the guilt passed quickly. I settled down on the wooden bench under the eaves of the vintage red barn, sipping coffee from my Yeti that I had made earlier that morning in the cottage. I was thankful that it was still hot. God bless the Yeti.

I was relishing a rare moment of quiet. I closed my eyes. My book sat on my lap unopened for several moments as I listened to the Southern summer noises—the cicadas, the breeze rustling the lush green canopy all around me, water rushing through a creek in the distance. It was so still and so peaceful, yet these small sounds could be isolated and elevated if you listened hard enough. It was like nature's symphony orchestra.

But when I opened my eyes, I saw something else. Beneath the beauty of this place, something sinister was lurking. As I looked out into the distance into the dense forest that lined the mountain, I was acutely aware that a missing woman was out there somewhere, enveloped by the darkness of the trees that surely barred the sunlight in many spots. I pictured her clawing at the brush, her skin dirty, bruised, covered in scratches and cuts, trying to survive, praying that she would get out alive.

"Is this seat taken?" a thin, older man with gray hair asked me. He had the name "Wilson" embroidered on his work shirt. He sat down beside me before I could answer. When I glanced at his outfit, I realized that he and Nelly were wearing the same uniform. We both sat silently for a moment, taking in the little sounds. I wondered if he, too, was noticing the juxtaposition of the beauty with its dark core, a core that could swallow someone whole if they made a misstep in this rugged environment. I tried not to think about the boys navigating a steep mountain trail on horseback. I said a silent prayer that their guide would surely not put them in a dangerous position.

"So, what do you do here, Wilson?" I said, expecting him to be shocked that I had noticed his name so quickly. It was part of my training as a journalist to notice details. I liked it when people wore their names on their shirts so I could address them more personally right from the beginning. I sometimes imagined how much nicer the world would be if we all wore name tags.

"Little of this, little of that. Mostly that," he said with a snicker. "I shoe horses, help with the skeet shooting range, run the archery class. Sometimes, I even carry rafters down the river. Whatever they need me to do. Lately, been helping a lot with the search. Even volunteered some after hours."

"The search" I took to mean the search for the missing hiker. I was amazed at how casually Wilson had mentioned it, like he assumed I already knew about it. I saw my opening immediately. This happened to me all the time when I was interviewing someone. I could usually tell right away if they were going to open up to me or shut me down. Wilson was ready to talk.

"Tell me about it," I said casually, trying not to make eye contact with him. "The search, that is."

"It's tough, rugged land up here. Last cell phone ping was on Overlook Trail before the phone died. Folks around here call it Deadman's Pass. But the resort isn't very fond of that name. It's pretty fitting if you ask me. Not the first time someone's lost their footing up there. That's the one she told her husband she was heading out on. Bad omen. It's rated 'difficult.' Lots of incline. Lots of steep, craggy rockface. And the drop-off, well, it's real high. One misstep and you're heading straight down into the gorge. No one could survive that. Problem is, you can't see the drop through all the foliage, which makes some folk, especially visitors, complacent. They don't understand what they're up against."

I was impressed by Wilson's use of the word "complacent." Maybe he wasn't as grizzled and country as he appeared. People surprised me all the time. It was a constant reminder not to think you had someone figured out based on their appearance. I took in everything Wilson was saying, trying to think of how to respond in the best way to get more information without spooking him.

"That seems like a lot for a woman to take on by herself," I said, thinking I might potentially play into his Southern chivalry.

"Yes, ma'am. But from what I hear, she isn't just any woman. She's a champion athlete, does races all over the world. Smart too. She is one of them lawyers who swoops in on companies that are in trouble and fixes them. Big wig in Washington. At least, that's what I'm told. Started out as a prosecutor, assistant district attorney years ago, somewhere not far from here, and rose up through the ranks."

I knew at this point I was not going to be opening my book today. All I wanted to do was research this woman. I looked down at my phone and saw that I had no bars. I decided Wilson would have to be my Google for the moment.

"Do you know her name?"

"I only know her name because we yelled it a lot in the woods when we were looking for her, before the cops got involved. Her name is Pamela, last name Stevens. I'm hoarse from screaming it so much. I sure hope they find her. Feel like we're all pretty invested in this whole thing now. We've put in a lot of hours and covered a lot of ground. It's a crying shame we haven't been able to find her. But I've still got hope. Smart, powerful woman like her, bet if she wanted to disappear, she could make it happen. I hope for her sake that's what this is."

Wilson then turned away from me and walked toward the barn without saying goodbye. I stared down at my book, knowing I wouldn't be getting any reading done today.

I could hardly contain myself as I paced the front porch with a glass of wine, waiting for Matt to return from his fishing trip. The boys had discovered they could play video games on the large flatscreen television in the den and were happily ensconced in their digital dueling. Playing video games was the only time they were not in perpetual motion. Their obsession with gaming gave me a rare moment to breathe.

I had finally gotten an internet signal when I returned to the house and connected my phone to Wi-Fi. I immediately started searching for information about Pamela Stevens. The regional newspaper had a short blurb about her disappearance that contained a brief interview with the local sheriff, Aubrey Lansing. Sheriff Lansing told the reporter he called in the state police when he felt like the search got overwhelming. They were searching roughly fourteen thousand acres on the Bingham Reserve, the resort property, concentrating on the area around the trail I now knew was called Deadman's Pass by the locals. This is where investigators got the last signal from Pamela's phone. But the phone was most likely dead by now, and she could have easily strayed from the trail. There was no telling how far she was from the last known location of her phone, but at least it gave searchers one known area to focus on. I kept thinking about Morris saying that looking for someone in the summer here was like searching for a needle in a green haystack.

The article also talked about the rough terrain and how easy it was to get turned around on the mountain, where everything looked the same, just an endless sea of massive trees. When I looked closely at the trees that surrounded the cottage, they seemed to be mocking me with their long, spindly branches and their delicate leaves that swayed in the breeze. *Come in, come in,* they beckoned. *Come in, but you can't leave. We just might swallow you.*

The article also pointed out that there were bears and rattlesnakes in these parts that could be deadly for a person who came in contact with them in the woods. There was a particular danger in startling a mother bear with her cubs. I closed my eyes and imagined stepping on a rattlesnake or being cornered by an angry mama bear. I shook my head, trying to get rid of these horrible images, but they stayed with me even with my eyes closed.

I learned from my online research that Pamela Stevens was an attorney who started her career, ironically, with a short stint in the Annandale County District Attorney's Office, right after she finished law school at Duke University in Durham, North Carolina. She quickly headed into private practice with a firm that restructured companies going through bankruptcy. She had worked for multiple firms up and down the East Coast, and now, she was the senior partner in her own firm that billed tens of millions of dollars a year. Her rate was nearly $2,000 per hour according to Law.com.

After reading this, there was no doubt in my mind that Pamela Stevens had the ability to disappear if she really wanted to. She was clearly brilliant and connected to powerful people. That's all it would take to vanish into the ether, never to be heard from again. But the big question nagging at me was *why*? Why would she want to vanish? And why here?

I found her headshot on her LinkedIn profile; her wavy brown hair cascaded around her shoulders and framed her long, thin face with its angular features. She had full lips and dark eyes. She wasn't classically beautiful, but she was interesting-looking and intriguing. Something about her appeared strong even in the small, slightly grainy photo. She looked directly into the camera without apology as if to say, "This is who I am, world. Don't mess with me."

Where are you? I thought as I stared at her LinkedIn photo, thinking about the fact that most people never expected their headshot to be plastered on a missing person poster. I slammed my laptop shut just as Morris pulled up in front of the cottage in the van. Matt practically rolled out, wet and muddy, with a small, red cooler held high in his right hand and a big grin on his face.

"This was so cool. You really should have come. I actually caught some fish," he said, holding up the cooler triumphantly. "Did the boys have fun horseback riding? Did you enjoy some downtime for a change?"

I could tell Matt had had a few beers. He was giddy and chatty. His face was ruddy from a combination of sun and alcohol, and he smelled like fish. I was sitting in a rocking chair on the front porch. My empty wine glass sat on the small wooden table next to me. Unlike Matt, the alcohol did not make me giddy, but pensive. I wanted so badly to tell him what I had learned about the missing woman. But I knew that he was in no mood to talk to me about something serious right now. So, I smiled and closed my eyes before I answered.

"Yes, they had a ball. I got to read a little. It was a nice day. Now, why don't you get cleaned up, and we'll go to the lodge for dinner. We don't want to miss our reservation."

I tried not to sound distracted by the case or frustrated by his impaired state. Luckily, he was too excited to pick up on my lack of interest in his fishing stories.

"What are you talking about? I caught dinner!" he said with a hearty laugh.

Matt held up the cooler again in the air above him, gazing at it. I shook my head vigorously and playfully pushed him inside to take a shower. I wanted him to take a shower to erase the fish smell that stuck to every part of him. I also wanted the hot water to sober him up so that we could talk about what I had just learned about Pamela Stevens.

I knew a lot about working in restaurants. I had worked as a waitress all through college and graduate school. I knew the best way to get a good tip was to strike up a conversation with the customers and find some common ground. If they liked me and felt like we could relate to each other, they were more likely to tip me well. It was a pretty simple equation. I could never understand my coworkers who didn't offer this kind of personal service and then complained about poor tips.

As a customer on the other side of this equation, I always appreciated it when wait staff made a sincere effort to have a conversation with me. I made sure my tip reflected their graciousness.

Bentley, our gregarious waiter in the lodge dining room, was a little rough around the edges. His vest was too big, his shirttail was untucked, his beard unkempt. But right away, I could tell that he was a talker. From the moment he greeted us, he was telling us about Bingham and all the things we should do while we were here. From hiking to mountain biking to kayaking, he explained the possibilities with great enthusiasm.

"So, Bentley, how far away do most of the people who work here live? It sure is a long way up the mountain," I asked, genuinely curious.

"True. Most of us commute to work anywhere from thirty-five minutes to an hour. There's just not much in the way of a town near here. Laurel is the closest one. We park in an employee lot at the base and take a shuttle up to save our personal vehicles from wear and tear. When the weather's bad, we get to stay here, essential personnel that is. Which is pretty much everyone," he said with a good-hearted chuckle.

Matt was giving me a side-eye. He could tell I wasn't just shooting the breeze with this man. I was on a thinly veiled mission. As a journalist, I was goal-oriented in a lot of my conversations, looking for something specific. Being subtle about it was the key. Sometimes, it took me a little time to get there, especially if I wanted to catch the person off guard. Most of the time, I got the information I was looking for by just being good-natured and letting people talk. I found that most people liked to talk, especially about themselves. They also liked to fill the silences, so it was important to listen patiently and wait for them to speak.

The boys were oblivious to our conversation. They were aggressively ripping open sugar packets and pouring the contents into their glasses of ice water and then stirring them with a knife. Normally, this would have supremely annoyed me, and I would have dragged them out of the restaurant and found a bench where they could sit and reflect on what they had done. But tonight, their actions barely registered on my radar. I wanted to pick Bentley's brain so badly. If he wasn't waiting on other tables, I would have invited him to join us for dinner.

"Wow, they must pay very well for everyone to commute so far," I said, trying to sound nonchalant.

Matt had now graduated from giving me the side-eye to

lightly kicking me under the table to tell me to knock it off. His beer buzz had subsided, and he knew exactly what I was doing. I deftly ignored the shin kicking. It wasn't the first time I had ignored him in my pursuit of information.

"They do pay well. They do. It instills a certain amount of loyalty here for sure. Especially because there's not much work in this area. We know we're lucky to have these jobs. And the customers here tip well too. So, it all works out. Most of the time, that is."

I took the mental note that we needed to leave Bentley a good tip for his friendliness and candor.

"That's good to hear. Sounds like you are all like one big family. I mean, I heard you guys even helped search for the missing hiker."

With that, Matt kicked me so hard under the table that I almost screamed. I gritted my teeth and gave him a quick cut-it-out look. Matt turned away from me just in time to see the boys trying to tip over their sugar water glasses. He reached across the table for the glasses awkwardly, just as they sloshed water onto the white linen tablecloth. He grabbed both of them just in time to keep them from spilling everywhere.

Bentley stopped pouring water into my glass from the silver pitcher midstream, tilting it upright and cradling the base in his palms. He looked around cautiously before he answered my question about the search. I wondered if the woman's family might be in the restaurant at this very moment. But I didn't dare scan the room yet. I kept my eyes firmly on Bentley, waiting for him to respond. Like me, he ignored the drama with the boys and their water glasses. He hung his head and then looked up at us again.

"We did the best we could. This has never happened here before. It's just so devastating for everyone," he said slightly above a whisper. "They've asked us not to say too much for obvious reasons. But I can tell you they're still out there looking for her. And no one is going to stop until they find her. One way or another."

I read between the lines, returning Bentley's solemn gaze. They were calling it a rescue mission, but I knew from my experience that it would soon turn into a recovery mission.

2

MAJOR JACK SORRELLS

I COULD BARELY BREATHE AS I HOOFED IT UP THE SAME hill one more time, looking for something, anything that might help me find her. I had been gaining weight for years, and now, it was catching up with me. I was sweating right through my uniform. I had to stop and brace myself against a tree. There were so many potential pitfalls on this trail—rocks, twisted roots rising out of the dense soil, and masses of tangled brambles with prickers that could tear right through your pant leg. Deadman's Pass. Anyone who'd spent any amount of time on the mountain knew how easy it was to imagine someone falling to their death from here.

Even though I was from here, I had a healthy respect for the danger on the mountain. I knew that I was no match for the steep, rugged terrain and the thick, dark forest that went on for miles, making it possible for even the most experienced hiker to become disoriented.

But what if she fell and that fall didn't kill her? What if she was lying in the brush somewhere on the side of the mountain with a broken leg, a shattered pelvis, or a smashed collarbone, waiting for someone to come and rescue her? Someone like me.

I couldn't get the thought out of my head. What if it were my wife, my sister, or God forbid, my daughter?

No. I had to push through. This old body would have to deal with the heat and the intense terrain. I would leave the rock climbers to scale the face of the mountain into the gorge looking for a broken body, but I would do the common-sense thing. I would look a few feet off the trail in either direction, hoping to find some clue that she was still alive, fighting to be seen. I would be the hero of the story. Then maybe everyone would finally take me seriously again. I saw the way the other deputies still looked away from me sometimes when I spoke to them, even though my mistake had taken place more than ten years ago. I saw the pity in my wife's eyes sometimes when she quickly looked away from me mid-conversation, even in the eyes of my daughter. But I would show them all I was worthy of their respect. If it was the last thing I did, I was going to find Pamela Stevens dead or alive.

We were eating dinner when I got the call from Sheriff Lansing to join the search. I knew the Overlook Trail. It was treacherous topography with big drop-offs that involved sheer rock formations that extended hundreds of feet into the gorge. At this time of year, the mountainside was covered with so much foliage and brush that it was deceiving. You couldn't see the edge of the mountain when you were walking on the trail. But if you had ever been up there in the wintertime, you knew the edge was there. You had seen it with your own eyes, and you knew just how treacherous it was.

Even at the peak of summer, there was a darkness on the mountain, something that was hard to describe. The trees blocked the light, and it made the trail almost impossible to traverse in certain spots.

"Okay, I hear you. How many hours has she been missing? Why didn't they call us in earlier? Ridiculous. We're behind the eight ball now. But I'll get my team out there right away."

My wife, Cindy, looked up at me with concern. She put down her fork, which was holding a small lump of mashed potatoes. She crossed her arms across her chest. Her forehead wrinkled like it always did when she was anxious or worried. Kelli, my daughter, was engrossed in her phone as usual, even though Cindy had told her repeatedly that the dinner table was a no-phone zone. Kelli was a good kid, but she still liked to push our buttons and defy the house rules like a typical teenager. Plus, she was an only child, which by default made her spoiled. We had wanted more, but it wasn't in God's plan.

"What's going on, Jack?" Cindy asked me with deep concern in her voice.

"Missing woman. A hiker, or trail runner, something like that. Anyway, she went out to Overlook this morning and never came back. Sheriff wants me to get a team up there right away."

Cindy brushed a stray piece of hair from my forehead, a small gesture to acknowledge she understood that duty called, and that as a result, I would have to miss yet another home-cooked meal. She was used to it by now, but it didn't mean that the interruption was any less annoying. If anything, over the years, it had become more annoying as she believed my seniority should keep me from having to respond to emergency calls after hours. Yet, in a county as big as Annandale with so few deputies, we had no choice. We were all on deck when something big happened.

"How about I pack you a little food to eat on the drive? It will take a while for you to get there. You need to eat something. Who knows when you'll get a break."

For the first time during the conversation, Kelli looked up

from her phone. She toggled her head from me to her mother and rolled her eyes in a grand gesture as only teenagers can do. She then buried her gaze back in her phone, probably realizing that her mother was too distracted to scold her. Just that split-second little shake of her head made me feel guilty, like she was outing me as a bad father who consistently missed family dinners. I knew that I was being too sensitive, but it bothered me, the thought that my family got upset when I put work in front of them.

"Thanks, hon. You're the best," I said, standing from my seat at the table and kissing the top of Cindy's head. It was small gestures that did make me feel appreciated by my wife, where my insecurities about being an average cop, an average husband, and an average father melted away. But it was a fleeting feeling of contentment. The self-doubt would creep back into my brain in a few short hours. And if for some reason it didn't, Kelli would be there to remind me of how I had failed her and everyone else I loved in my life.

When I finally got to the top of the mountain at the staging area, there were about thirty people milling around—deputies from my department, state police officers, and volunteers from the community. It took a skilled and brave group of people to traverse this dangerous landscape, especially at night. And while I appreciated all the local volunteers, it was also my job to make sure they didn't get hurt, or God forbid, lost. That's all we needed, another missing person.

"What do we have so far?" I asked my lieutenant, Barry, who had gotten there shortly before me.

"Nothing, sir. It's like she vanished into thin air. Was one of those extreme sports types, training for some crazy thirty-four-mile race in Jackson, Wyoming, called the Teton Circ, according to the husband."

"Can't understand people like that. What have they got to prove?" I said, thinking about how Cindy would never do something like that. Her idea of taking risks was going on the upside-down roller coaster at Disney World with Kelli. And even then, she closed her eyes, screamed, and held on, white-knuckled. Afterward, she would say she felt like she was going to throw up for at least an hour.

"My thoughts exactly. But, anyway, we're thinking she either had a medical emergency, or she tripped and fell off the trail and rolled down the mountain. Easy to do on Deadman's—I mean Overlook. Would just take one misstep on an exposed root or a rock."

"Got it. Tell me something I don't know. Did she have water or a cell phone?"

"She had a racing belt on with several bottles of a sports drink, according to her husband. And we pinged her cell phone and got an initial hit. We lost the signal, so I think it's probably dead by now, but the original hit was in the vicinity of Big Rock, the highest point of the trail. Still haven't found the phone. Honestly, we haven't found much of anything at all. We even set up a roadblock at the bottom in case she was disoriented and wandered out to the road for help."

"What about the husband? Have we spoken to him? Any funny business going on there? Troubled marriage? Fighting?"

When a woman went missing, we always had to rule out her husband or boyfriend first. It was nothing personal, just standard operating procedure. We started with the people closest to the missing person and worked our way out in concentric circles. This didn't sound like a case of foul play to me, but I still had to cover all my bases.

"He seems clean so far. Name is Darwin Stevens. He says he's an investment banker in DC. They're both in their early forties. He's got a child from a previous marriage, a teenager. They have no children together. Surveillance video shows him reading on the porch here and then watching tennis on the television in the bar and having a few beers. Multiple witnesses saw him throughout the day. He was always within sight of the cameras since she's been gone. Pretty airtight alibi if you ask me."

"What's his demeanor?"

"Shocked, stunned. I think it's not registering for him yet. He keeps saying how strong she is and that she'll be okay, that she's probably injured somewhere, and that we have to find her before it's too late."

"Any chance she disappeared purposely? Maybe she was unhappy with the husband and saw this as an opportunity to get out." This was another path that I had to go down. Sometimes, missing people were missing on their own accord—walked away from their lives.

"Not getting a sense of that. But you know how it is, it's too early to truly figure out exactly what's going on here. Anything is possible," Barry said with a shrug.

Barry was green, but he had good judgment. I had no doubt that he was going to be a solid investigator. This case would be one of his first big tests.

Darkness had descended quickly on the mountain. Only the moonlight illuminated the peaks jutting into the sky in the distance. They looked ominous, like someone had painted them an even darker black than the sky. My investigators rolled in large LED lights and brought in folding tables where they could spread out maps in the parking lot. It looked like a carnival with the bright lights slicing through the inky black sky and frenetic activity swirling beneath them.

"Who is in charge here at the resort?"

"Woman by the name of Evelyn Sparks. She's pretty freaked out. Doesn't want this to reflect poorly on Bingham. I think that's why it took them so long to call 9-1-1. They thought they could handle it themselves, sending out their own teams of searchers. Then they realized they were in way over their heads. Think she's under a lot of pressure from the owner to keep this all very low-key. I've overheard her on lots of heated phone calls with someone. Probably him, I'm guessing."

Barry gestured to a woman with a black shawl wrapped tightly around her body. She looked like a butterfly in a cocoon. She was pacing nervously at the edge of the parking lot and speaking quietly into a cell phone. I was proud of Barry for assessing Evelyn's state of mind so quickly. Being a good investigator was about noticing the details that other people ignored.

I made a mental note that I needed to speak with Evelyn Sparks next. I had to make sure she understood who was in charge here, that this was a law enforcement operation, and we couldn't have any interference from the resort. It wasn't our job to protect their reputation.

"What about wildlife? Any bear sightings or rattlers recently?"

"Nope, but you know as well as I do this mountain is full of both. I'm not saying one of them got her—but if she's injured, bleeding, on the ground out there somewhere, there's no telling what could happen."

I knew even in the early moments of the search that it would be my mission to find Pamela Stevens no matter what I had to do to make it happen. The first thing I intended to do, however, was to have a word with Miss Sparks. She might not want to cooperate with us, but I was going to make it very clear that she didn't have a choice.

3

EVELYN SPARKS

As soon as I saw the overweight cop ambling toward me beneath the bright, artificial light that was now bathing the parking lot, I tried to act like I was still on the phone. I had just hung up with the owner of the resort. Martin Bingham lived in California. He was a tech giant who made millions in Silicon Valley and created the retreat as a very private and exclusive getaway for people who liked the outdoors but wanted to experience it in a luxurious setting. He was furious that I had called in law enforcement to help with the search.

I tried to explain to him that I didn't have a choice—that the entire staff had searched for hours and come up empty, that we needed the resources that the sheriff's office and the state police had at their disposal. They had brought in drones with infrared capabilities that could pick up body heat. They had search-and-rescue dogs and professional rock climbers who could rappel deep into the gorge. The state police had a helicopter that could cover more ground in an hour than we could cover in a week. We needed them. But Martin didn't see it this way. All he cared about was the precious reputation of the resort and what this might do to our bookings. He was trying to micromanage the situation from three thousand miles away. He obviously didn't trust me.

I cared about our reputation too. This job was my world. I had worked so hard to get to a position in the industry where I was running a high-end resort. I had earned this life, but at the same time, I never forgot where I came from. I had climbed out of poverty and a dysfunctional childhood to be the person I am today. I couldn't bear the thought of losing it all because I had pissed off Martin.

Still, above everything else, I was a human being, and I was not going to let a woman die because of foolish pride. I had met Pamela when she arrived the day before. We had a very formal but lovely conversation on the front steps when I handed her a welcome glass of champagne. I remember she said, "This is so delightful. what I need right now," as she swiveled her head in every direction to take in the perfectly blended rustic tones and luxury of the resort. I recalled that her husband, Darwin, put his hand on the small of her back and guided her into the lobby while a valet put their bags on a rolling cart. That gesture, the slight touch of her back, made me feel like there was real affection there. It was something I didn't see every day from the wealthy couples who stayed with us.

"Evelyn Sparks?" the large officer said with an almost shrill tone as he got within range of me, purposely ignoring my pretend phone call.

"Yes, excuse me a moment," I said, putting up a finger to continue the ruse. I pretended to hang up and slipped the phone into the back pocket of my jeans. I looked at the man directly in his eyes, holding his gaze with my intensity. "What can I do for you, Officer?"

"Major Jack Sorrells. You can call me Jack. I know you've probably told the story a million times, but I am now the person in charge here for the sheriff's office, and I need you to go through it one more time with me. I'm sorry to make you repeat yourself, but I need to make sure we are doing everything we can to find Mrs. Stevens."

In a reflexive gesture, I put my hand to my forehead. I was so tired. And this man was on my last nerve. I knew he was just doing his job, but after all the tense phone calls with Martin, I didn't know if I had the strength to be interrogated again.

"Really, can't you just look at someone else's notes? I'm exhausted. We've been at this for hours."

The officer looked at me with disdain now. I had seen this look from the townies before. Even though we were the biggest employer in the area and paid far above a living wage, some of the locals still thought of the management at Bingham as elitist snobs. If he only knew where I came from, he probably wouldn't be lumping me together with them. We probably had a lot more in common than he suspected. But I could see the judgment in his eyes, and it wasn't going away anytime soon.

"So, you don't have the time or energy to help with the search for a missing woman?" he asked incredulously, clearly intending to get a rise out of me. I didn't like his tone, but I guess I deserved it.

"No, I'm sorry. I didn't mean it that way. It's just, well, it's been a very emotional day as you can imagine," I said, stopping there. I didn't want the officer to start getting suspicious that we were covering up anything from my nervous rambling.

"Okay, so start from the beginning," he said, not giving me an option. "Should I call you Miss Sparks or Evelyn?" He gestured to a stone bench in front of the lodge, where we both sat down. I didn't realize just how weary I was until I was sitting. I suddenly felt all the energy drain out of my body. I could have curled up right there on the cold, hard stone and gone to sleep for the night.

"Evelyn is fine." He nodded for me to continue. "Well, Mr. Stevens came to us at about 2:30 p.m. and said he was worried about his wife, that she had gone out for a hike, or a jog, not sure which one. Anyway, she should have only been gone about two hours, or two and a half at the most. I mean, this happens from time to time. We get a lot of city dwellers here who think they know how to navigate this mountain terrain, and they really don't. It takes real training. They often get a little turned around. Honestly, we usually just send out a couple of guys on a golf cart, and we find them pretty quickly. So, I told him not to worry. I told him that if another thirty minutes passed, we would send out a search team to look for her. I told him she probably just got a little disoriented in the woods, maybe stepped off the trail a few feet, and got confused. Cell phones don't work very well up here, so it's likely she wouldn't have had GPS or even the ability to call for directions. I assured him that she would probably figure it out and be back any minute, that this kind of thing happens a lot and usually ends well."

"So, what happened next?"

"Well, that's when he told me she was an extreme athlete and was training for some major race that was coming up in a few months. He also told me she had excellent survival skills, that she had camped in remote places where she hiked by herself all the time, sometimes even nailed her sleeping bag into the side of a mountain on a ledge. Can you imagine that? Sleeping on the side of a mountain? I've seen photographs of stuff like that—terrifying. He made it clear that she was no wallflower, and that if she was missing, something bad must have happened to her."

"What did you do?"

"I got all my available personnel on the radios. Cell phones, like I already said, are iffy up here. The service is very spotty. I told everyone to meet at the lodge immediately for a search. We have these rough-terrain vehicles. They're super rugged, can handle steep, muddy mountain passes. I divided my employees up into teams, gave them maps, and sent them out to Overlook, where she told Darwin, the husband, that she was headed when she left him at the lodge. She wasn't planning on doing the whole trail, just an out-and-back, meaning she would go for a certain amount of time, and then turn around, allowing the same amount of time for coming back."

"So, why didn't you call us right away when the husband came to you?"

"Like I said, this kind of thing happens all the time. We were a little more concerned than usual this time, given her skillset, that she should have been able to make it back, but we still felt pretty confident that we could handle it," I said, my voice shaking. I knew he would think I was lying. But I wasn't lying, I was just nervous. Talking to someone with a gun and a badge made me anxious. It reminded me of all the times officers had come to our apartment when I was a little girl with arrest warrants looking for my father.

"What was his demeanor like, the husband's?"

"I mean, he was really worried, but not frantic. Just very concerned. And, of course, his concern grew the longer she was gone. I would say he's acting the way any normal husband would act in this situation. I don't think anyone really knows how they would act in a situation like this. It's a nightmare."

I suddenly regretted adding that last line to my statement. I was saying too much out of nervousness. I needed to stick to my script and not add in any opinions that might make the investigator think I was lying.

I wondered immediately why he had asked me that question. Did he think her husband had done something to her and then lied to us about her going out on the trail? I hadn't even considered that. It also didn't seem likely to me based on my interactions with him throughout the day. But what did I know? I had just met the man. I certainly didn't know him well enough to say whether or not he could have done something bad to his wife.

"So, what made you eventually call 9-1-1?"

"I don't know. It was starting to get dark, and my guys came back muddy and exhausted after finding no sign of her. These guys are tough; they're modern-day cowboys. They grew up in these mountains. They know how to navigate the terrain. And, so, when I saw them defeated like that, I realized we needed more help, that we couldn't do it alone. It was the right thing to do to ask for help."

Stop it, Evelyn. You're rambling. Just answer the questions.

I finally stopped talking and sat there quietly as the cop scribbled furiously with a ballpoint pen in his little black notebook. It reminded me of a scene from a Netflix detective show. I had watched enough of those shows to know that I didn't need to offer up any extra information. I just needed to answer his questions in a straightforward way and stop there. Rambling always got people into trouble on those shows. I was not going to be that person.

"Thanks so much for your time. Can I have your contact number so I can get in touch with you if I have more questions?"

"Sure. Absolutely."

He scribbled down my number in his little notebook in the corner of a full page. I wondered why he didn't just put it in his cell phone. I guessed he must be old-school. Everything about him looked old-school, including how the buttons on his uniform strained to hold in what appeared to be a well-honed belly, developed over many years.

"I'll give you my direct line at the lodge too. Like I said, cell service is not great up here."

"Perfect, and we'll need a copy of all the surveillance footage around the time of Mrs. Stevens' absence. My lieutenant told me it shows the husband reading on the porch and then sitting at the bar watching tennis?"

"Correct. I can give that to you on a USB if that helps. I'll get my staff working on that right now."

I was warming up to this Jack person. I realized that my judgment of him in the beginning was not totally fair. He seemed like a person who was genuinely concerned about doing a good job. I liked people who cared, even though my icy exterior didn't always reflect that.

He shook my hand, thanked me, and then drifted back in the direction of the massive LED lights, disappearing into their blinding glow.

I felt my phone vibrate. I looked down and saw that it was Martin calling again from California. It figured that I would have cell service at this very moment when he was trying to harass me about how I was handling the situation. I let the call go to voicemail. I didn't have the energy to deal with him. Martin would have to wait a little bit longer to berate me.

4

DARWIN

I stared at the magnificent mountain peaks in the distance that were illuminated by the moonshine. Their beauty was undeniable, but at the same time, I had an ominous feeling that they were hiding something. Evil lurked stealthily beneath the magical forms that resembled a picture on a postcard. I imagined Pamela somewhere up there in pain, scared, trying her best to get back to me. I'm pretty sure I told her not to go. At least that's what I recalled saying.

I had a change of heart. Everything I thought I wanted, to be free of our constant bickering and her control over me, had evaporated. I wanted her back now. Everything about the day was so fuzzy, it was like I was watching an old home movie on a projector that glitched every few seconds.

"Come on, we're on vacation. Can't you lay off the training for a few days?" I think I said to her. "We're here alone, no work. Let's have a few drinks and watch tennis and have some laughs like we used to. Let's reconnect with the old us. Remember them? They were a lot of fun," I had said with a sly smile, a smile that used to make her melt way back when. Not anymore.

She had given me a perfunctory peck on the cheek, more for the other people around us than for me, and then she waved me off with her hand and a devilish grin, acting like this was the craziest idea I had ever had. Pamela was always like that, making fun of me right to my face. She was a hard person to love. She was also a hard person to live without. Instead of making me hate her, her dismissiveness only made me crave her attention more.

"Training doesn't take a vacation. You have to be consistent, silly. Even you know that!"

Back in the day, I had been quite the triathlete and marathon runner myself, but life and work had gotten in the way, and now, I was still fit, but not in crazy good shape like my wife was. My idea of exercise these days was a four-mile run or a ten-mile bike ride. This kept me healthy enough and sane. But Pamela was so competitive. She used every opportunity to remind me that she was stronger and tougher than I was. And she was both.

"Okay, well, make sure you take plenty of water, or whatever that blue stuff is that you're so fond of. And make sure your cell phone is charged."

Even as I said these things, the things a concerned husband is supposed to say to his wife, I knew I didn't mean them. Deep down, I was manifesting what was about to happen, picturing my life without her, a life where I could do whatever I wanted to do, be whoever I wanted to be, without Pamela's constant judgment. An imaginary life with someone else, someone more like Victoria.

"Aye, aye, captain. I won't be long, I promise," she said, laughing. She tussled my hair, pulling me back into her sticky spiderweb that I could never truly detach from, no matter how hard I tried. She always had a way of pulling me back in. This was her superpower.

"Okay, so where are you going and how long? You know

you're supposed to tell someone your plan when you go out into the woods."

"It's a trail called Overlook, about six hundred feet of elevation. Supposed to be quite challenging. I've heard the locals call it Deadman's Pass. It's a couple miles long. Should be a breeze. I'm going to do an hour out and an hour back," she said with a wink and took a swill of the blue liquid in a small bottle that she then replaced to a loop on her running belt. It looked like antifreeze to me, the kind you put in your car. In fact, you could probably mix a little radiator fluid in with a sports drink, and no one would be able to tell the difference until it killed you.

I reached for her hand one more time, but she waved me off again and headed out of the lodge in the direction of the trailhead. I watched her swagger across the manicured lawn. She knew that my eyes were on her the entire way. This was the quiet behind-the-scenes push and pull of marriage, the waning and ebbing of love and hate, the adoration, and the resentment, the blurring of the emotional lines drawn indelibly on a makeshift battlefield. It was hard not to love someone as beautiful and accomplished as Pamela was. Sometimes, it was equally as hard not to hate her.

As she disappeared into the woods, I clicked on my Friend Finder app so that I could follow her route. I wanted to know exactly where she was at all times.

"Mr. Stevens, is there anything I can get you?" a woman's voice said tenderly. I could feel a light touch on my shoulder. I turned on the barstool where I was sitting to see the manager, Evelyn. I thought she was a little standoffish when I first met her, a typical luxury resort manager, sucking up to the rich people, hoping for big tips at the end of the week. But she had grown on me throughout the afternoon, constantly checking in with me and reassuring me. She told me my room would be comped and that I could stay as long as I needed to. She also told me that if other friends or relatives came here for the search, Bingham would also put them up free of charge. I knew this was bad optics for them, to have a guest missing at a fancy place like this. Yet, she had been nothing but gracious to me. She also had a quiet elegance about her, a delicate and fragile beauty that was different from Pamela's brash, in-your-face personality.

"No, Evelyn. I'm good. Thanks for checking in. To be honest, I'm not sure what I should be doing. I keep expecting her to walk out of the woods, muddy and tired, and tell me some crazy story about how she got turned around, and then we'd go have a shower, a meal, and a big laugh about it."

Evelyn looked at me cautiously, as if she were trying to assess my credibility. Naturally, as the husband of the missing woman, I would be under suspicion. But I knew my alibi was airtight. I was here all day, here in the lodge the entire time. The only time I left the barstool was to go to the bathroom. Everyone saw me. I had nothing to hide. I saw the tiny surveillance cameras with their blinking red lights in every corner of the resort. I knew they would support my alibi. But a few more looks like the one Evelyn was giving me right now, and I would have to hibernate in my room. I couldn't afford to crack in public in case the investigators were looking for a scapegoat to pin Pamela's disappearance on. I had to appear calm.

"Maybe you should go upstairs and try to get some sleep. I promise I'll come get you if they find anything, anything at all. The search is going to be much easier to do during the daylight. There's not a whole lot anyone can do tonight."

With this, she squeezed my shoulder gently. I wondered what it would be like to have a woman like her in my life, a kind, nurturing soul—an un-Pamela. Even Victoria was not as perfect as Evelyn.

While I agreed with Evelyn about needing a break, I also thought about what it would look like if the missing woman's husband just called it a night and went to bed. It didn't seem right. But I did have some important calls to make. I had to call Pamela's parents in Charlotte, North Carolina, and let them know that she was missing. I didn't want them to see it on the news or read it online. I also needed to call my mother, who was staying with my fifteen-year-old daughter, Polly, and let her know what was going on. Polly's mother, my ex, Geni, happened to be on her honeymoon in the South of France with her new husband, Derek. Otherwise, Polly would have been with her. My mother had uncharacteristically offered to stay with Polly, and I had accepted her offer. She rarely did anything for me, so I felt like she owed me this time. It was the least she could do for a son who had been nothing but devoted to her.

I certainly didn't want my mother to tell Polly anything about Pamela being missing. Polly didn't quite love Pamela, but she had grown to like her. Geni, to her credit, had encouraged their positive relationship. Geni said that there was enough love to go around and that Polly needed to be part of both of our families. Still, this news didn't seem appropriate to share with Polly quite yet. Eventually, everyone in the family would need to know what was going on. We would circle the wagons. I'd need their support to get through this.

5

CELIA INVESTIGATES

You would have to be living under a rock not to feel the sea change at the lodge the next day. The air was thick with all that was not being said. The employees were sporting over-the-top fake smiles, trying so hard to appear pleasant that it looked physically painful for them to hold their faces this way.

Matt and I had rented paddleboards for an excursion at the local reservoir. The boys were staying behind in a sports camp that went from nine to noon. I felt a tiny bit guilty about leaving them alone with all this chaos swirling around the property, but the counselor assured me they would have a ball and would be nowhere near the search. First, they would swim, then they would play a mean game of croquet, then they would have a ping pong tournament, and finally, s'mores over the firepit on the lodge's back patio. I took her reassurances to heart to make me feel justified about leaving them. Truthfully, they exhausted me. I just needed a break. The expression "family vacation" had always been such a paradox to me. There was nothing about traveling with kids that amounted to an actual vacation in my mind. Plus, Matt and I needed some alone time—something we rarely ever got.

Matt and I met the paddleboard guide at a designated location at the top of a steep hill. He told us to jump into his work truck, and we would head down to the put-in site. We started down the steep, muddy embankment with hairpin turns. Reflexively, I put my hand to my chest. I felt like I was on a roller coaster ride that wasn't going to end well.

"Don't worry," the guide said. "I've been driving around here since I was ten."

The fact that he had been driving since he was ten was no reassurance. I immediately wondered what kind of parents let anyone drive at ten.

The truck would intermittently get stuck in deep pockets of mud that seemed to be dripping off the edge of the trail. The guide would then simply throw the truck into reverse, spin the tires, and pull out of the muck with such force that it sent brown goo spewing all over the sides of the vehicle and covered the windows with spiderweb-like brown trails. The trees all around us were blocking the light, giving the whole scene a horror movie feel. I could practically hear the audience yelling, *What are you doing? Are you crazy? Turn back!*

I looked at the name embroidered on the guide's work shirt: "Eddie."

"Also shot my first doe around here when I was five," Eddie said to no one in particular, without being prompted.

I wasn't sure that killing an animal at the tender age of five was something to brag about. But I quickly realized that Eddie embodied the mountain man narrative. He was one with this land in a way that visitors could never be. He was exactly the type of person I needed to probe about the hiker's disappearance. He was of this place, someone who knew exactly how things worked on the mountain.

While we drove, Matt and Eddie made small talk about hunting, guns, car racing—all things Matt knew very little about, but he was a chameleon in social situations, always changing personas to make himself more relatable. Eddie didn't seem to notice Matt's lack of actual knowledge about the subjects they were discussing. It was clear that Eddie liked to talk and didn't really listen too closely to what other people were saying. He just kept on telling stories, getting the truck stuck in the mud, throwing it into reverse, spinning the wheels to get out, and then leaping forward within inches of us going over the edge of the mountain. My heart was beating out of my chest now. I realized I was holding my breath and decided to concentrate more on breathing so I wouldn't pass out as I gripped the handle on the ceiling above my seat.

I pictured the headline: "Pennsylvania Couple Dies After Their Vehicle Falls Off Mountain." Once again, the sinister feeling I had been having about this picturesque place crept back into my mind. There was something dark here beneath the shiny natural exterior, dark and brooding, something that had swept Pamela Stevens into its clutches.

We finally got to the reservoir in one piece, and it was stunning. It looked like a postcard. I forgot everything I had been thinking about this being a dark place. The reservoir was filled with deep, blue, calm water as far as the eye could see. Tall, fluffy, green pine trees dotted the rocky shoreline. Eddie gave us no instructions. He just propped our boards at the edge of the water and handed us each a life jacket and an oar. Luckily, we were experienced paddle boarders and didn't need much instruction. We often paddled with the boys at a lake near our house in Pennsylvania. Matt paddled in silence until we got to the middle of the reservoir, away from Eddie.

"Weird dude," Matt said too loudly as I shushed him and turned to see if Eddie was close behind us. Matt's voice carried across the water in an echo. Eddie was stretched out in a kayak floating in our direction, but I figured he was too far away to hear us talking. At least, I hoped so. I thought he even might be sleeping.

"I think he's a character," I said in a loud whisper, just loud enough for Matt to hear me over the sounds of our paddles breaking the surface of the water. "Unapologetically himself. It's refreshing. It's so boring when everyone is so predictable."

"That's one way to put it," Matt said with a sneer as he paddled harder in the direction of a dam that Eddie had pointed out at one end of the reservoir. This had been Eddie's only instruction, to go toward the dam. Matt looked like he wanted to race me, but I was in no mood for a competition. I gave him a stern look to make it clear that I was not racing—not today, not ever.

"Seriously, he's a mountain guy. That's just the way he rolls. How old do you think he is, anyway?" I asked Matt as I casually turned around again to see if Eddie was within earshot again. He lay completely still in the orange kayak with just his work boots peeking above the front end of the vessel.

"I don't know, eighteen? Thirty-two? It's hard to tell with a guy like that."

Matt was right. Eddie was ageless. A boy, a man—who knew? I turned around to see the kayak suddenly gliding up next to me. Eddie was still lying down, but he was paddling from a prone position. He slid up parallel with our boards.

"Ya'll okay?" Eddie said in a flat voice, a tone somewhere between total boredom and annoyance. How many times had he taken snooty city couples out on the reservoir and dealt with their arrogant demands? I didn't want to be those people. I sensed that he kind of liked us in his own way because we were low maintenance compared to the others.

"Absolutely. This is gorgeous."

"Yes, ma'am, it is."

The "ma'am" made me think Eddie was closer to being a teenager than a full-fledged adult, but then he just might have good Southern manners. I casually glided through the water, letting Matt get ahead of us. I couldn't see Eddie without fully turning around, but I could hear him paddling just a few feet behind me. This was my chance to talk to him about Pamela Stevens away from Matt. Matt was fed up with what he perceived as my obsession over the case. It was my nature to be curious and ask questions. I couldn't just turn it off because I was supposed to be on vacation. Matt knew who he married. This was not a surprise. He needed to get over it.

"Eddie, can I ask you something?" I said, slowing down to let him catch up to me again.

"Of course, ma'am. Anything."

Eddie's tone seemed to be warming to me, as if getting away from Matt somehow softened him. I continued paddling straight ahead, keeping my gaze on Matt in the distance, who was apparently taking part in an Olympic paddleboarding trial. He was paddling like his life depended on it.

"What do you know about the missing woman, Eddie?"

For a second, Eddie was silent. The only sound was the whoosh of our paddles in the water. He was sitting up now, paddling properly, paying close attention to me in a way that he had not paid attention to Matt in the truck.

"It's real sad. I was part of the original search team. We looked everywhere. But it's too dense, the brush. No way we could find her if she went off the trail. They even looked from the air, with a state police helicopter and drones that sense heat, but they couldn't find anything. If they don't find her soon, something else will."

"Something else?"

"Yes, ma'am. I hate to say it, but if she's hurt or dead, she'll be scavenged by buzzards or maybe even a bear."

The way Eddie told me this, so matter-of-factly, made my

skin go cold even though it was seventy-five degrees and the warm sun was peeking through a blanket of brewing storm clouds. I scoured the shoreline of the reservoir that had looked so beautiful to me when we first got here. I imagined buzzards picking apart a body somewhere in the dark forest, not far from where we were on the water.

Matt was now paddling hard in our direction. I willed him to move faster as I didn't want to be alone in this place any longer with Eddie. The conversation about animals scavenging dead people was a little too much, even for me. It was amazing how beauty could turn dark with just a few words. But that's how it was here, a constant contradiction, a beautiful but dark place that could swallow a person whole like it did Pamela.

"Eddie, is there any possibility she could still be alive? I hear she's a tough lady, in great shape. Maybe she just fell, broke some bones, and is trying to get back to civilization, hoping someone will find her and rescue her."

I turned to look at Eddie, who was scratching his chin while he appeared to be contemplating my question. I realized for the first time that he had braces. They caught the sunlight at just the right angle and gleamed. *Young*, I thought.

"Possible, but highly unlikely. You would have to be a seriously amazing survivalist to stay alive in these woods for more than a few days. But I guess you can never completely rule anything out."

I thought about the possibility once again that maybe Pamela Stevens wanted to disappear, that she used this opportunity to walk away from her life with the help of her powerful connections. I recalled Wilson's casual mention of the idea. But this didn't seem like a conversation I needed to be having with Eddie.

Eddie lay back down in his kayak and continued his lazy-man paddling. Just then, Matt slid in close to my board like he had just crossed the finish line at a grand prix.

"What are you guys talking about?" Matt asked breathlessly —like a man in his forties who was trying to exercise like a twenty-something.

"Nothing," I said, trying to sound casual. "The weather."

Just then, the sky opened up and the rain started coming down in buckets.

6

JACK, MAKING AMENDS

When I first picked up the cigarette butt from the ground just outside Rosa's bedroom window with a napkin that I happened to have in my pocket from breakfast at the local diner that morning, I told myself it was just an insurance policy, that the crime scene investigators would arrive with a search warrant in a few hours and legally seize all the evidence they could find. It was more of an impulse than anything else. I was sure that Billy Barnes was the one who stalked and raped Rosa Sampson, and quite possibly other women. I would have staked my life on it. All I needed was the DNA to prove it. I believed the cigarette butt would contain Barnes' DNA.

So, I had reached down with the clean napkin, scooped up the cigarette butt, and put it in my pocket. When I got back into my car, I pulled a clean plastic bag from the glove compartment and put the napkin with the cigarette butt inside. I sat there for a minute, staring at the bag in my lap, knowing what I was doing was technically illegal; it was not how the chain of evidence was supposed to work. The search warrant signed by a judge had to come first. But somehow, I convinced myself that there was a greater good at stake. What I did may not have been legal, but in my mind, it was the right thing to do. I needed to ensure that Barnes would pay for what he had done to Rosa. Intellectually, I knew this evidence would not be admissible in court because of how it was taken without a search warrant, but I did it anyway.

I had a buddy at the state crime lab who I knew would probably run the DNA test for me if I promised not to ever reveal that he had helped me. This case had torn me apart—the photos of poor Rosa's injuries, her face beaten to an unrecognizable mush that reminded me of hamburger meat, the scrubs she was wearing ripped into shreds, tears that looked like they were made by an animal's claws, not a man. Barnes *was* an animal, and I intended to make sure justice was served for what he did to Rosa, a young nurse who was just doing her job, minding her own business, not asking for any trouble. She had just gotten home from the overnight shift in the emergency room at the regional hospital when he attacked her in her bedroom. Sometime before dawn, he had climbed through the unlocked window and waited for her in the dark, crouched in her walk-in closet. He sat quietly waiting for just the right moment to pounce—just like a beast.

Billy Barnes had already been on my radar for a string of rapes involving drug addicts and sex workers—victims that many people didn't seem to care about. No one would listen to me when I told the other investigators we had a serial rapist on our hands. Then, he had attacked one of us, a woman who could be our sister, our daughter, our wife. Now, Barnes would finally pay for his crimes, even if he only went to prison for this one case. It would be enough to put him away for life, or at least something close to that. I felt like this would be vindication for all the women he had violated, even if he was never charged in the other crimes. That's how the justice system sometimes worked. You couldn't always get someone for everything he'd done, but if you got him for at least one egregious crime, you could put him away so he couldn't hurt anyone else. That was the goal.

I didn't think through the ramifications when I picked up the cigarette butt. If I had, I would have never done it. I wish I had had a crystal ball that could have shown me how my actions would play out in the future. I wish I had a time machine that would allow me to go back to that moment and leave the stupid cigarette butt on the ground. I should have just stepped over it and kept walking, left it for the crime scene technicians. But what if they didn't find it? What if they missed it? What if they didn't get the DNA evidence that we needed to find probable cause to arrest Barnes?

My buddy did test the cigarette butt for me, and as I suspected, the DNA was a match for Billy Barnes. I kept it to myself because, by that time, other items of evidence—a ripped piece of his T-shirt on the windowsill, the victim's dried blood beneath his fingernails, and a surveillance photo of him from a gas station close to the crime scene—had pretty much sealed his fate. I didn't need the insurance policy anymore. I forgot about it. I stuck the bag containing the cigarette butt along with the lab report in the little safe I kept in the corner of my garage.

When I was called to testify at trial by the prosecution, they asked me a series of standard questions about the crime scene and then moved into specifics about what happened to Rosa. Then it was the defense attorneys' chance to cross-examine me. I was confident at that point that there was nothing they could ask me that I couldn't answer. Billy Barnes was going down no matter what. I had helped make that possible.

"Investigator Sorrells, is it true that you took evidence from the crime scene without a search warrant and had it tested on your own?" The defense attorney asked this with a smugness that reminded me of a scene right out of Perry Mason. The only difference—this was real life. I had screwed up.

I felt my heartbeat speed up. My breathing became shallow.

My vision turned gray and fuzzy. There was a ringing in my ears. I couldn't focus on anything but the attorney in front of me, who had a face like a weasel and a distracting hipster goatee on his unnaturally narrow chin. I had a choice in that moment, and I blew it.

"No, I did not," I said without hesitation. I was shocked by how quickly the lie rolled off my tongue. As soon as I said it, I knew the lie was far worse than anything that I had done with the cigarette butt. Law enforcement officers didn't lie in court. I had lied on a witness stand in a court of law after I had placed my hand on the Bible and promised to tell the truth.

"Your honor, I believe this witness has just perjured himself. I have a witness who can prove this did in fact happen. We respectfully request a mistrial in this case. If the state's star witness lies about this, what else is he lying about?"

Everything that happened after that was a blur. There was a flurry of motions from the attorneys and legal phrases that I didn't totally understand. The judge sent the jury out and did something called "voir dire." He put a witness on the stand outside the presence of the jury to see what evidence the defense had against me. As soon as I heard the defense say "witness," I saw the director of the state crime lab sitting in the back of the courtroom. He was a bald, stout man in a baby-blue suit and a red tie. He was my buddy's boss. There had been an audit of DNA tests run at the lab within the past year. My buddy had no choice but to come clean when the test I asked him to run was discovered in the audit. He had been put on probation and suspended without pay for a month. He never contacted me to tell me what was going on because he was trying to keep his job. I knew in that moment that it was over for me, or so I thought.

As expected, the judge ordered a mistrial and granted Barnes bond. Less than twenty-four hours later, he was back on the street. Less than twenty-four hours later, I was handing in my badge, my service revolver, and my patrol car keys to Sheriff

Lansing and heading home to Cindy. I was suspended without pay for six weeks and told there was a possibility I could come back if the internal disciplinary board recommended that I be reinstated after some counseling and re-training. Thankfully, the district attorney, Mimi Vaughn, who knew me well and knew I had good intentions, chose not to charge me with perjury even though I was clearly guilty of this crime.

Mimi was Annandale County's first black district attorney—no small feat in a predominately white hillbilly area like ours. She had a reputation for being firm yet fair. I respected her for that. She gave me a pass this time, but I knew it was a one-time deal. If I screwed up again, she would have no mercy on me. I was indebted to her for life.

Even though it was a big relief that I did not get charged with perjury, what mattered to me the most was that a rapist was now a free man, walking the streets, free to attack again, thanks to my mistake. Mimi also chose not to re-try Barnes. Because I, as the lead investigator, was deemed not credible, the case was forever tainted. It would have been impossible for her to try the case without me as a witness. I had let her down. I had let everyone down. Mostly, I let Rosa down.

Barnes left town, but Rosa couldn't handle what happened. It was too much for her to imagine that the man who violated her was free to do it again to someone else. She couldn't live with the pain. She took her own life a few days after Mimi Vaughn announced her decision not to re-try the case. She took a handful of pills that she stole from the hospital pharmacy and died in her own bed, the same bed where Barnes had taken her soul from her. Rosa's death felt like a direct result of my mistake. It became my forever cross to bear. She was with me every moment of every single day. I even carried a copy of her obituary and the article about the mistrial from the newspaper in my wallet to remind me of my sins and the fact that they had cost a woman her life.

Every once in a while I would take out the worn piece of newspaper, unfold it, spread it out on my desk or my kitchen table, and look at it. Even though it was faded and creased, I knew the words of the article by heart. The headline read, "Suspected Rapist Walks after Investigator Lies on Witness Stand." I knew that I would spend the rest of my career trying to atone for what I had done to Rosa. Her death would not be in vain.

The search for Pamela Stevens was about me failing Rosa. It was about me making amends. I couldn't bring Rosa back, but I could be a better investigator, a better human, and finally make a difference that people would recognize. It was about me getting back into everyone's good graces—the sheriff's, the community's, my family's.

Even though I got my job back after a month of counseling and going through a criminal justice ethics and procedure class at the local community college, I was humiliated. Prior to the fumble, I had been skyrocketing up the chain of command and was well on my way to being a high-ranking officer in the Major Crimes Unit. After my suspension, they made me start from the bottom again. I was a patrol officer rescuing cats from trees and helping old ladies who fell getting out of the bathtub.

It took me ten years and a lot of hard work to regain my seniority, to get back to where I was supposed to be years prior. I was finally the head of my unit—the unit in charge of finding Pamela Stevens. I had no intentions of letting her down. I decided it was time to talk to Evelyn Sparks again. This time, I would pitch the idea of holding a press conference about the case. The more eyes we had on it, the better the chance that we might solve it.

As I rapped lightly on Evelyn's office door in the lodge with my knuckles, I could hear her on the phone with someone, speaking in her upper-class lockjaw. I suspected she wasn't as uptight as she came across at our first meeting, but hearing her talk like this behind closed doors confirmed for me that she was an intense woman. Obviously, this situation was putting a lot of stress on her, a lot of stress on everyone who worked at Bingham.

"Martin, I'm doing the best I can. No, I don't need you to come here. I hear you, but we have to help find this woman. It's the right thing to do. Even if you don't get that from a humanity perspective, you must get it from a business perspective—we need to appear transparent and caring."

Then there was a long period of silence behind the door. I assumed Evelyn was listening to the owner of the property further berate her. It was not hard to imagine that this Martin guy was unhappy about the negative publicity his precious resort was getting as a result of the situation. I admired how hard she was trying to convince him this was the right thing to do, to support the search effort, even if she had to appeal to his wallet. I knocked again, this time a little bit harder.

"Okay, I will keep you posted. I've got to go. I think someone is at my door," Evelyn said, sounding relieved to have an excuse to hang up.

A second later the door swung open, sending a wave of warm air in my direction. I scanned Evelyn's office and saw a small space heater next to her massive desk, which I assumed was to compensate for the subzero air conditioning in the building.

"Can I help you, Officer?" she asked with clear disdain in her voice, as if we had never met before. Maybe I had judged her correctly the first time.

"Yes, and, as a matter of fact, we might be able to help each other."

7

EVELYN STRADDLES

When I saw Major Sorrells standing at my office door, I couldn't think of a way that my day could get any worse. Martin was threatening to get on his private jet in California and fly here so that he could "handle things." That was the last thing I wanted or needed. Now, I had this good-old-boy from Mayberry who was trying to use reverse psychology on me to get *me* to help *him*. All I really wanted to do was lock my office door, lie down on my couch, and pull the colorful blanket a client had knitted for me over my face. I wanted to block out the midday light streaming in through the ceiling-to-floor windows in my office that overlooked the green, rolling valley below and the mountain peaks in the distance.

I knew he was probably a good guy with honest intentions who was just doing his job, but he had no idea what kind of pressure I was under from Martin to keep everything beneath the radar. I couldn't figure out how to satisfy Martin and do the right thing at the same time.

This man also didn't understand that despite my appearance —my pressed linen pants, exquisite silk blouse, perfect makeup, and diamond stud earrings—I was a country girl in disguise, a scrappy hustler just like him. I asked him what he needed from me in an abrupt tone. I knew that my tone was too sharp, but I was being triggered every other moment by people wanting something from me: first Martin, and now this guy. Then the investigator told me something that almost made me laugh out loud: that he was there to help me.

"I'm pretty sure that's not the case," I said curtly. "You need something from me, not the other way around."

I tried to steady myself. The more I pushed him away and refused to cooperate, the more it looked like the resort had some culpability in Pamela Stevens' disappearance, which couldn't be further from the truth. And I reminded myself that despite his disheveled appearance, his gut straining at the buttons of his uniform shirt, the sweat beads forming at his brow and above his upper lip, he did seem to care about his job, about this case, and about this woman. I took a deep breath.

"Miss Sparks, I mean Evelyn, can we chat for a moment?"

"Yes, that's fine," I replied with less edge in my voice, feeling somewhat softened by his politeness. "Come in, please."

I motioned for him to sit on the couch next to my prized throw blanket. Although I cringed a little as he rested his big, beefy forearm on it. I made a mental note to have it sent to the laundry service after he left.

"Evelyn, I think it's time to ask for the public's help, to hold a press conference to see if anyone out there knows something or has seen anything that might be helpful to the search. Sometimes, people have information that they don't realize is valuable to an investigation. Even a small tip can lead to big results."

I was still standing, pacing back and forth in front of the couch, imagining how Martin would take this if I held a press conference about Pamela Stevens' disappearance. My gut told me that Martin wouldn't take it well at all. I was torn between doing the right thing—cooperating with this cop—and doing the safe thing—whatever Martin told me to do. But Martin was not a good person. I knew that. It wasn't that he was evil or anything, he was just a narcissist. He couldn't help reacting the way he did to situations where he felt threatened.

"So, Major Sorrells, you mentioned this is a way to help me too. I don't see how that's possible. As you can probably understand, all this negative publicity is very bad for business," I said as I felt the edge creeping back into my tone despite my efforts to sound neutral and professional.

The major crossed his other beefy arm across the one that was already pressing into my precious blanket. I was definitely washing it as soon as he left.

"First of all, let's drop the formalities. Please call me Jack. Any good public relations person knows that getting out ahead of something and being transparent is the best way to forge goodwill with the community. I'll let you take the lead on this one, like it was your idea. Maybe we can even get Darwin to say a few words. The goal is to shake the bushes a little—metaphorically and literally. I mean, who knows, a hiker, a fly fisherman, or a hunter may have noticed something that could help us find her."

I could tell that Jack was good at his job. He was trying to convince me to do something that I knew with every fiber of my being would send Martin over the edge. It might even cost me my job. Yet, I was feeling the pull of his argument tugging at me.

I thought about being hungry as a child. I thought about my mother working three jobs to support us—me falling asleep on the couch after licking a jar of peanut butter dry with my fingers, the television blaring as I waited for her to come home from the graveyard shift at the cosmetics factory, take a quick nap and a shower, and then get go to her next job at the convenience store down the road. I vowed as I saw her coming through the door, a halo of early morning light silhouetting her weary body in the small hallway, that I would never live like that as an adult, that my life would be different. I had worked so hard to make this happen. Martin had given me the opportunity that took me to the next level. He had plucked me from relative obscurity as the manager of a busy hotel chain in Maryland and specifically groomed me for this job. He gave me a shot. He believed in me. I had proved myself to him over and over again in the four years I held the position, even when it meant doing Martin's dirty work on occasion. I owed it to him not to screw this one up despite his obvious shortfalls as a human being. More importantly, I owed it to myself.

I had given perks to guests at the resort who I knew were bad news at Martin's direction—mostly white-collar criminals who had come here to hide. I had fudged the numbers in Martin's books on occasion, under his orders, to shield us from massive tax liability. And I had drastically underpaid my staff per Martin's instructions because they were financially desperate, vulnerable, and lived in a region where few jobs were available. I did these things without looking back, without weighing what doing his evil deeds meant to my sense of self-worth. Now, I felt like I was suddenly being given the opportunity to save myself.

"Of course. That does sound reasonable. What do I need to do to make it happen?" I asked with confidence, already acting like it had been my idea all along to have a press conference, which was absurd.

As I heard the words come out of my mouth, I knew that I was risking everything. But there was a voice inside my head that was stronger than fear. It was a voice that told me I had to do whatever I could to help find this woman. I wasn't sure why it was suddenly so important for me to do the right thing after so many years of doing the wrong things. I decided I would listen to this new voice. I liked how it made me feel about myself, like, after all that I had been through, I was still capable of being good.

8

DARWIN TAP DANCES

I COULD TELL BY THE LIMP HUG JOAN GAVE ME THAT she thought I had done something to Pamela. It was the kind of lame hug you give someone who has the flu, and you don't want to catch it, so you try not to get too close to the person. Inside I was screaming for her to be honest with me and not just dance around what she was thinking.

Alex, Pamela's father, didn't pretend. I put out my hand to shake his, and instead, he handed me his bag and ordered me to take it to his room even though there was a valet ready and waiting at his side with a rolling cart to do just that. There were no pleasantries exchanged between us, no chit chat, no consoling me over my missing wife, just shrewd judgement that we both understood could only mean one thing. The line had been drawn in the sand, and it was clear that we were on opposite sides.

Hadn't they considered the fact that their daughter was a daredevil and quite possibly got herself into a dangerous situation? They knew Pamela had a penchant for taking risks. She was also a strong woman, one of the strongest women I knew.

Pamela did what Pamela wanted to do. No man, including me, had control over her or her decisions.

My brother, Dallas, took an overnight flight from New York City so that he could be here to support me. He told me not to worry about Joan and Alex, that they had always been uptight and unwelcoming and that this situation just gave them more of an excuse to be even colder to me. Either they thought I did something to her, or they believed I was careless and allowed my wife to put herself in an unnecessarily risky situation. Either way, I was sunk in the eyes of my in-laws.

"I told you so," Dallas said in a mock high-pitched female voice meant to be Joan speaking to Alex in the privacy of their luxury suite. "I knew he was trouble all along. One failed marriage and a child—too much baggage."

I knew Dallas was probably right about how they viewed me, but then I thought about the fact that they were scared parents who needed someone to blame for their daughter's disappearance. I was an easy target. I tried to put myself in their shoes. I couldn't imagine what I would do if something happened to Polly. After all, they were right to blame me. It made sense. It's always the husband when something bad happens to a woman. Even I knew that, as much as I wanted to deny it.

So, when Evelyn first came to me about speaking at the press conference, I thought she was crazy. Why would I put myself in a position to have more arrows slung in my direction? Everybody would be analyzing me, waiting for me to mess up. But Evelyn had been kind to me in a way that no other woman had been in a very long time. She comped my room and the rest of the family members' rooms. She checked in with me about how I was doing. I at least owed it to her to listen to her proposal.

"So, you know Jack, he's the lead investigator from the county. I'm sure you've spoken to him a few times already. He thinks it would make a strong impression if you spoke at the press conference. It doesn't have to be long, just say something that might motivate people to want to help. You would be putting a literal face on the tragedy for the public—it might get people who could be wrestling with their consciences to come forward. Or even just spark someone's memory of something that might be helpful to the search. What do you say? Will you do it?"

Evelyn gazed at me hopefully with a soft smile on her small, perfect face with its chiseled cheekbones. I wondered again what it would be like to be with a woman like Evelyn, someone demure and sophisticated, the opposite of Pamela. But these were the same thoughts that had led me into the Victoria situation, a situation that almost tanked my career.

As much as Evelyn's approach was wearing me down, I wasn't sure that I wanted to be the face of Pamela's tragedy. She rested a hand on my shoulder as she talked, looking directly into my eyes. I was sitting on my favorite barstool again, two-and-a-half beers in. She looked so sincere, like she really wanted to help me. I wanted to believe her beautiful, piercing eyes, but I was also a little buzzed and not confident I could truly assess anyone's credibility in this moment. Could I trust her not to make me look like a fool?

"I really don't like to speak in front of groups," I stammered. "I don't know what I would say. I think I might make it even worse than it is already if that's possible."

"I can help you with that. I do a lot of public relations for the resort. I just think it could be very powerful to have you there saying a few words. It will have more of an impact than anything the rest of us could possibly say. She's your wife. You're the one who is in the most pain."

Was I? I thought. Not so much. I was more numb than anything else. I didn't know what to feel. Evelyn squeezed my shoulder and again looked at me directly in the eyes with her pleasant, unhurried gaze that suddenly put me at ease. It felt good to be touched, especially by someone like her.

"Okay, I'll do it," I said and then took a long swig of my third beer. "When?"

"First thing tomorrow morning."

"Well, then, I better get some good sleep tonight. Her parents, Joan and Alex, just arrived this afternoon. They might want to speak as well. You should ask them."

Evelyn studied me for a moment. She had walked by when I was greeting Joan and Alex in the lobby. She must have sensed the awkwardness in the encounter. But despite what they thought of me, they were Pamela's parents, and they should be allowed to speak to the public if they wanted to, even if I might not like what they had to say. It was the right thing to do to extend the invitation to them.

"Of course, we'll include them. I'll let them know where and when the press conference will be and that they can speak if they decide they want to say something. No pressure, of course. They seem like pretty private people."

"That's one way of putting it," I said a little too flippantly. "Thanks for this. I know you're just trying to help. I appreciate all you're doing," I said as I saw Dallas out of the corner of my eye coming in my direction with a big silly grin on his face about to blow up this very cordial conversation I was having with Evelyn.

"Great, I'll be in touch with you about the details this evening."

As Evelyn turned to go, Dallas slid into the barstool next to me and slapped me too hard on the back.

"Already getting some action from the ladies, I see. Body's not even cold yet."

"You're unbelievable," I said, not trying to hide the disdain in my voice.

Dallas could tell by the horrible look on my face that I wasn't in the mood for his inappropriate brand of humor at this moment.

"Sorry, that was in poor taste."

"You think?"

"You hangin' in there, buddy?"

"Yeah, sure, best I can under the circumstances."

Dallas ordered a vodka and soda and then turned to look at me.

"Who's the chick?"

"The chick? Oh, you mean Evelyn?"

"Yes. The lady who had her hand on your shoulder. Hate to throw this down, brother, but it's a little too early to start dating."

He just couldn't help himself. With that, Dallas slapped the palm of his hand on the bar and started belly-laughing so hard that he almost spilled his drink, which was in his other hand. It sloshed a little onto the bar, making a small puddle near his elbow. I watched and waited for him to get his button-down shirt wet. I refused to warn him.

"She's the manager of the resort. She asked me if I would speak at a press conference tomorrow and plead for the public's help in finding Pamela. It's a huge property, a lot of land to cover. We need more people in the mix, and we need to know if anyone saw anything that might help us find her."

"I trust you said, 'No way, Jose'? Because that is not smart, brother. You already have all eyes on you. Why make it worse?"

"I told her I would do it. Why not, if it helps find Pamela?" I said, not believing my own words. Dallas was right: the last thing I needed was more attention, people poking around in my marriage, trying to find dirt, trying to topple my alibi. If they looked hard enough, there were things to find.

"Dude, you need to tell her that you changed your mind.

You'll be nervous. You'll ramble. They'll pick apart everything from how you look to each wrong word you say. They will crucify you. They'll use your own anxiety against you to make you look guilty. It's a very bad idea. Trust me."

Dallas' elbow finally grazed the spilled drink on the bar, making a dark stain on his light blue shirt. I grinned at my little victory. He ignored my grin and the puddle and took another swig of his drink and then rattled the ice in the glass. I stared down into my empty beer bottle and considered what he was saying. I understood that he had good intentions to protect me, but at the same time, I had to prove that I had nothing to hide. Everyone saw Pamela say goodbye to me at the bar. They saw me sitting here all afternoon waiting for her to return. I had the best alibi that anyone could have. I was on surveillance tape, and video doesn't lie.

"Well, I didn't do anything wrong. So, I have nothing to be nervous about. I'm going to do it. End of discussion." I lifted my empty bottle and motioned for the bartender to bring me another beer.

"Okay, bro, it's your funeral. But don't come crying to me when every reporter is analyzing your facial expressions and picking apart what you said. Hey, by the way, based on what you told me about how things had been going lately, any chance she took off, walked away? If anyone could pull that off, she could. I mean, I know you guys had your differences, but any chance she found out about your troubles at work and freaked out?"

I shook my head in frustration again. I couldn't believe he was bringing up the Victoria situation at a time like this. I regretted ever telling him. I was desperate to speak with someone right after it happened and trusted him against my better judgment. We had one conversation about it, and then I told him I never wanted to speak about it again. It had been nothing but a meaningless flirtation that went very wrong.

Pamela was never supposed to find out. And as far as I knew, she never did.

Dallas then clinked his glass with the neck of my beer bottle in a cheers motion. I wasn't sure what we were cheering to— finding Pamela or my eventual demise.

9

CELIA REPORTS

I watched Matt pack the car with his fishing gear and the boys' suitcases. He was not happy to be cutting our family vacation short, but he also saw the writing on the wall. My editor had given me the green light to do a story about the missing hiker, which meant I was now officially working and not on vacation. Matt said this environment, with the search swirling all around us, was not a good one for the boys. I agreed. So, he was leaving me here to work and heading home to Philadelphia.

In the distance, another storm was brewing. Inky black clouds hovered low over the mountain. I could hear the deep growl of thunder getting closer by the second. An occasional bolt of lightning came down from the dark clouds, threatening to split the mountain peaks in two. I imagined a terrified Pamela trapped in some cave by the angry weather, waiting for it to pass.

"Okay, so, drive safely," I said, embracing him from behind as he closed the tailgate of the SUV. He was stiff as a board and didn't return my affection. He pulled away from me like I was radioactive. Just then a thunderbolt clapped in the distance, startling both of us a little. The mountain was glowing with rage and indignation.

"I mean, don't you have the information you need already? Why can't you just write the piece at home, remotely, do your interviews over the phone, and turn it in?" Matt stood in front of me, his arms crossed in a defensive posture. Even though he understood my job after being together for so many years, he still didn't like it. He especially didn't like how it constantly interrupted our family time.

Little pellets of rain started prickling my skin. I ignored them even though I could tell I was going to get soaked.

"You know I can't do that. This is a developing story. I need to be here as it unfolds. I need to interview people in real time, face to face, when things are fresh, not over the phone."

He grunted and shook his head. It was a speech he had heard a thousand times before.

"A 'developing story'? That's comical. We all know that she's dead. You could write this from anywhere. It's just a recovery mission now. Woman goes hiking and falls to her death from a mountain ledge. End of story. Even I could write it!"

The wind had picked up, and it was making my hair blow in every direction. I had to keep brushing it out of my eyes. Matt knew how much I hated storms, yet he ignored my discomfort and continued the standoff. I could feel him getting under my skin like he often did in these situations. I just wanted him gone so that I could concentrate on the story. I wanted to run back into the cottage and get away from the approaching storm. I also wanted to get away from the tension between us. Yet, I didn't want him to leave on bad terms. He was going home to take care of our children. I had to temper my rage, something everyone who stays married for a long time must learn how to do. I inhaled and exhaled deeply, just like my meditation app told me to do. I wanted to come across firm but calm.

"First, we don't know that she's dead. Second, whether she

is found dead or alive, it's still a story. You know how this works. I'll be back in a few days. I promise. I appreciate you taking the kids home. I agree, this is not a good environment for them to be in."

I reached out and kissed him gently on the cheek, cupping his face lightly with both of my hands. He didn't pull away this time. Another loud thunderbolt. It lit up the entire driveway. I could feel my damp workout shirt beginning to stick to my skin as the rain picked up.

"Boys, let's go," Matt yelled through the open door of the cabin, averting my gaze. "It's about to pour."

Suddenly, they rushed out of the door and practically tumbled down the wooden steps, barely stopping to let me give them a quick squeeze before they catapulted themselves into the backseat. Matt gave me a half-hearted wave without turning around as he headed toward the driver's seat. I watched them drive down the gravel road as the tires kicked up small pebbles behind them. Then, like someone pulling a rope on a bucket of water above my head, the angry skies let loose, and a deluge of rain poured down on me.

I ran inside to get out of the rain. I looked at my watch as I trailed water across the hardwood floor and realized it was almost time for the press conference. I had just enough time to jump in the shower and get ready. I couldn't let Matt's frustration get to me. I had a job to do. I would deal with him later.

When Carol Lee first went missing, people thought maybe she fell down a well. There were lots of old, unused wells across the farmlands of Pennsylvania. They were supposed to be sealed off and clearly marked, but over the years, the harsh winter weather and curious teenagers had uncapped many of them, leaving them exposed to any unsuspecting passerby who might wander across them and fall in by mistake. Once you fell down a well, there was no way to get out, and unless someone else just happened to come along, no one could hear your cries for help.

As the search for Carol went into its sixth day, we all knew that there was little hope she would be found alive. Her mother had been at work when she disappeared. Carol was supposed to be waiting for the school bus. Her mother had dropped her off at the corner where the other kids were already waiting with their parents. Heather was a single mom who couldn't afford to be late for work. She felt like it was safe to leave eight-year-old Carol with the other children and parents at the stop as the bus was due in about five minutes—five minutes Heather didn't have if she wanted to be at work on time and keep the job that put food on their table and a roof over their heads. Heather told Celia she would regret this decision for the rest of her life. It was five minutes she desperately wished she could rewind, so that she could do it all over again. She would have stayed at the bus stop with Carol and been late for work. Carol would have been safe, and she would have gotten a little flak from her boss. In the whole scheme of life, what was more important, her daughter's safety or being late for a job she didn't really care that much about?

There was no way she could have anticipated that the bus wouldn't come or that Carol would go back to the house, take the extra key from beneath the potted plant on the front porch, and open the door. She couldn't have known that at that very moment someone was breaking into the back of her home and was startled by the child's appearance, that Carol saw his face, and that he didn't think he had a choice but to put a single bullet in the little girl's head, right between her eyes.

Heather explained to me what the police had told her about the investigation. We were sitting across from each other in her small yellow kitchen, drinking honey and turmeric tea. I was scribbling furiously on my notepad, a small digital recorder on the table between us. I was fine. I was holding it together, listening intently as her voice cracked beneath the weight of her tremendous grief. But when she described how police found Carol, squished into an old suitcase like a pile of dirty laundry and left in a cornfield, that's when I lost it. I tried to keep the tears from rolling down my face. I narrowed my eyes and squeezed them tightly, as if I might will the tears back inside. They came anyway, dropping like a rainstorm onto my pad, mixing with the ink and creating blue murky pools on the paper.

Who was I to share Heather's grief? I was a reporter. I was supposed to be a professional. I was so ashamed by my display of emotion that I turned away from her and wiped my tears on the back of my sleeve. When I finally left Heather's house that day, I cried all the way home. The way she had described her daughter curled up in a ball in the suitcase—the dried blood on her pink hair ribbon, her little hands with their fingers laced, clutching her chest—made me ache to my core.

I decided that day I couldn't do this anymore. I couldn't cover crime stories, especially stories about missing and murdered children. When I thought of Carol Lee, I thought of my own boys. How could this happen to any family? How could any parent survive such a tragedy? If something like that happened to one of my boys, I didn't think that I could. How was Heather still upright? Still talking? Still breathing?

When I finished writing my article about the case, which included Heather's emotional interview, I went home, closed the blinds, and got into bed, pulling the covers up tightly over my face. I stayed that way for ten days, only getting up to use the bathroom or get a sip of water. I didn't shower. I didn't eat, I just lay there in the dark bedroom, thinking about how this could have happened to a child. Matt was so worried that he didn't know what to do. His mother came to help out with the boys. They were babies then, and Matt had no idea how to take care of them without me. He also didn't know how to take care of me. It wasn't really his fault. He was so used to seeing me strong. This devastated version of me stunned and terrified him. It was not what he thought he was signing up for.

Then one morning, I just snapped out of it. I got up and decided to live again. I decided that if I let Carol's death be the end of me, then the murderer took two lives. The pain was Heather's burden to bear, but somehow, I had taken it on as my own. From that day forward, I told my editor I didn't want to cover missing person stories that were likely to end with a dead body. He had agreed to my terms.

When I asked to do a story about Pamela Stevens, he didn't hesitate to say okay. It was like he conveniently forgot our agreement, but I had too. It was my agreement to make, and therefore, mine to break. I convinced myself that a missing woman was completely different from a missing child. There was no way Pamela's disappearance would hit me as hard as Carol Lee's did. I was back in the fire, and I liked it, but it was about to get very, very hot.

The storm had passed, but everything was still soggy. Staff from the lodge were frantically wiping down the chairs with towels in front of the podium that had been set up for the press conference. The podium itself was beneath a rustic-looking portico that had thankfully shielded it from the storm. I imagined it was something that was frequently used for weddings and doubted it had ever been the centerpiece of a press conference about a missing person.

The list of characters gathered for the event was like something straight out of central casting—the burly cop, the demure resort manager, and the nervous husband. Evelyn, the manager, kicked things off with a terse statement about doing the right thing and coming forward if anyone knew anything about Pamela's disappearance. She was saying all the correct words, but they were devoid of any real passion. I wasn't moved or convinced that she actually cared. It felt more like a public relations ploy than a show of sincere concern.

She was an attractive, diminutive woman dressed impeccably in black pants that flared out at the bottom. She wore a crisp gold silk shirt with a loose bow around the neck. Her dark hair was swept back in a tight bun that revealed her high cheekbones. Small, elegant diamond studs adorned her ear lobes. When she spoke, it looked like she was in pain, as if someone were holding the barrel of a gun to the back of her head while she talked. Though, based on her fancy outfit that screamed extravagance, I wondered if she had ever really experienced a bad day in her life.

The black clouds had receded, but there was still a gloomy, gray pallor across the sky hanging over us. The rain had stopped, but the air was damp and cold. It was like the mountain understood this was a solemn moment. Or maybe it was gloating at the fact that we couldn't figure this out, that it had successfully taken one of us into its dark, secret world to a place where our human skills were no match.

"We here at the Bingham Reserve stand prepared to do whatever we can to bring Pamela Stevens home to her family. Please help us do this," Evelyn said, pointing in the husband's direction and beckoning him to come to the podium. As he walked up, I could hear the camera shutters all around me clicking as blinding flashes went off like a series of tiny explosions. Likewise, television cameras swiveled on their tripods in his direction and followed him from his seat to the podium. Darwin Stevens shielded his eyes from the lights as he reluctantly ambled up to the microphone. Like Evelyn, he also looked like someone was holding a gun to the back of his head, like someone very persuasive was making him do this. I assumed they probably were. I couldn't imagine that he had volunteered to speak in front of this group with everyone's accusing eyes on him.

"Thank you all for being here today. I really don't know what to say except thank you to all the officers, all the volunteers who have already put so many hours into the search for my wife. Thank you to the resort for hosting me and my family during this difficult time. I will never be able to repay all of you for what you've done. I know Pamela. I know my wife. She's tough, and if she's out there somewhere, and she's able to, she is trying to get help, trying to get home. So, please don't give up on her. That's all. Thank you from the bottom of my heart."

Darwin ran his hand through his unruly hair and turned away from the podium as the crowd of reporters shouted questions at him. It was clear to me he would not be answering any of their screams. He sat back down in a folding metal chair next to Evelyn. She placed a hand on his shoulder and gave it a little squeeze to say good job. Honestly, he hadn't done a good job. He had come off aloof, distracted, and very anxious. This wasn't exactly the impression you wanted to make when your wife was missing. I strongly suspected after this performance that Darwin Stevens had something to hide.

Next, Major Jack Sorrells got behind the podium. He readjusted the microphone to bring it up to his height and then read what appeared to be a verbatim statement from a piece of paper in front of him, cataloguing everything they had done since the beginning of the search to find Pamela.

"We have covered about seven thousand acres overall, thirty-six miles of trail, and had forty-six officers from multiple agencies and dozens of local volunteers helping with the search. So far, we've come up empty, but we are not giving up. We will not stop until we find Pamela Stevens."

Sorrells was heavyset, and sweat was starting to form on his brow. He pulled a cloth out of his pocket and wiped his forehead before continuing. Evelyn then handed him a bottle of water. He slowly unscrewed the top and took a big, long sip as if he didn't have a crowd in front of him waiting for him to speak again.

"Let me be clear. If you have information about this woman's disappearance and you do not share it with us, you could be charged with obstruction of justice. Everything is relevant, even something you might think is unimportant. Think hard about where you were and what you saw in the last few days. We've set up a number you can text anonymously and report information. You don't have to use your name. It's completely confidential. Please help us bring Pamela Stevens home to her husband, her parents, and her friends. Thank you."

When the major mentioned her parents, he gestured in the direction of an older couple in the front row, who I assumed were Pamela's mother and father. Based on their body language and the embarrassment on their faces, they did not want to be singled out. At the same time, I also believed they wanted to know what happened to their daughter and were willing to suffer through this public humiliation for that reason. There was a coolness between Pamela's parents and Darwin. They sat on separate rows and didn't interact at all. I filed this observation away. I would investigate it later.

The major paused and looked at the audience as if he were waiting for someone else to speak. It was so quiet you could hear the leftover raindrops pitter-pattering off the trees around the portico.

"I will take a few questions if you have any," he finally said as arms shot up in every direction and the journalists started yelling to be heard over one another. "One at a time. I can't hear anything if you're all screaming."

"Major Sorrells, Ashley Benson from the *Charlotte Observer*. Do you think she had some kind of accident? Or a medical emergency?"

"That's our best guess right now. The problem is that the brush is so thick this time of year that if she fell off the trail and is hurt, it could be very difficult to spot her. That's why it's so important that we keep searching. The more eyes we have out there, the better chance we have of finding her."

"Investigator Sorrells, Janice Poynter, *CNN*. What about wildlife? Could she have come in contact with a bear or a venomous snake?"

"Anything is possible. But we are hoping that's not the case. We're hoping that she's just laid up somewhere with an injury and we will eventually find her. We understand that she's a pretty tough cookie. She has wilderness survival experience based on what her husband has told us. She has a better shot than most people of making it out there."

The major scanned the crowd, and his finger landed on me. I was startled at first that he had picked me out of the throng, but I jumped right in to avoid having my moment hijacked.

"Sir, Celia Finch, *Philadelphia Inquirer*. When does this search turn from a rescue mission into a recovery mission? Who makes that decision?"

The major looked stunned by my question. He put both hands on the podium, splayed his fingers, and rocked back and forth in his black army boots for a few seconds. Finally, he adjusted the microphone again, bringing it closer to his mouth, and leaned in to speak.

"Well, young lady, I'm not sure how they do things in the big city of Philadelphia, but down here in North Carolina, we don't give up looking for someone and hoping to God they're still alive just because it's hard or inconvenient. Last question."

The investigator swiveled his head away from me dismissively, turning to a male reporter from a local television station on the other side of the crowd. My pride was a little bruised by the way he reacted to my question, but at the same time, he gave me an incredible quote. I had stumbled into the perfect storm of a story. People would be following this even if it didn't happen in their backyards, which is the main goal, to make people care about your story.

I had promised Matt that I wouldn't get in too deep, that I would simply do my job and separate my emotions from the story, no matter the outcome. Unfortunately, every time I closed my eyes, I pictured Pamela Stevens alone in the brush at night with a broken leg, calling out for help, hoping that a bear wouldn't get to her before rescuers did. Today, I imagined a cold, wet Pamela cowering for cover as the dark clouds and lightning hovered above her. I pictured her shaking with every clap of thunder, begging the dark mountain to give her a break, to release her from its clutches.

And then I thought of another scenario—her body at the bottom of a craggy ravine, bruised and battered from hitting all the rock tails on the way down after falling from the edge of the mountain trail, her lifeless eyes wide open, staring up at the starry sky that she could no longer see.

I tried to stop myself from thinking these things as I watched Darwin Stevens slink away from the event alone, leaving the couple I assumed were Pamela's parents behind. They stood quietly to the side, speaking with the investigator in hushed tones. Occasionally, they would glance over their shoulders as they talked. I realized right away they were making sure they were out of earshot of Darwin.

"He's an odd one, that husband, don't you think?"

I turned to see Nelly, the lady from the stables, standing next to me in her brown work shirt with her name on it, her construction boots coated in muck from the horse barn. Her arms were crossed, and she was shaking her head as stray strands of her grayish-blonde hair swept across her weathered face.

"Odd in what way?" I asked, genuinely curious about what unique insight this hardened mountain woman might have.

"He's not upset that she's gone. You can see it in his eyes. They're dead eyes. No feeling at all."

"Everybody handles grief differently. Maybe he's just emotionally drained."

"Think what you want, but I'd put my money on the fact that he had something to do with her going missing."

With that, Nelly turned and walked away. She seemed like a person who had the kind of life experience that led to real wisdom. This meant she also probably had good instincts. I had every reason to believe that she might be right.

10

JACK PUNTS

THE PRESS CONFERENCE WENT WELL, AT LEAST UNTIL that snooty Philadelphia reporter asked me that insensitive question as Pamela's parents sat right there in front of me with their sad, pleading eyes. What in the world was I supposed to say? She's probably dead? Even though that's the truth, it wasn't the right thing to say, at least not yet. It had only been forty-eight hours. I wasn't about to give up yet. There was still a slim chance we might find her alive. I had to hold onto some shred of hope so that I could do my job.

I knew it was only a matter of time before we found her, dead or alive. She had to be out there somewhere. The question was where? The husband didn't do himself any favors with that awkward speech. I was pretty sure he didn't have anything to do with his wife's disappearance, but I couldn't rule out anyone at this point.

His alibi was ironclad. The poor guy was on the resort's surveillance video drinking at the bar while his wife was hiking. An alibi on video was just about the best defense you could have. I still thought he was a jerk for letting her go on that treacherous trail alone, but being a jerk didn't mean you were guilty of murder.

And that Evelyn, man, she was wound tight. She looked like she was being forced to walk over hot coals with bare feet when she spoke. I had tried to let her take the credit, like it was her idea to step up to the plate and do the right thing, but it had to be obvious to anyone who was watching that she was hosting the event under extreme duress, and I was the duress.

Now, I had an even bigger problem. The state police told me they were pulling out their resources—their helicopter, their dogs, their drones, and their rock climbers. They told me they couldn't invest any more time or people into what appeared to be a recovery mission, the words the Philadelphia reporter had dared me to say.

I understood why the state police were pulling out. We had zero leads. At least if we had a specific area that we could concentrate on, it would be time well spent. But right now, we were just spinning our wheels, and they had other things to do than search thousands of acres of dense forest for a woman who was likely dead.

I hadn't told Evelyn, Darwin, or Pamela's parents that the state police were exiting because I didn't want anyone to lose hope. I was now in charge of the entire case, and it was my responsibility to come up with a plan to keep the search going. With such a small staff at the sheriff's office to cover such a large county, I didn't have enough people to make this work. I knew I could get volunteers. People in this community wanted to help. But I needed guaranteed bodies every single day. I decided the only option was for me to ask the ice princess, Evelyn, if she would lend me some of her staff members to help with the search.

"What can I do for you?" Evelyn said as I rapped on the door with my knuckles. She was sitting ramrod straight at her desk, staring at her computer screen like she was trying to figure out a complicated math equation. She didn't look up. Her glasses were perched on the bridge of her nose, her brow furrowed in concentration.

"Well, I need a favor," I said in my most bashful voice as I plopped down in the armchair in front of her. Her gaze stayed on the computer screen.

"I thought I just did you a favor by holding the press conference?" she said, finally looking up to meet my eyes. She pulled her fingers away from the keyboard and pushed back from the desk in her rolling chair, crossing her arms across her narrow frame.

"True, you did. But now I need another one."

"How many favors do you think I should give you?" Evelyn responded in a coy voice. "Three? Like a genie in a bottle?" Her dry wit was a breakthrough. She was finally warming up to me.

"Well, see, here's the deal." I leaned forward and wrung my hands. She was no doubt making fun of me, but I had to ignore her sarcasm and try to get her to give me what I needed. That was my gift: convincing people to do things they didn't want to do.

"There's a deal?"

"The deal is that the state police are done with this whole mess. They're pulling out. We're losing the helicopter, the drones, the dogs, the guys that rappel down the side of the sheer rockface. So, if I'm going to continue to do this and do it right, I need your help."

Evelyn looked amused. Oh, how I wished I weren't dealing

with this stuck-up woman. She knew how we operated here in the mountains. There was an unwritten rule that we helped each other out, no matter what. She probably never needed help a day in her life, and she certainly didn't appear eager to offer me any help.

"What kind of help?" Evelyn asked, her tone softening just a little. Or had I imagined it?

"Help with the search. I need bodies. Can you lend me some of your people each day so I can cover some real ground? I just don't have enough people on my team to make it work. And time is running out. Every single day that passes that we don't find her, the lesser the chance that we will find her. I want to find this woman, and I think you do too."

With that, I sat back in the chair and folded my arms to mirror her exact pose. I stared at Evelyn, waiting for her to speak. She broke our silent standoff, uncrossing her arms and leaning forward on her desk.

"Yes," she said just above a whisper.

"Yes, what?" Even though I understood her, I wanted to hear it loud and clear from her lips.

"I will help you."

I had achieved the impossible. The ice princess was melting. I needed to take advantage of her graciousness before she changed her mind.

"Great. Let me tell you about my plan."

She rolled her eyes but kept my gaze. Progress. The melting was underway.

11

EVELYN PITCHES IN

As soon as Jack closed the door behind him, I regretted that I had offered to help with the search. Martin was already insanely mad at me, and I was on very thin ice with him. Now, I was offering to allow people on his payroll to help the local sheriff's office look for a missing woman. Had I lost my mind? I had. This was the only explanation.

I wasn't sure if it was the way he looked at me, but I believed that Jack Sorrells saw an uppity, intense woman when he sat across from me. He had no idea where I came from or what I had to do to earn this life. He and I had a lot more in common than he thought—humble, country beginnings. The difference was that I had made the choice to have a different life, and he had simply carried on with the cards that he was dealt. But there was no way he could know that about my background. He just saw what I looked like on the outside and made an assumption about who I was. This was how most people operated, judging people by their appearance without really knowing them. I did it too.

I agreed to give Jack six bodies a day to help with the search. I told him it was a temporary arrangement, that we would go day by day depending on the availability of my staff and their willingness to participate. Although I knew they would all be more than willing to search for the missing woman versus shoveling manure out of the barn or driving around picking up soiled sheets from the cottages. Despite the horror of what had transpired, this was still the most exciting thing that had ever happened here at Bingham, and for most of these ordinary people with their ordinary lives, it was the most exciting thing that had ever happened to them, period.

"It's a deal," he had said too giddily, shaking my hand so brusquely I felt like he might pull my arm right out of its socket.

I sat back down after he left and thought about how I would have to keep this from Martin, how he was just itching to jump on his private jet and fly here from California and to take control as he had threatened to do numerous times over the phone in the past few days. And then, just as this thought crossed my mind, speak of the devil. I saw Martin's name flash across the screen of my cell phone. I toyed with the idea of not answering it, but I knew that to keep him at bay I had to keep talking to him.

"Evelyn, it's Martin," he said formally, as if I didn't have his number programmed into my phone. "I just want to know what has transpired since we last spoke. What's this I'm hearing about a press conference? One of my employees here saw it online and sent me a link."

I sat up straight and laid the phone down on the desk, putting him on speaker. My heart was racing. My palms were sweating. Of course, he knew about the press conference. It was all over the news. I just didn't think he would find out this fast. I had to make a choice to turn the ship around. I took a few deep breaths in through my nose and out through my mouth just like my online yoga instructor had taught me to do.

"Martin, I did exactly what you asked of me. I got out in front of it. I tried to show everyone that we're being transparent, that we're cooperating with authorities. I decided this was the best way to position ourselves in the media spotlight given the circumstances. This is what you pay me to do. To make decisions in our best interest."

My tone was measured and calm even though I was shaking on the inside. But Martin didn't know I was falling apart. As long as I kept my voice neutral, I could get away with this false bravado.

"You *decided*? Since when do you decide anything without consulting me?"

"I really didn't have a lot of time to think about it. The investigator came to me and asked if they could do it right away. I honestly think it went well. I've gotten a lot of good feedback about it online, about how we appear to have nothing to hide, that we're fully cooperating and giving the authorities all the support they need."

Martin was quiet for such a long time that I thought we might have gotten disconnected. But then he spoke. This time he was the one who was calm and measured.

"Do we have anything to hide, Evelyn?"

"No, of course not," I said, no longer able to keep the shaking going on inside of me out of my voice. I honestly wasn't sure if we had anything to hide. Was I protecting Darwin Stevens by supporting him? Was I protecting the reputation of the resort by denying the potential dangers our guests faced on the trails that we encouraged them to hike? Or was there something even worse going on that I didn't know about? Anything was possible at this point.

"Good, let's keep it that way. And no more press conferences without consulting me. Do you understand?"

"I understand," I said, feeling defeated by his condescension even though I had technically won this round.

When he hung up, I sat there for a long time looking around my perfectly appointed office, wondering how a girl like me had scored this life. I watched the white, fluffy clouds roll by the floor-to-ceiling windows in the perfect blue sky. Was I willing to give it all up, this view, this job, the paycheck, just to do the right thing? I honestly didn't know. But I did know one thing: someone was hiding something. People didn't just vanish without a trace. Someone knew what had happened to Pamela Stevens, and I intended to get to the bottom of it before the situation imploded my life.

12

DARWIN CRUMBLES

Alex and Joan were full of disdain every time they saw me. They weren't even trying to hide their scowls, and their dark, accusing eyes pointed right at me, the man they deemed responsible for their daughter's disappearance. Could I have been a better husband? Sure, I could have. Could I have tried harder to give Pamela the life that she wanted without going into debt? Absolutely. But I did love her. I knew that now more than ever. I loved her and missed her. I didn't want her dead. I had a lot of regrets. I especially regretted Victoria. It should never have happened. Just like me letting Pamela go.

I replayed the moment over and over in my head as she walked out of the lodge to the trail. I thought about the casual way she had waved back at me and then strolled across the field in the direction of the trailhead. It was part of the formality of marriage, the polite civility that you showed to each other even in challenging times that said, *We're in this together*. Should I have stopped her? Pamela had never needed protecting. But maybe that was the problem. She always seemed so strong, so in control of everything. I had always wanted her to need me, to make me feel like the man I was supposed to be. But she didn't need anyone.

Sometimes, when we argued, especially about money, I felt like she needed to be protected *from* me. After one too many whiskeys, she would say something that triggered me like no one else could. I felt an intense hatred welling up inside of me. In those moments, I sometimes pictured doing bad things, like taking the lamp next to me and smashing it over her head. But I never did anything like that, and I never would—at least, I didn't think I would.

For most of our marriage, I had felt emasculated by her confidence, her success, the way she lived her life independently as if I were an afterthought. But the truth was that Pamela was a force of nature, and she had chosen me. That had to mean something. It had to mean that I was someone worth choosing. I had just never looked at it this way, until now, until it was too late.

The events of the day she disappeared were foggy. I knew I had too much to drink while I was waiting for her at the bar. I was annoyed that she decided to go for a run instead of spending time with me. At one point, I got so impatient, I went outside and walked toward the trail to see if she was on the way back to the lodge. The next thing I remembered was being back at the bar, looking up at the clock and realizing she had been gone for a very long time. Panic surged inside of me.

"Hey buddy, how's it hanging?" my brother Dallas asked, slapping me too hard on the shoulder with his hand, bringing me swirling violently back into the present moment.

"Not well. My wife's missing, if you haven't heard."

Dallas casually ignored my passive aggression, sliding in next to me at the table and pouring himself a coffee from the pot the waitress had set down. Then he took a piece of my toast and slathered it with butter and jelly. The dining room was almost empty, but there were a few tables of people that were within earshot.

"Things are not going to get better just sitting here and stewing about it. Let's go do something. Take your mind off it."

"I should be out there searching with everyone else."

"No, you shouldn't. That cop, Jack something or other, said it's not good to have family searching for a loved one. They're too emotional. There's no telling what you might come across. And then you can't unsee it, ever. I don't think it's a good idea. You need to take his advice and let the professionals do their thing."

Dallas grimaced and then took a big bite out of the toast, crunching loudly. While I appreciated his support, his flippancy in the face of this obvious tragedy was beginning to wear on me. It had been the constant dynamic of our relationship since we were kids. I was the realist; he was the dreamer. He saw the glass half-full, where I saw it half-empty. Most of the time, our differences were about unimportant stuff like which sports teams we liked, or whether it was okay to date a woman smarter than you were, but this time, our different perspectives mattered. I was not going to allow him to give me a bunch of false hope with his positive platitudes.

"How about golf?" he suggested in between loud bites.

"Golf? Did you say golf?" I replied, not bothering to keep the incredulousness out of my tone.

"Yep, golf."

"You really think it's a good idea for me to play golf when my wife is missing?" I said between gritted teeth as quietly as I could. "You were the one who told me everyone is watching me, waiting for me to mess up, to prove that I had something to do with Pamela's disappearance. How would it look for me to just go play a casual game of golf while my wife is missing?"

"You got a point, bad optics. Okay. My bad."

I shook my head and stood up from the table, throwing my napkin down on my chair. At this point, I wished that I hadn't called Dallas—that he hadn't come, that he had stayed at a safe distance from me in New York. The last thing I needed was him making me look guiltier to Alex and Joan than I already did. But I also needed someone in my corner. He would have to do for now.

"It's not about optics, Dallas. It's about doing the right thing. Have you seen the way Joan and Alex look at me? Like they want to kill me? They think I did something to Pamela. They're convinced of it. What if they start convincing other people?"

"Look, ignore them. They're just upset and looking for someone to blame. You're an easy target. Like I said before, it's always the husband."

"Great, just great. Thanks for your insight, little brother. Maybe you should go share your theory with the investigators. I'm sure they would appreciate your help!"

I stormed out of the dining room, almost knocking over a chair in my wake. I didn't look back to see if Dallas was following me or still sitting there oblivious, eating my cold, hard toast. I wasn't paying attention to where I was going. Suddenly, as I was rounding the corner from the restaurant into the hallway, I walked almost directly into Alex and Joan, who were on their way into the dining room for breakfast.

"Wow. So sorry," I said, startled, putting my hands up in a surrender gesture. Then I heard Joan whisper under her breath in an almost imperceptible voice, "Sorry for what?"

I wasn't sure what came over me. Maybe it was the lack of sleep, maybe it was stress, maybe it was how fed up I was with their glaring faces. I spun around as they passed me to enter the restaurant and summoned a courageous voice from somewhere deep inside me.

"Why don't we talk about what you really think instead of

just tiptoeing around this thing, pretending there's no elephant in the room between us?"

Joan turned back first with daggers in her eyes. I thought she might take her long, red fingernails and rake them across my face. Alex must have thought the same thing because he grabbed her arm and pulled her back in his direction toward the restaurant.

"We're upset and under a lot of stress, Darwin. This is not the time or place for this," Alex said in his baritone voice of reason, still clutching Joan's twitching arm with its red talons ready to strike.

"When is the right time, Alex?" I said, my voice getting louder and drawing the attention of the other diners. "I didn't get a copy of the what-to-do-when-your-wife-is-missing playbook. Maybe you could order one for me on Amazon." I knew I was out of line, but I couldn't stop myself. Alex had set me off, and I was in pain. To be fair, I knew he was in pain too, I just couldn't understand them blaming me instead of supporting me. It didn't make any sense. There was no evidence that I had done anything wrong, and they wouldn't find any. I was sure of that.

Just as I was about to step closer to them, I felt a hand on my shoulder. I looked back to see the young guide from the paddle boarding excursion that Pamela and I had taken the day before she disappeared. His name was Tony, or Danny, or Eddie, or something like that.

"Mr. Stevens, sir, let's get a handle on ourselves. Okay?" the boy said with a mountain drawl, gripping my shoulder and trying to turn me away from Alex and Joan.

Then another guy appeared on the other side of me. He was also an employee—an older, thin man with skin like leather and grizzled features like he might have been raised by wolves and lived in the woods for most of his life. His work shirt read Wilson. I remembered seeing him at the stables when we took our orientation tour of the property after we arrived.

"Ya'll don't want to do this. There's a lot of tension in the air. I get it. But let's all calm down for a minute and take a deep breath," the older man said.

I could feel the two men steering me in the opposite direction from the dining room. I was struggling to pull away from them, but they were strong, especially the young one, who I could now see was Eddie from the name embroidered on his tan work shirt.

"Thanks, gentlemen. Sorry for all the commotion," Alex said with a little wave as he turned around and steered Joan back in the direction of the restaurant by her elbow. Like me, she struggled to get out of his grasp. I imagined she wanted to run back and punch me in the face. Alex acted like he was apologizing for cutting a driver off in traffic instead of what he really did, which in my mind was to imply that I killed his daughter.

"Jerks," I said under my breath as Eddie and Wilson led me to a bench across from Evelyn's office. One of them ran and got me a bottle of water. The young one sat down next to me, unscrewed the top, and handed it to me.

"Mr. Stevens, I can see you're in a bad way. I can't pretend to imagine what you're going through, but you gotta figure they're going through something too. Their daughter is missing. They need someone to blame, and it's you. Don't give them any more ammunition."

"That's exactly what my brother said," I exclaimed too loudly after downing the bottle of water in a few short gulps. I punched the air triumphantly to emphasize how much I appreciated what the kid was telling me. Hearing it from him made all the difference. I needed an outsider's point of view, someone other than Dallas. This kid was reasonable, and he was making sense.

"It's just not worth it. With all you got going on, I would suggest you just lie low and stay out of their way," Wilson, who was now standing next to the bench, chimed in.

The boy stood and gave me a little pat on the shoulder and

then left, trailing behind Wilson. I sat there a little stunned that I was taking advice from two mountain men who probably didn't even graduate from high school. Yet, they definitely had degrees in social intelligence. They were one hundred percent right. I couldn't let Pamela's parents get the best of me. No one had any proof that I had done anything wrong. There was proof of my innocence, the best kind of proof, video proof. If there was any actual evidence that I had done something to my wife, Major Sorrells would surely be shaking me down by now. Yet, he'd been nothing but professional and kind to me. I was in the clear, at least for the time being.

As I was about to get up, the newspaper reporter turned the corner and looked at me suspiciously as she walked by. She was the arrogant one who had asked the insensitive question at the press conference about when the search became a recovery mission. No tact. No wonder people didn't like the media. She turned around to look at me sitting pitifully on the bench, like she was thinking about sitting down next to me. I turned my head away to show her that she was not welcome. She got the message and kept walking.

"Mr. Stevens," another woman's voice said. I looked up to see Evelyn standing over me with her hands on her tiny hips. "What's this I hear about an altercation at breakfast between you and your in-laws?"

Suddenly, I was nine years old in the principal's office after a fight on the playground. The last thing I wanted to do was get in trouble with Evelyn. She was one of the few people whose opinions of me I cared about.

"I'm so sorry. I don't know what came over me. It won't happen again."

13

CELIA BEARS WITNESS

As soon as I heard the commotion, I put down my coffee. I was standing at the complimentary hot beverage station in the middle of the lobby, filling my cup with honey and cinnamon to help wean me from my white sugar addiction. I could hear voices being raised at the entrance to the restaurant. One of them I recognized as Darwin Stevens, Pamela's husband. I decided I needed to get closer to find out what was going on.

When I rounded the corner, I made it a priority to stay behind a large potted tree next to the massive stone fireplace. Peeking through the branches, I watched as Darwin approached an older couple with an angry stance and a loud voice. I couldn't hear exactly what they were saying, but I could tell it was getting more heated by the second. As I studied the couple more, I realized they had been in the front row at the press conference, and the major had referenced them as being Pamela's parents. It was all making sense to me now. Pamela's parents must think Darwin had something to do with her disappearance. And they just might be right.

Suddenly, the encounter was getting very intense. Pamela's mother looked like she was going to scratch Darwin's eyes out with her long red fingernails. Her husband was holding her away from him, gripping her elbow. As Darwin inched closer to the couple, I saw two employees approach Darwin: the kid from the paddle boarding adventure Matt and I had gone on and the older man from the stables whom I chatted with while I waited for the boys. For some reason, I recalled their names were Eddie and Wilson. I never forgot a face. I wasn't quite as good with names, but these guys I remembered.

It looked like Darwin was getting ready to lunge at the couple when Pamela's father put his hand up in a stop gesture and appeared to be trying to calmly talk him down. But Darwin was having none of it. He wrestled in Eddie's and Wilson's grips until Pamela's parents finally turned and walked away from him and into the restaurant. The men wisely led Darwin in the opposite direction down a hallway where they disappeared from my view.

I went back, got my coffee, and sat down for a minute in a cozy, overstuffed chenille chair to replay what I had just seen. Darwin was obviously losing it. Was he losing it because he did something to his wife, or was he losing it because Pamela's parents *thought* he did something to his wife? It was hard to tell, considering I was not within earshot of their conversation. Either scenario seemed possible.

I couldn't blame Pamela's parents for looking at Darwin suspiciously. He hadn't exactly presented himself as the most authentic and empathetic husband at the press conference. He flatlined. His words came out monotone, like he was reciting his grocery list instead of talking about his missing wife. This, of course, didn't mean he had anything to do with Pamela's disappearance, but it certainly didn't help create a positive impression of him. He came across as anxious, someone who seemed to be hiding something.

Could he have done something to Pamela that made her want to run away? To disappear? Maybe he was abusive, or maybe he was unfaithful? Maybe she took this opportunity to get away from this man?

The only way to know for sure what had just happened between Darwin and the couple was to go straight to Darwin and ask him. However, I figured this tactic was probably not going to work. When I asked my question about the recovery mission during the press conference, I saw him glaring at me. Sure, I knew it was an insensitive question, but I was trying to get the investigator to tell us the truth about what was really going on here. There is a very good chance Pamela Stevens is already dead. This is the truth. But in hindsight, I guess it wouldn't have hurt for me to be a little more diplomatic about this perspective in front of her husband and parents.

I reluctantly pulled myself out of the cozy chair and went in the direction I saw the men taking Darwin. I was looking at my phone as I walked down the long hallway and almost bumped straight into Eddie and Wilson.

"Hi guys. Looks like you just broke up a potential wrestling match," I said, hoping my sarcastic barb would encourage them to share some information with me.

"Oh, nothing like that, Mrs. Finch. Just a few words exchanged, that's all," Wilson said, taking the lead and giving Eddie a stern don't-you-dare-say-anything look. "Nothing to worry about. We got it under control. You know how families can be, especially during a stressful time like this."

"It's a lucky thing you were there. Who knows what would have happened if you hadn't been?" I said, trying to keep them talking with me. But my witty banter was not drawing them in. They both just stared at me like I had said something grossly inappropriate. After a few seconds of silence, Eddie finally spoke.

"Mrs. Finch, you have a good day now," he said, tipping the brim of his camouflage baseball hat in my direction as he and Wilson walked away. It was obvious that they did not want to speak with me one second longer than they had to. It was not prudent for them to share dirty laundry about another guest. I had found them to be so chatty when I met them out on the property doing their jobs. Today, that chattiness was gone.

    I continued down the hallway until I spotted Darwin sitting alone on a bench. He was in front of the resort manager's office. I wondered if he was waiting to see the principal, a.k.a. Evelyn, about his little outburst in front of the restaurant. I walked slowly by him and looked back, wondering if I should just plop down next to him and start talking. Then, he abruptly turned his head away from me, a sure signal that he was not interested in anything I might have to say. I kept walking and sped up my pace. *Don't worry, Darwin,* I thought to myself. *I'm not done with you yet. Not by a longshot.*

When I got back to the cottage, I decided to give Matt a call and fill him in on what had been going on. His anger had subsided. That's how relationships worked. One day, you were so mad at your spouse you wanted to spit at him; the next day, you forgot all about it, or at least buried it, because life kept moving on—there were meals to make, bills to pay, children to care for, and jobs to do. There was no time to allow minor disagreements to deplete your precious energy or focus. Matt and I were pretty good at putting trivial stuff behind us. This was one of the biggest secrets to our success as a married couple.

    Matt's emotions about the situation had morphed from anger into concern over how deep I might be getting into this case. He didn't want to see me go down a dangerous path again, like I had with Carol Lee. But I could tell he was reticent to bring it up, scared to unearth that bad chapter in our lives—as if saying it out loud might summon the ghosts.

"So, Pamela's husband almost came to blows in the lobby a little while ago with her parents. Two workers had to pull him away to keep it from getting physical. I swear, I thought he was going to take a swing at them. It was wild."

"That's crazy. Sounds like he's got something to hide," Matt said like the wannabe detective he always played when I was working on a complicated case and shared the details with him.

"Not necessarily. I think it's only natural for the parents to put some of the blame on him in a situation like this, even if it's unfounded. But he's certainly not handling it very well. He should just ignore them and chalk it up to them being terrified about what might have happened to their daughter."

"Look, I just want to make sure you're not getting too involved, like you did with . . ."

Matt stopped midsentence. I knew he did not want to say Carol Lee's name out loud, as if the mere act of saying her name might send me right back to that dark bedroom where I spent ten days, not knowing if I could ever function again.

"Say her name, Matt. Carol Lee. It's okay. I'm okay. That is not happening again. I'm focused on getting the facts, getting my story, and getting out of here, then getting home to you guys. I promise things are different now. I can handle this. How are the boys?" I said, trying to reassure him and deflect his attention.

Just as I asked the question, I heard what sounded like an explosion coming from somewhere in the distance behind Matt.

"Video games," he said bashfully.

"What did I tell you about that?"

"Look, I needed a couple of hours to get some work done. They've been all over me every minute. I haven't been able to get anything done. Don't forget, we used to park them in front of the TV when they were little. This isn't going to permanently damage them."

"That was different. They were watching cartoons. They

weren't playing games where they were killing people. I'm telling you, I've read a lot about this. It makes them more aggressive. I don't like it."

"Okay, I'll make them stop when I get off the phone. But listen, Celia, be careful, honey. Okay? Take care of yourself, and come home to us soon. I need you! I'm drowning here."

At that moment, there was another explosion in the background, and the sound of the boys cheering in tandem. At least they were cheering together and not fighting.

"I promise I will. I love you."

"Got to go!" he said abruptly, and then the line went dead.

I sat on the edge of the patchwork quilt neatly folded at the end of the bed and wondered how I had gotten so lucky. I also wondered if Pamela had been unlucky when she married Darwin.

14

JACK CAVING

If it weren't for Cindy, I probably wouldn't be alive. Even though sometimes I secretly thought she believed I was a loser. The words that came out of her mouth continued to amaze me and contradict this extreme insecurity. She lifted me out of the darkness on a daily basis.

"Look, the state police pulling out means nothing. This is your case, not theirs. Good riddance, frankly. You can handle this. You will do a better job than they ever could because you care. This is your community. Your home. You have a personal stake in finding this woman."

I watched as Cindy twisted the spaghetti neatly around her fork and brought it up to her delicate mouth, a delicate mouth whose toughness continued to impress me even after so many years of marriage.

"I know, but I just hope we'll have enough people to continue the search."

"You will. Believe in your powers of persuasion. You said that woman, Evelyn, was going to give you some bodies. There are also plenty of people in the community who will volunteer. I know it's going to work out. I know you're going to find her.

Now, eat up. You need your fuel to keep going at this intense pace."

I knew she was right. I looked down at my plate and realized I hadn't touched a thing. Steam was still rising off the tomato sauce as I cut into a meatball and started to slice it into small pieces. I had no appetite, but I didn't want to offend Cindy. She always said that if someone bothered to make you a meal, you needed to appreciate it no matter what. I had taken that mantra to heart based on the size of my expansive gut.

When I closed my eyes and tried to imagine where Pamela Stevens might be, all I could see was Rosa: Rosa being brutally raped by Billy Barnes, battered Rosa in her shredded scrubs, Rosa lifeless in her bed after taking all those pills. I had blood on my hands for what I did to her. Nothing would ever make it right, not even finding Pamela. I knew this, but I still believed it would bring me some solace to find Pamela, solace that I had been missing for so long.

"Jack, this case isn't about Rosa," Cindy said in her uncanny tone that let me know she had always been able to read my mind. "This is about finding Pamela Stevens. You have atoned for Rosa's death for so many years. You're a good man. You work hard. You care. You need to believe in yourself the way I believe in you."

I wanted to hold onto Cindy's words and wipe away all the pain I had gone through for the last decade over my lie that led to Rosa's death, but even Cindy's faith in me couldn't change the fact that when I looked in the mirror, I saw only the lie. It hung over me like a lingering storm cloud, the voice of self-doubt in my head always mocking me and taunting me, telling me I wasn't good enough, that I would never be good enough.

It was dark now, and the house was quiet. Cindy was sleeping next to me, her face looking serene and calm on the plump pillow. I tried to focus on her rhythmic breathing, to let it lull me to sleep. This time when I closed my eyes, I didn't see

Rosa. Instead, I saw Pamela covered in bruises and cuts, dragging an injured leg through the forest, stopping to lean against trees as she struggled slowly to make her way through the dark night. Suddenly, I knew beyond a shadow of a doubt that Pamela Stevens was still out there, alive, waiting for me to find her. I had to make it happen for her and her family, and for me. I had to find a way to become the hero I always wanted to be.

15

EVELYN REMEMBERS

I CAN CLOSE MY EYES AND REMEMBER THAT FEELING like it was yesterday—feeling so hungry that I thought the acid in my stomach might start eating away at my organs, devouring them one cell at a time, and eventually, make its way to my skin until I dissolved into nothingness. This seemed like a better alternative than lying there in pain starving to death.

I would curl up in my tiny bed under a pile of blankets in a fetal position and try not to think about it. *Mama will be home soon. She will bring food with her.* And sometimes she did bring something from the food pantry—canned meat, beans, peanut butter, bags of rice. Even today, I can sit with a spoon and scrape a jar of peanut butter clean, savoring each creamy delicious bite as if I were eating some gourmet delicacy.

In my new life, I had found discipline. Now, because I could afford to eat whatever I wanted, I chose to eat healthy, fresh foods in moderate portions. This was what kept me looking so svelte—that and yoga. Sometimes, I pretended I was a ballet dancer, flowing elegantly down a hallway like I was about to take the stage. As a child, when I looked in the mirror and saw my gaunt frame, it screamed poverty. Now, my lithe appearance tells a different story. *She's a woman who really takes care of herself because she has the means to do so.*

Still, it didn't take much to bring me back to my childhood angst. I remembered standing on the countertop in the kitchen when I was just three or four and looking in all the upper shelves of the cabinets to see if, by chance, my mother had hidden some food there and forgotten about it.

During the school year, because I was from a low-income family, I received free breakfast and lunch in the cafeteria. So, even if I had to skip dinner because there was no food in my house, I could make it until the next morning. But on the weekends and during vacations, my stomach growled in constant pain, turning itself inside out until I felt so weak that I just wanted to sit in a chair and watch television. And that's exactly what I did day in and day out for many of my formative years.

I learned my lesson about keeping our family's secret at school one Monday morning when I let it slip to my physical education teacher that I hadn't eaten all weekend and couldn't possibly run four laps around the gym with my classmates. The PE teacher told the school guidance counselor. The guidance counselor called my mother. The next day, a social worker came to our house to interview my mother and see for herself what the situation was. Luckily, my mother had anticipated this scenario. She cracked open my piggy bank, scooping up all the quarters I had found and saved over the years into a plastic grocery bag. She came back with three bags of groceries and put them away like this was normal for us. Right before the social worker arrived, she made me pork chops, green beans, and mashed potatoes. She set the plate full of hot food in front of me just as the doorbell rang.

"Eat this slowly, you hear, not like an animal," she scolded me through gritted teeth. "And don't eat with your hands."

I did as I was told. In truth, I was savoring each bite because I had never had a meal like this before. I pretended this was the way we really lived, putting my napkin on my lap and sipping the iced tea in front of me like a lady who had all the time in the world to lounge at the scratched wooden kitchen table and eat a delicious home-cooked meal prepared just for me. The social worker looked at me with interest. She wrote notes in her little blue spiral notebook. My mom opened the refrigerator and cabinets to show her that we had plenty of food. Then, she told her I was just a picky eater, and that my comments about not eating over the weekend involved a particular meal where I refused to eat what was on my plate, and she made me go to bed hungry. That was all, my mother said: no crisis, just some tough love.

By the end of the hour-long visit, my mother had sufficiently charmed the social worker into believing that everything was fine in our house, that she was a good mother, and I was simply a fussy little girl with a big imagination and an even bigger mouth. They were so friendly toward one another that I thought they might hug when the woman finally left.

"Don't you *ever* pull a stunt like that again, young lady. I'm doing the best I can. I'm working three jobs to keep a roof over our heads. If you don't like it, you can go to foster care. That's what will happen if a social worker comes around again. And I promise you, foster care will be a whole lot worse than living here."

My mother turned and walked down the hallway to her bedroom. I sat quietly, chewing a bite of my pork chop, trying to make it last as long as possible.

When I saw Martin's text, I felt like that little girl in that dingy apartment, crying and holding my belly.

"I'm on my way. I'm coming to clean up the mess you've made," it read.

I stared at it, reading it over and over again, as if I had missed something. Maybe he didn't really mean it the way it sounded? Maybe he was being sarcastic? But I knew better than that. Martin had no sense of humor. He was coming to North Carolina to take care of business. He was coming here to fire me.

I knew it was crazy to imagine that losing this job would plunge me back into a life of poverty and despair. I had saved plenty of money in my years working at the Bingham Reserve. I could even afford to take a few months off in between jobs. And with a fancy position like this one on my resume, I could probably write my own ticket. So, why was him coming here sending me into such a tizzy? Why couldn't I just be rational and face whatever he had to say to me? I already knew the answer. I was taught by my mother that even when you did get something you thought made you special, it could be taken away in a second. She reminded me every single day that I was not special, certainly not good enough to be rewarded with things like a fancy job with a title and a nice paycheck.

My mother walked back down the hall that night after the social worker left to see me still in the kitchen, chewing on a piece of pork chop. She grabbed the plate and poured the contents down the disposal in the sink, letting the grinding sound go on for what seemed like an eternity. When it stopped, she calmly wiped her hands on the dish towel and slowly turned to me and said, "That will show you not to tell lies to your teachers again. If you do, there will be no food, not even from the food pantry."

I slunk away to my room and cried myself to sleep, imagining all the fresh food that was still in the cabinets and the refrigerator. At least there would be something to eat in the morning. But when I woke up, the house was quiet. My mother was gone, and so was the food. She had taken it all away. My stomach rumbled as hot tears began rolling down my face, stinging my cheeks.

There was a faint knock on my office door. Could it be Martin already? Did he send the text and then hop right on his private plane? It would still have taken him several hours to get here between the flying time and the ride from the airport. Reluctantly, I pulled open the door to see Darwin looking weary and slightly drunk.

"Evelyn, I wanted to let you know I am leaving, heading home to DC to be with my daughter. I just can't take the stress of being here anymore."

I ushered him into my office and motioned for him to sit down on the couch. The poor man looked like he might just collapse and fall into a deep sleep right there in front of me. But he managed to stay upright and silent for a moment. I waited for him to speak again.

"I know this looks bad for me to leave in the middle of the search, but the way everyone here stares at me, like I've done something wrong, it's all too much. I need to be home with people who love and support me. I need to be away from all this. I especially need to be away from Pamela's parents. I hope you understand."

Darwin motioned to the window, presumably indicating the search that was taking place deep within the woods, beyond the large field, in places we couldn't see from here. Even though the view was beautiful, the mountain was like a living, breathing animal that could swallow a person whole if they didn't watch their step. I turned away from the window and tried to erase the thought of the mountain winking at me, asking me to keep its secrets.

I almost felt sorry for Darwin, but at the same time, I did think it was very strange for him to leave right now. Pamela had to be here somewhere. Chances were that we would eventually find her—at least her body. And the thought that he would not want to be here to identify her and put closure on this nightmare made no sense to me. Unless, of course, he was guilty of something.

"Darwin, I understand where you're coming from. But maybe we could put you in a more remote residence where no one will bother you, where you can get some rest, but still be close if they find something."

"If they find *something*? If they find something, it will probably be my wife's dead body. I don't think I can handle the thought of it."

Darwin put his head in his hands and began to cry. At first, it was just quiet whimpering, but then the whimpers turned into sobs that made his entire body heave and shudder as he gulped for air. I handed him a box of tissues with one hand and put my other hand on his shoulder.

"You can't think that way. We need to have some hope. *You* need to have some hope. That's the only way you're going to get through this. Ignore those people and their looks. Who cares? This isn't about what other people think. It's about finding Pamela and bringing her home. Screw them."

When I said the word "screw," Darwin looked up at me through his tears and grinned. I had touched a nerve. Hearing that word coming out of such a proper woman's mouth had made him smile. He dabbed his eyes with a tissue and then blew his nose.

"Look, I appreciate everything you've done for me. I really do. Letting me and our family stay here indefinitely, trying to make me comfortable, but I've just got to go. I can't explain it. The longer I stay here . . . my mind is starting to play tricks on me. I'm starting to wonder if maybe I really *did* do something to hurt Pamela, but I've just blocked it from my brain. I know that sounds crazy, but I don't know what's real anymore. I just need a break for a few days. I'll be back. I promise."

I did think it was odd that he was hallucinating the fact that maybe he did hurt his wife when we all knew where he was the entire time she was gone—at the bar, drinking, watching tennis. *He must really be losing.* If he started talking this way around Jack, he might get himself into real trouble. And if that nosy reporter got a whiff of any of this, it would be the headline the next day. No, Darwin Stevens should not be here. He needed to leave as soon as possible, and I would help him do that.

"I guess you're right. You do need a break. I'll make arrangements for your flight and get you to the airport. How soon can you be ready?"

"Fifteen minutes."

"Good. I will text you when it's time to meet Morris on the side of the inn, near the bike area. We don't want to cause a commotion when you leave. Best to just let everyone think you are hibernating in one of the remote cottages on the property."

I knew Darwin's leaving would raise suspicions about him, especially when Jack heard about it.

16

DARWIN RETREATS

EVELYN PATTED ME ON THE BACK AS I LEFT HER office. She was a kind person. I almost felt bad for the way I had acted, crying like a baby on her couch, making this whole thing about me when it was really about Pamela. Still, I knew I played it just right. I had to get her blessing to leave. It was selfish of me to be thinking about my feelings when Pamela was still out there somewhere alone, injured, fighting to get home. Yet, somehow, I made myself look pitiful to Evelyn instead of selfish. That was the goal, and it worked.

I wasn't sure how she would react when I shared with her my fears that maybe I did do something to Pamela and just didn't remember it. It was a spur-of-the-moment thing to say. I just blurted it out without really thinking about the consequences. Thankfully, she reacted very calmly, but maybe that was just an act. Maybe she picked up the phone and called that hillbilly cop the minute I left her office and told him what I had said. Maybe her offer to get me a flight and a ride to the airport was just a ruse to make me feel comfortable so I wouldn't suspect that she was sending the burly investigator to arrest me.

Or maybe, just maybe, I was overthinking everything. Maybe

Joan and Alex had made me so paranoid that I was constantly on edge, starting to doubt myself and my ability to keep it together. Evelyn seemed like a nice person, an honest person, not someone who would pretend to be compassionate and then double-cross me. I didn't have anyone I could talk to. I certainly couldn't talk to Dallas. He had a way of making everything worse, smiling and slapping me on the back and saying all the wrong things. For some reason, Evelyn just felt like someone I could talk to, but confiding in her was a risk. I knew that with clarity now. I only hoped that she would have some mercy on me and keep it to herself, that she would just think it was the crazy ramblings of a grieving and confused man.

One thing I was not confused about was what happened at work: the texts between Victoria and me. The texts that had been taken out of context and used against me by my manager. I had worked so hard to keep Pamela from ever knowing about the whole debacle. I was pretty sure I had succeeded, but now I was beginning to doubt myself. Maybe Pamela found out, and maybe she disappeared intentionally. Was that even possible? Could she pull something like that off? I was pretty sure Pamela could do just about anything she set her mind to.

It was definitely time for me to go back to DC, to blend into the cacophony of the city streets where no one would stare at me or even pay attention to me. I would once again become a faceless person in a sea of urban chaos. This was exactly what I needed right now. Even if it was just for a day or two so I could regroup and figure out my next move.

As promised, Evelyn booked me on the first available flight, which left the next morning from Charlotte at 8:00 a.m. This meant we had to leave the resort at 5:00 a.m. to make the hour-

and-a-half-long drive to the airport. Dallas had decided to leave as well. Even though he was thoroughly enjoying his all-expense-paid vacation with its luxurious perks, he realized, wisely, that it was also time for him to get out of town, that it made no sense for him to be here without me. His flight to New York was later in the day, so I traveled in the van with only Morris, the driver, for company.

"Surprised to see you leaving so soon, with the search still going on and all," Morris said in the dark van as I was starting to doze off in the backseat. He said it with more curiosity than judgment. I looked up to see us driving through a gauntlet of tall trees lining the winding road. They were silhouetted against the early morning sky, still bathed in moonlight. I felt like they were crowding us, coming in closer with every bend in the dark road that seemed to be no match for the van's headlights. I couldn't wait to get out of this place. There was a darkness beneath all the radiant beauty, a darkness that had taken my Pamela away.

"Well, it was getting pretty hard to stay."

"I get it. Lots of people looking at you, I guess."

I was taken aback by his boldness. It seemed to me that an employee of a fancy resort might want to keep his mouth shut at a time like this. He was starting to annoy me, but I knew I had to keep myself in check. I couldn't risk revealing myself to Morris or anyone else. I knew better than to take any more risks. The situation with Victoria had taught me that.

"Yes, it was pretty rough."

"I imagine it was."

I sat with his statement alone in the dark as the van wound around the hairpin turns—any single one could result in us plunging to our deaths over the edge of the mountain. The skeletal-looking trees that loomed above us seemed like they might reach out and grab the van with their spindly branches and crush us into oblivion. Morris held the wheel loosely with one hand, maneuvering the vehicle adeptly down the treacherous road like he had done it a hundred times before. He probably had done it a hundred times before. I decided I would use the darkness as a protective cloak and get up my courage to ask him about what people were saying.

"What do you think happened to her, to my wife?"

"What do I think?" Morris asked with surprise in his voice, suddenly not so bold, as if no one had ever asked his opinion about anything in his entire life.

"Yes, I'm curious. You're from here. You obviously know this area, these people. You know how people think here. What's your gut telling you?"

"Well, no disrespect, Mr. Stevens, but I think she probably fell. It's real easy to fall off the edge of these trails if you don't know the area well. It happens from time to time. And it's a long way down. Not survivable, I'm sorry to say."

"Okay. That sounds logical, but then what? Where is she? How come no one can find her? Shouldn't we at least be able to locate her body and put an end to this nightmare?"

"You would think so. But that's where it gets a little more complicated," Morris said as he finally reached the bottom of the mountain and pulled onto the flat highway that would take us to Charlotte. "I mean, it's rugged terrain out here. Lots of craggy rocks sticking out that you could hit on your way down. Then you have to consider the wildlife, the scavengers waiting for a feast. You'd be surprised how far a buzzard can spread the remains of a human body. There's a legend that a man fell from the trail here about forty years ago, and they found his femur near Charlottesville, Virginia, in a vineyard about three hundred fifty miles away. Turkey vultures, that's what buzzards are, can fly up to two hundred miles a day. They say one of them carried that man's femur bone for at least two days and then dropped it in Virginia."

Suddenly, I felt like I was going to be sick. Why did this man think it was okay to talk about human remains like it was nothing in the context of my wife's disappearance? I yelled at Morris to pull over to the side of the road. He did, and I jumped out of the van onto the gravel right-of-way just in time to vomit in the grass at the edge of the pavement. Morris stood over me and handed me a towel to wipe my mouth and a bottle of water.

We got back in the van and rode in silence the rest of the way.

As I slept on the plane, my head coddled by the luxury of the first-class seat that Evelyn had booked for me at the resort's expense, I dreamed of Pamela. I watched her walk away again, off on her hike, a wry smile on her face, giving me her signature beauty queen wave. Gone were all the feelings of resentment between us, the fights over money, the disagreements about our future, and how my daughter, Polly, fit into that future. Instead, I felt only warmth and genuine love toward her. Her disappearance had healed me from the little bits of anger that had woven themselves into our marriage without me even realizing it. Before you know it, you wake up one day angry at your spouse for no reason, and then just stay that way. It goes on for so long, you don't even remember what you were mad about in the first place.

It was this anger that had led me to Victoria. Pretty, simple, easy Victoria. The texts were just words, banter. They meant nothing. It was just a game. First, I wanted to get her attention. I did that. Then I wanted to keep her attention. And that's where things went very, very wrong.

But I wasn't mad at Victoria anymore for getting me in trouble at work, and I wasn't mad at Pamela for the many years of mutual transgressions. I was mad at myself. I was more sure than ever that I still loved Pamela, that if I had another chance, I was determined we could get rid of all the stupid baggage we were carrying around and go back to basics, just the two of us.

I startled awake when the flight attendant came over the loudspeaker to tell us we would be landing soon. I wiped some drool off my mouth, ran a hand through my messy hair, pulled my seat back up, stowed the tray table in front of me, and looked out the window at the swirling clouds below. I wondered for the hundredth time where Pamela had ended up, and I wondered if maybe she was looking at the same clouds I was. It strangely comforted me to think this.

My dream had been an epiphany. I realized that I truly did love my wife, and I missed her terribly. More than anything, I wanted her back. Now awake, I had another epiphany. I knew it was too late.

17

CELIA CONTINUES

THE MISSING HIKER STORY HAD GONE NATIONAL, AND other newspapers were picking up my reports with my byline. So, I stayed at Bingham and continued working. Stories like this came around very rarely in a journalist's career.

Matt was not thrilled with my new gig, but he wisely kept quiet and gently reminded me every time I talked to him not to get too obsessed. Under his breath, I imagined him whispering the cautionary words—*Carol Lee*. Even though it had been only a few days since Pamela's disappearance, everyone knew that she was probably dead. But where was her body? Why had no one found her after so much intense searching? It didn't make any sense.

I wanted to pick Jack Sorrells' brain, but we had gotten off on the wrong foot at the press conference, and I wasn't sure how to patch things up with him. He had been cordial enough to me after that, professional for sure, but there were obviously some feelings stewing beneath his words when he spoke to me through visibly gritted teeth. Somehow, I needed to penetrate his coolness and make him realize that I wanted exactly what he wanted: for the searchers to find Pamela, dead or alive, and bring some resolution to this nightmare for everyone involved.

I texted Jack and then called him as soon as I got back to my cottage on day three of the search, exhausted from spinning my wheels all day long, talking to volunteers who had come up with nothing. I had borrowed a car for the day from the resort and gone to the closest town, Laurel, to interview locals about their thoughts. When I returned that evening, I parked the car at the bottom of the serpentine road and let Morris take me back up in the van. Shadows of the imposing trees with their skeletal branches were just beginning to form on the asphalt beneath the full moon. Once again, I was reminded that this place held secrets far beyond the disappearance of Pamela Stevens. It was an imposing, unforgiving ecosystem that we were no match for.

When Morris delivered me to my cottage, I asked him to come in and look at my television remote. Without Matt or the boys to help me, I couldn't figure out how the complicated thing with a gazillion buttons worked. I had spent the last few nights squinting through my reading glasses as I watched Netflix on my phone. Given that Morris was younger, I assumed he probably understood the complex technology of smart televisions much better than I did.

He was more than happy to help, either out of sheer boredom or the expectation of a big tip. Too late, my radar went up thinking how it was not so smart to invite a man I didn't know into my remote cottage at night. But after a few minutes of friendly banter, during which he stared intently at the TV and then occasionally looked down to study the remote, I became more comfortable.

"Morris, how do you think the search is going? I mean it's still pretty active, right?"

"Yes, ma'am," Morris replied, his eyes still fixated on the screen as he went through a series of buttons on the remote.

"Are there a lot of people still searching?" I asked. Even

though I knew the answer to this question after my day spent with the volunteers, I wanted his take on it.

"It's slowed down a bit. I mean our boss, Miss Evelyn, she's still making us do it every day—well, at least some of us, but nothing's coming of it. So, not sure how much longer we'll do it."

"She's *making* you do it? I thought the employees here wanted to be part of the search?"

"Oh, sure, it's great to get out of work and walk the trails all day. But it gets a little old when you don't find anything, plus there's no love lost between us and them."

Morris smiled as he finally figured out how to pull up my Netflix account on the screen. I could see the triumph in his eyes. Man against television. Man wins. He then turned to look at me for the first time during our conversation.

"Who is 'us and them'? What exactly do you mean by that?" I asked now that I had his full attention, and I assumed he was patiently waiting for his tip.

"You know, the locals and the guests. No disrespect, Mrs. Finch, but some of the visitors here aren't exactly cordial to us. There's a lot of friction. We do our jobs the best we can, hoping for some good tips, as you can imagine. But there are people you just can't please, no matter what you do. It can be really frustrating. And frankly, sometimes they're downright ugly to us. And we still have to smile and take it. Miss Evelyn tells us never to confront a guest."

He looked toward the door, certain he had said too much. He then looked back and handed me the remote. I reached into my pocket and pulled out the first crumpled bill I could find. It was a twenty. I handed it to him.

"Oh, that's too much," Morris said, looking like the bill might burn him if he touched it. "I just figured out your TV for you, that's all. I was glad to do it." It seemed like he was trying to walk back spilling too much information by rejecting the tip.

"Nonsense, just consider it extra for all the times I should have tipped you and didn't. Plus, you don't realize how happy you've made me. Now, I don't have to balance my phone on my knees and squint in the dark if I want to watch something."

He smiled and took the bill, smoothing it out before folding it in half and sliding it into his back pocket.

"If I were you, I'd just leave that television on all the time while you're here and turn the volume down. That way, you don't have to mess with it again. And by the way, I wasn't talking about you when I said that thing about visitors not being cordial. You've always been real nice to me, to everyone. Hope I didn't insult you or anything. If I did, I'm sorry for that."

"No worries. You didn't. I promise. I get it. I meet a lot of jerks in my line of work too. Why can't people just be kind? It's not that hard to do."

He nodded at me knowingly. I was surprised to hear Morris talk so much. It was the most words he had ever said in my presence at one time. He turned toward the door to leave, but I had one more question for him. I knew that if I didn't ask it now, I might never have the chance to do it.

"Morris, one more thing."

He turned back to look at me, his pale skin turning pink beneath his red mop of unruly hair, as if I might be about to make a pass at him. This was the furthest thing from my mind, but it was still kind of flattering that he might be thinking this.

"Was Pamela one of those guests?"

"Ma'am?"

"The difficult kind, the kind that rubbed the locals the wrong way?"

"I'd rather not say, Mrs. Finch, if that's okay. Have a good night. Thanks again for the generous tip. I really appreciate it."

Morris' chatty demeanor evaporated as quickly as it had arrived. The screen door slammed shut behind him. As I watched the taillights of the van scream down the driveway, the back tires kicking up gravel in its wake, I realized that Morris had just given me a very important clue without saying anything at all.

I locked the door behind him and grabbed a blanket from the couch to wrap around me. As I looked out into the dark forest, I suddenly had a chill. I wished that Matt were here with me. There was something so unsettling about being alone in a cottage surrounded by the dark place that had taken Pamela.

The next morning, I headed to the lodge to see who might be around to talk to. I needed to find someone who would confirm my suspicions that Pamela was not the most gracious resort guest. Evelyn had already told me that her interaction with the missing woman was "lovely," but I expected nothing less from the hoity-toity manager of a swanky resort trying to keep a story from ruining their reputation.

I figured most of the other employees would act the same way Morris did if I probed them—skittish about criticizing a woman who was most likely dead. Logically, the fact that she was less than kind to the workers here probably had nothing to do with her disappearance, but it might have something to do with how much effort the staff was putting into the search. I figured the person who most needed to know this was my pal Jack Sorrells. As if I had summoned him through a crystal ball, he suddenly appeared, coming out of Evelyn's office as I rounded the corner.

"Investigator Sorrells, can I have a word?"

He turned to me with an audible sigh. I thought I saw an eye roll as well, but I was not deterred. I had turned tougher people than Jack Sorrells before, ultimately winning them over with my humor and authenticity, even if our first meeting was a little heated.

"I'm in a hurry, Miss Finch."

"I called you *and* texted you."

"I know, but we have nothing new to share. That's why I didn't return your calls or texts," he said with exasperation in his voice, like he might be ready to blow up at me.

"Can we make a truce?" I asked, jutting my hand out in his direction for a shake.

"A truce?" he asked, looking bewildered.

"I think we got off on the wrong foot, and I'm sorry for that. We both want the same thing, for Pamela Stevens to be found."

He shook my hand tentatively and shook his head at the same time.

"Miss Finch, if you think I've been stewing over a reporter's insensitive question while I am conducting a major search for a missing woman, then you don't know me at all. I haven't given it a second thought. I'm a little bit busy if you haven't noticed."

"I understand. And I'd like to tell the story behind this massive effort, an effort that you seem to be single-handedly leading. You never know, it could help generate some leads. I'm pretty sure there's no such thing as bad publicity in a missing person case. Can we just get a cup of coffee? I promise I won't take up a lot of your time."

He looked down at the file in his hand, and then back at Evelyn's office door. Despite his large stature, Jack Sorrells had a soft quality about him, like his tough cop exterior was a costume he put on for work every day. Off the clock, I imagined he was a kind, sensitive person who ate dinner with his family each night and revered his wife.

"Okay, one cup of coffee. But I can only talk on the public record about things that will help move this case forward. I'm not giving you anything off the record, even on background."

This was not Jack Sorrells' first interaction with the media. I had googled him and read the articles about the Billy Barnes rape case that had been thrown out because Jack botched the chain of evidence protocol and then lied about it in court. I learned about his subsequent suspension and fall from grace and the victim's eventual suicide. But I also learned that over the past decade, Jack had worked his way back up the ranks instead of quitting like most people would have under the circumstances. He could have left his job with his tail between his legs and started over in another community where people didn't know about his mistakes. But he didn't. He stuck it out. In my eyes, that made him even more tenacious and honorable because he stayed to atone for what he had done. And even though he did make some serious mistakes, I firmly believed he didn't cause that woman's suicide. Billy Barnes did.

"Have you heard anyone say that Pamela Stevens was not the nicest guest?"

The major put his coffee cup down with his big, beefy hand. He looked up at me, studying my face. His hand looked like it could crush the delicate cup on the gold-rimmed saucer in front of him with one swift movement. He sat silently for a moment, staring at me as if he were assessing my credibility with his special detective superpowers.

"Can we go off the record?"

"I thought we weren't going off the record."

"I changed my mind. Can't a person change his mind?"

"Of course. Yes, we can go off the record."

"So, the brief answer is yes. She was apparently a bit of a diva despite her outdoorsy persona. Short with some of the staff, overly demanding, but nothing that rises to the level of someone wanting to hurt her. Why? What have you heard?"

"Not much. Basically some of the same," I said, stretching my interpretation of what Morris didn't tell me.

"I'm not sure it's relevant," he quipped.

"It might not be, but it might be. Especially since the staff is part of the search team. They may not be trying very hard if they don't like her."

"True. I hadn't thought of that. But that's a pretty big leap. Most people want to do the right thing, even when it's hard."

The major folded his hands and looked up at the heavy wooden crossbeams of the vaulted ceiling as if the answer to all these questions might be dangling there from a fishing line.

"Look, I'm a journalist. But I'm also a human being. I would like to see you solve this case. We might be able to help each other, off the record, of course, sharing information that could be beneficial to both of us. I promise I won't burn you. That's not who I am or what I do. You can check with my law enforcement sources in Pennsylvania. They'll vouch for me."

The major picked up the fragile porcelain cup, took another sip of his coffee, and then set it back down delicately on the table. He smiled at me for the first time since I met him. We had a deal.

18

JACK, GIVING UP

THE PHILADELPHIA REPORTER MADE ME THINK I could still do this. She acted like we were in some conspiracy together, like it was me and her against the world, that together we would find Pamela Stevens. I almost believed her.

Frankly, she was growing on me. I had misjudged her in our first encounter. I had mistaken her Yankee brashness for a lack of caring. It was clear that she did care; she just went about it in a different way than we did here in North Carolina. But even with her passion for solving this case, I was up against a wall. Sheriff Lansing was running out of patience. Even though it had only been a few days, he didn't want to invest any more resources in the search.

"Jack, you've done the best you could. We just can't keep sending people day after day out there into the woods to search for this woman and leave the rest of the county uncovered. We've got a big job to do and lots of people depending on us." I could hear the old leather in his swivel chair crunch over the phone as he leaned back into it. I had seen him in person so many times like this, pensive, looking up at the ceiling as he cradled the phone at the nape of his neck. He didn't like uncomfortable conversations.

I tried to explain to Sheriff Lansing that I was using volunteers from the community and from the resort, that only three of our guys were being tied up on a daily basis. But three was too many when we had so many miles to cover here in Annandale County.

"You know even three is too much on a shoestring budget like ours, Jack," he said. The leather crunched again, and the wheels of his chair squealed as he slid on the parquet floor of the old office. I closed my eyes and pictured him there like something from another era. "It's time to let this go. You fought hard. I'm proud of you. Eventually, someone will stumble across her. A hunter. A hiker. It may be next week, next month, or even next year. But we can't keep this going. It's just not feasible. You know it, and I know it."

I sat there silently in my patrol car, looking at my hands, knowing that Aubrey Lansing was thinking the same thing I was thinking—that finding Pamela Stevens wouldn't make up for letting Billy Barnes go. It wouldn't make up for letting Rosa down. I knew he wouldn't say it out loud; he was too good of a man, but he was thinking it, and his thought hung there between us, moored in the silence.

I ended the call feeling defeated, wondering how I was going to keep the search going without his blessing. The truth was that I couldn't. It would be impossible. The proverbial writing was on the wall. It was time to give up, to let go. I had failed again, and this was my fate, my punishment that I continued to live through over and over, every single day. I simply couldn't get ahead of it. I was doomed to repeat my mistakes.

I knew it was Martin the second he walked down the hallway. Evelyn had described him to me—a rich, young, hipster techie from California. It wasn't hard to spot someone like that in the mountains of North Carolina. He stood out in his fitted pants cuffed at the ankles, his fancy leather slip-on shoes, and his skin-tight, pink golf shirt tucked into his waistband and cinched with what looked like a snakeskin belt. I wouldn't be caught dead in that outfit. But it caught my attention, and that's exactly what he was going for.

"You must be the investigator in charge," the hipster said, thrusting a hand in my direction. At least he had manners.

"Yes, and you are?" I asked, catching him off guard as I pretended not to be awed by his presence. I really didn't want to be, but this guy screamed high society. I was more than just a little bit awed. I also couldn't ever remember properly meeting someone from California. This was a first for me on many levels.

"Martin Bingham, the owner. This is my resort. I just got in from California. Exhausted, but I needed to be here to handle this situation. Can we chat?"

I followed the hipster into a large office next to Evelyn's. It was luxurious with a massive fireplace, floor-to-ceiling windows, a formidable, polished mahogany desk, and two leather couches separated by a marble coffee table sitting atop an Oriental rug. The whole thing looked like something out of one of those HGTV shows Cindy was so fond of, where they featured spaces owned and decorated for the rich and famous.

"Please sit down," the hipster said and motioned to one of the couches.

I sat down and immediately regretted it as I sank deep into the cushion. I wondered how I was ever going to get up. I had to put the thought aside so that I could concentrate on what Martin was about to say. I would deal with the awkward exit when it was time.

"Major Sorrells—Jack—may I call you Jack? You can call me

Martin," the hipster said in a passive-aggressive tone, sitting down on the couch opposite from where I was sitting. His skinny frame barely made a dent in the cushion.

"Sure," I said, shifting uncomfortably in the sinking cushion that I was silently battling. Luckily, Martin appeared to be such a narcissist that he wasn't paying any attention to me at all. Instead, he was thinking about the words he had prepared for me.

"As you can imagine, this situation is not good for my business. It scares people away. I think we've been very gracious, allowing it to go on as long as it has. And transparent—God knows that press conference was about as transparent as it gets. But now, it's time to wrap things up. I'm sorry about this poor woman going missing. I do empathize with her family. I really do, but we've got to get back to work. We need to make our guests feel comfortable and safe again. I can't have my resort be a crime scene forever. I need your help. Actually, I need your word that you and your people will vacate the property immediately."

Suddenly, I didn't care about the fact that I was sinking into the cushion. I couldn't believe the lack of humanity in this guy, the gall of him asking me to call off the search for a missing woman because it was inconvenient for him. What a jerk.

"This is an official law enforcement operation. I can't just call it off because it doesn't suit your business model."

"Jack, I was hoping we could work this out so that I don't have to go over your head, to the sheriff. I know that Evelyn has given you free rein, but I'm here now to take back control of the situation. Don't make this difficult on yourself."

I stared at the hipster wide-eyed. He was so thin I wondered if he ate anything at all. I could easily take him out with one hand, grab him around the neck and slam him to the ground. Of course, I wasn't going to do that, but in the moment, it felt very tempting. I knew that if he called Sheriff Lansing, I was sunk.

Lansing had already told me to back off, he wasn't going to defend me to this rich little clown. I would just have to tell Martin I would do what he wanted me to do, and then do what I knew was right, but do it under the radar.

"Okay, we'll pull out. But the investigation isn't over, not by a longshot. If I get any leads and need to come back on this property for any reason, I will do it. I'm sure I can find a judge to sign a search warrant."

"We'll cross that bridge when we come to it, but for now, I want you and your people and all evidence of this search off my property by the end of the day. Am I making myself clear?"

"Very clear."

I pictured myself again throttling his skinny little neck with both my hands but then realized I would have to get up off the couch first to do this. I suddenly remembered what a challenge this was going to be. I struggled to pull myself out of the soft cushions, making my exit look awkward and pitiful instead of commanding and strong, the way I wanted it to appear. I turned at the doorway and looked back at Martin, who was still sitting on the other couch with his legs crossed, now staring at his phone like everyone else of his generation. He had already dismissed me.

"But let me be very clear as well. If we don't find this woman, the blood will be on your hands," I said, my voice booming from some confident place deep inside me. I didn't wait to see his reaction. I just kept walking with a commanding stride. *Take that, little man.*

19

EVELYN RISES

When my assistant, Simone, told me that Martin's private plane had just landed at the airport, I immediately had a panic attack. I pictured him, Armani-clad, swaggering into my office, sitting down in my white leather chair, crossing his legs, staring out the window, and then telling me that I was fired in his most dismissive tone, one that I knew too well. When Martin was done with people, he discarded them like a piece of trash. He never looked back. I had heard many stories about seemingly close relationships that Martin ended without a second thought.

I figured the best thing I could do was not to be here when he arrived. This would hopefully give him time to cool off before we talked. It was a beautiful day. Uncharacteristically, I decided I might go for a little hike. It was something I hadn't done in weeks because I was always too busy. At least, that's what the voice inside my head told me whenever I thought about it. Being outside was one of the things that made me fall in love with Bingham, and I had lost that connection because I was such a workaholic who refused to take even short mental health breaks. If I stopped working even for a second, I felt like my dreams might slip away like sand through my fingers, like I might suddenly wake up and be that poor, hungry little girl praying for her next meal again.

I closed my office door, slid off my dress pants and my heels, and pulled on some jeans, socks, and hiking boots that I kept in my desk drawer. I used to love to slip away and go hiking when I first got the job, before the tourist season got busy. Eventually, I stopped permitting myself to take a break. But today, I was allowing myself this interlude, especially if I was about to be fired. It didn't make sense for me to waste one more minute stewing about Martin and my dire situation when I could be enjoying this gorgeous mountain possibly for the very last time.

I pulled on a T-shirt, grabbed a water bottle and my phone, and headed out the back door of my office that led to a path that wound right down the side of the lodge. I didn't really have a plan. I just wanted to be gone so that Martin would not be able to jump down my throat the second he arrived.

I made my way down the trail, watching my footing closely as I stepped over small rocks and tree roots. I remembered how much I had loved this when I first came here. I was still a country girl at heart. In the worst moments of my life, when my stomach was rumbling, and my mother was ignoring me, I would sometimes run off into the woods and wander aimlessly for hours. It took my mind off the hunger. We didn't go to church, but I knew other kids at school who did, and this seemed like the closest thing to church to me. It was so quiet and peaceful—honestly, it was sacred. All I could hear was the breeze gently rustling through the branches and the persistent hum of the invisible orchestra of cicadas serenading me with their summer symphony.

It was the light that always convinced me the woods were like church. Instead of pouring in through the prisms of the stained-glass windows, it descended in thick beams through the branches, fracturing as it danced on top of the leaves like it was breaking through some invisible barrier. The effect was breathtaking: a thousand points of light sprinkled across the trail. As I trekked along the path down to a creek, I could see shafts of light forcing their way through the trees around me, like they had been sent directly from heaven to guide me.

There was also a power in nature, an unspoken spiritual force that was at once beautiful and something to be feared and respected. I knew the mountain in all its forms, and despite this shiny spectacle, I knew at night that it could be a dangerous place, a place with the power to crush you if you didn't truly understand it. I understood it. The mountain and I had an agreement. I honored it, and I did not dare wake the sleeping giant.

All the worry about Martin being angry with me and about what might happen to my job faded into the background with each step. The more distance I put between myself and the resort, the more distance I felt from my problems. Nature was a cure for anything that ailed a person, and I didn't realize I had been missing it so much.

I was in this silent reverie, my feet on autopilot, when I saw it. It was a glint next to a rock, beneath some brush. As I got closer, I leaned down to see what it was. I took a stick and nudged the small pile of brush. Out rolled a diamond ring, and not just any diamond ring, but a magnificent white gold band with the largest emerald-cut diamond I had ever seen in person encircled by smaller diamond chips. I brushed it off on my shirt and stared at it in the palm of my hand. It had to belong to Pamela Stevens. But what did it mean? If something had happened to her, why would her ring end up here, discarded in the dirt? Could an animal have taken it from her? Or a person? Or had she left it here herself as some kind of bizarre clue?

When I walked back into the lodge, I saw Jack coming out of Martin's office. He didn't see me, and I really didn't want to deal with him, so I stayed back, retreating into the shadows, waiting for him to make his way down the hall. He looked livid. I knew this feeling because I had experienced it many times before with Martin. It was his kingdom, and his word was gold. There was no democracy at Bingham.

What could Martin have possibly said to Jack? Did he tell him to call off the search? Was that even Martin's right to do so? Didn't the investigation trump the rights of a private property owner? I honestly didn't know the legal answers to these questions, but it seemed to me that a law enforcement investigation should outweigh a property owner's rights every single time.

I slipped into my office to put my work clothes back on. I figured if I had to confront Martin, at least I would try to look good. I gazed into my full-length mirror, smoothing down my hair and blotting the sweat from my face with a folded tissue. I didn't look perfect, but it would do. Just then, my phone rang on my desk. I hit the speakerphone button.

"Evelyn, where have you been? I've been trying to locate you for over an hour."

"Sorry, Martin, a problem with one of the cottages. I had to ride out there myself with one of the maintenance staff and make sure it was properly taken care of. The guest is a return customer whom we can't afford to disappoint."

I didn't feel guilty lying to Martin about my whereabouts. I needed the break. The short hike had cleared my head, even though I now had the small distraction of finding the ring to sort out.

"Okay, whatever. Just get yourself into my office right now. We need to talk."

I hung up the phone and checked myself in the mirror one more time. *This will have to be enough,* I thought. *I will have to be enough. And, if I'm not, too bad.*

"Sit down," Martin said, motioning for me to sit in the antique chair with gold brocade fabric on the arms and an elaborate needlepoint seat cushion. I knew it was an expensive antique, but I had always hated this chair. It was gaudy and uncomfortable. It wasn't a chair that was meant to be sat in. It was an interrogation chair. I sat down awkwardly against the stiff wooden back and then composed myself, crossing my legs and clasping my hands together at my knees to appear calm. I felt like I could hear the anxiety in my stomach churning beneath the fabric of my blouse. I was afraid Martin could hear it too.

"When did you get in? Did you have a good flight?" I asked, keeping my voice neutral.

"Okay, let's skip the niceties, Evelyn. You know exactly why I'm here. I'm here to clean up your mess, to do your job for you because, for some reason, you have failed to do it."

I sat quietly, thinking about the ring I had placed in the small safe in my office closet. I thought about how much money I might get for it if I sold it—enough to leave the job, leave the state, leave the country—enough to start over. Then, I shook my head a little to try and erase this awful thought from my mind. There was a good chance this was evidence in a missing persons case. I had to give it to Jack; that was the right thing to do. One person I was not going to be sharing this information with was the angry little man sitting in front of me, who insisted on making me feel as small as possible.

"Failed to do my job? That's interesting. I think I went above and beyond to preserve the impression that we were working hand-in-hand with authorities to bring this woman home safely."

"By now, it's obvious that she's dead."

"We don't know that."

"We do. It's the logical conclusion. So, I am now in damage control mode, waiting for her body to be discovered in a ditch by a hiker or float up to the feet of some fly fisherman in the river."

I contemplated giving in, apologizing to Martin, and promising to do whatever I needed to do to make it right. This was the sensible thing to do to keep my job. But that argument was getting strongly overruled in my head by a newfound confidence, determination, and indignation at all the little passive-aggressive ways Martin tried to gaslight me since we met four years ago.

No matter what the crisis was, Martin always seemed to manage to turn it around and make it about him. This wasn't about finding Pamela at all; it was about preserving poor Martin's reputation as a premier luxury resort owner. I had no pity for him.

"No matter how this ends, it's not going to look good for us," I said bluntly. "You might as well accept that now. A guest dying at our resort is not going to play well in the media. So, the only option is for us to get ahead of it, show the world we are doing our best to help the searchers locate her. That's what I've been doing. You entrusted me to do this job for a reason. You wanted to be hands-off and let me handle everything so you could concentrate on your company in California. That's exactly what I'm doing. So, if you'll excuse me, I've got a resort to run."

I stood up, walked directly to the door, pulled it open, and stepped out without looking back at Martin one time. I imagined him sitting there, his smug face contorted with confusion. I had either just burned my last bridge with him or secured my future as an executive in his empire. I wasn't sure which one it was, but I didn't have time to ponder it. I had a very important piece of evidence that I needed to share with Jack.

I took the ring from the safe and slipped it into my pants pocket, heading in the direction of the lobby. I was keenly aware of it brushing against the side of my leg with every step I took. It would have been so easy to walk out the front door, have Morris take me down the mountain to my car, tell him I was off to do an errand, and then vanish with the ring in my possession. It would be hours before anyone realized that I was gone for good. I would head across the country, find a jewelry dealer, and sell it. Before anyone traced it back to me, I would be in Mexico, or Canada.

But I knew that I was not going to do this. I was going to do the right thing and turn it over to Jack. I had called Simone at the front desk from my office and asked her to hold Jack for me. She told me he was just walking out when I called, and she had yelled for him to wait a few moments so that I could speak with him. She told me in a hushed tone that he looked annoyed but had agreed to wait for me.

As I rounded the corner with the ring tugging at the corner of my pocket, I asked Jack if we could step into a private room. I motioned to him, and he followed me as I walked down the hall and opened the door to a small conference room with my keycard that I kept on a lariat around my neck. I had the power to open every single locked door with my security clearance. It was a responsibility and a privilege that I took seriously.

I pointed to a chair across the conference table, and Jack slunk into it, looking like he had just been called to the principal's office for putting gum in a girl's hair.

"Evelyn, I hope this won't take long. Your boss has asked us to leave, so I'm in the process of pulling my team out. There are a lot of logistics I need to deal with to make this happen, so now is really not the best time for a friendly chat."

"Don't worry about him," I said, waving my hand in the air like Martin was a simple house fly I could swat away. "I'm in charge. You can stay. Ignore him. He doesn't know what he's talking about. He'll be heading back to California soon enough."

Jack studied me across the table and folded his hands. I imagined he was wondering if I was for real, if I really had the power, not to mention the guts, to make this unilateral decision against my boss' wishes.

"Well, he is the owner. I don't want to get in the middle of a boxing match here."

"You're not going to. You have my word. But that's not why I wanted to see you."

I slowly reached into my pocket and pulled out a small ball of tissue that I had wrapped the ring in. I gently opened it and slid the ring across the table for Jack to see.

"What is this?"

"It's a ring I found in the woods next to the trail when I was hiking today. It's a little offshoot trail along the side of the lodge that goes down to the stream. A lot of employees use it when they have a break. Not many guests know about it. The ring has to be Pamela's. Don't you think?"

Jack turned it around and around in his hand like he had never seen a diamond ring before. I could see the corners of his mouth starting to curve into a small smile. I could also tell that he was trying his best not to smile. It was like he didn't want to give me the satisfaction of owning this development. Or maybe I wasn't giving him enough credit. Maybe he was compassionate and didn't want to seem too excited about finding a dead woman's ring.

"It certainly is quite a ring. How do you know it's hers?"

"I don't, for sure. But it makes the most sense. No one else has reported a ring missing on the property, and surely, if you lost a ring like this, you would report it. It's got to be hers. It should be easy enough to find out. Take a photo of it and send it to Darwin."

"Can you show me exactly where you found it? We'll want to start a grid search in that area immediately."

I pulled a folded map out of my other pocket. I had anticipated this, so I had printed it from my computer and put a large red X on the spot where I found the ring. I slid it across the table, and he picked it up in his thick hands and studied it.

"Would you like me to put this back in my safe for the time being?" I offered even though I wasn't sure I fully trusted myself.

I stared hesitantly at the large diamond ring on the table between us. I wasn't sure what the protocol was for evidence like this, but I was pretty sure Jack didn't want to carry the ring around in his pocket while he searched the woods. He looked up from the map and stared at me for a moment, like he didn't know the answer to my question.

"Yes, that would be great for now. First, let me take a photo of it. I will get one of my technicians to pick it up from you tomorrow so he can take it to the sheriff's office and catalogue it into evidence."

He pulled out his phone from a holster on his belt and snapped a few photos of the ring from different angles. When he was finished, he slid the ring back across the shiny table to me.

"I'm not sure I want to show this to the husband. I haven't completely ruled him out as a suspect yet, and I don't want him knowing we found this key piece of evidence. I may run it by the parents instead, although I don't want to freak them out. It's a sticky situation."

I wasn't sure at this point if he was talking to me or talking through his predicament with himself to see if he might land on a solution. I had sympathy for his situation. I wouldn't last a day in law enforcement under this kind of pressure.

"You could look her up on social media and see if there are any clear photos of her wearing the ring. A ring that big is pretty easy to spot," I said gently, not wanting to overstep my bounds.

"Good idea. But no matter what we find out, I need you to keep this under wraps for now. Tell no one."

I nodded solemnly as I carefully wrapped the ring back in the tissue paper and slid it into my pocket.

"Got it."

"You didn't tell your jerk of a boss about this, did you?"

"Nope."

"Good. Let's keep it that way. The less he knows about this investigation, the better."

"I agree."

We both stood, and Jack reached out a hand across the table to shake mine. I wasn't sure what we were shaking on, but I took his hand.

"You're doing the right thing, standing up to that guy. No one should get in the way of finding a missing woman," Jack said.

He gave my hand a hearty shake and then turned to leave. Impulsively, I reached out and grabbed his arm to keep him from going.

"Major Sorrells—Jack, I mean, you're doing the right thing too. Keep at it. Don't give up on her."

This time, he smiled without trying to control the corners of his mouth.

20

DARWIN LONGING

Being back in DC, even for just a few days, was a mixture of good and bad. Good because I could blend into the chaos of the city and avoid all the accusatory looks people were giving me at the resort. The bad part was that everything in my house, everything I looked at, everything I touched, reminded me of Pamela. It was bittersweet. I didn't know I would feel this way. I thought I would feel relief, but that wasn't the case.

It wasn't her fancy dresses, suits, or high heels that made me think of her, it was the simple things. The little heart-shaped rock she found on a hike in Nevada, the painted coffee cup Polly made her at summer camp, the string of beads she liked to wrap around her neck three times and wear with a T-shirt on the weekends. Touching these things gave me an electric jolt, like I was literally connecting with her energy. No one told me grief would feel this way.

But I wasn't just looking at her things because I was nostalgic. I was looking for any evidence that she had found out about the thing with Victoria. Did she know that this foolishness, this inappropriate digital flirting, had cost me my job? That I had been pretending to go to work for weeks while I looked for another position? And the bigger question was, if she did know, why didn't she confront me? Maybe this whole thing, her disappearance, was a ruse to get away from me without her having to face this ugly truth, that her husband had done something unforgivable.

Pamela's friends had arranged a candlelight vigil for her in DC. I didn't like the idea of it because it felt so final, like saying out loud that she was dead. I especially didn't like the idea of putting myself in another situation where there was a silent inquisition going on in everyone's heads about me. Truthfully, I was dreading it, but at the same time, not going would create a gossip train so much worse than the one I would have to endure in person for just two hours.

On top of that, Geni was denying me visitation with Polly. She said it was for the best until things settled down. Her attorney explained to mine that they were afraid the media would try to talk to me or photograph me on the street while I was with her. They didn't want to put her through that. My attorney, Davon, told me not to fight it. He said this was not the time for me to be sticking my neck out in a custody case, that it would all work out, that Geni and I had a good parenting relationship, and she would eventually relent and let me see Polly. But this meant that my number one reason for coming home had been taken from me.

Deep down, I knew Davon was right. He wasn't just my lawyer; he was one of my closest friends. We had met in graduate school. He was already a lawyer but had decided to go on to get his MBA. He worked mostly with big companies now, doing corporate law, but he dabbled in family law, or just about anything else a friend needed help with. I knew that he always had my best interests at heart.

When I was asked to leave my company because of the Victoria situation, he negotiated a clean exit for me. They allowed me to resign and promised not to block my efforts to get another job. He told me this was the best I could hope for under the circumstances, and I trusted him. He also told me in no uncertain terms that I needed to tell Pamela before someone else told her about the scandal. This advice, I regretfully did not take.

And here I was, at his mercy again, and thankful for it.

Polly had a bedroom at my house and at Geni's house. We let her decorate them both herself, so she would feel at home wherever she was. I usually kept the door to her room closed when she wasn't at my house, so I didn't stew over her absence. Today, I opened the door and sat on the end of Polly's bed atop a crushed velvet comforter in an unusual color that she called "mango." I held her favorite blue stuffed pig from the hotel where we always stayed at the Jersey Shore and looked around the room at her things—her dance trophies, candid photos of her and her girlfriends from school, dried flowers in small vases from various events we had attended over the years. I wondered if she would ever be here in this room again. I had to put it out of my mind. I knew Davon was right. I didn't like it, but it made sense. I could not fight for Polly while I might be a suspect in the disappearance of my wife.

It would have been easier for me not to go to the vigil, to avoid the awkward side hugs of Pamela's friends and their accusing, smug glances at me. But I knew this would send the wrong message. It would expose me as a person who lacked character, who couldn't put aside his petty insecurities about what people were thinking to honor his wife.

The problem was that I still didn't know for sure if Pamela was dead. There was an energy swirling around in me that told me, against all logic, that she may still be alive. I walked out of the house that morning, and there was a red robin bouncing from limb to limb on the scrawny cherry tree in front of my townhouse. The bird was chirping wildly, like she was trying to tell me something. *I'll come back as a bird*, I remembered Pamela saying once, when we had a little too much wine and talked about dying. *I'll be red and wild. That's how you will know it's me.*

So, maybe she was dead. Maybe the bird was Pamela, or maybe she sent the bird to give me a message, but what was the message? I was still brooding over this dilemma when Dallas pulled up to the curb in his rented red convertible. The very next day after returning to New York from Bingham, when he heard about the vigil, Dallas had flown to DC. He said this was something I couldn't handle alone. I didn't dare tell him what I was thinking about Pamela still being alive, that maybe she discovered I was a liar and decided to vanish on her own. I knew how that would go. He would call me crazy, laugh at me, make me mad, and then we would ride in silence.

"Well, this is an appropriate car to drive to your missing sister-in-law's candlelight vigil," I said, strapping myself in while he screeched away from the curb so fast that I could smell rubber burning.

"Come on, lighten up. It should be a celebration of her life, a life well-lived, not a downer."

"Dallas, that's what you say when an old person dies, not when a person dies who still had a full life ahead of her. We don't even know if she's dead, by the way. This feels so wrong. I mean, what could they possibly hope to gain by holding this vigil, that a bear will come forward and admit to mauling her in the woods? I'm uncomfortable with this whole situation."

He took the turns so fast I had to brace my hand on the door handle to keep from pivoting into the driver's seat. The only thing good about the dangerous way Dallas was driving was that it was keeping me from focusing on what was about to happen at the vigil.

"You and me both, brother. You think I want to see Pamela's snooty friends again, how they're going to look at you with their Botoxed foreheads and their mean little squinty eyes? I do not. But I am going to support you and to support Polly. Polly is coming, isn't she?"

"No, Geni didn't think it was a good idea for her to come with all the media attention."

"That's out of control, dude. You need to put on your big boy pants and put her in her place. Tell her you need your daughter by your side at a time like this."

"Dallas, it's not the right time. Geni is holding all the cards. I don't want to blow it. I'm trying to work with her, not against her. Davon has been giving me advice on this, and he knows what he's talking about."

"Suit yourself," Dallas said as he once again pinned me against the door on another tight turn.

"Could you slow it down a little?"

"I could, but what fun would that be? By the way, what's this crazy talk about her not being dead? Of course, she's dead. It's been a week. There's no way she's still out there alive somewhere, dude. Sorry to break it to you. You've got to face reality."

"Well, until there is solid evidence of her death, until her body is found, I won't have closure. I need to see her body to believe it."

"You need to make peace with the fact that that may or may not happen. Chances are, a bear or something else has gotten to her by now. It's not going to be a pretty ending, no matter how it went down."

"You really know just what to say in trying times, don't

you?" I said, shaking my head in disbelief at his insensitive words, even though I knew this was what I could always expect from him.

We rode in silence for the next ten minutes as I thought about why my brother always seemed to bring up the worst possible image during a crisis. He had absolutely no filter, and I was over his sardonic little remarks. I preferred the silence to his brash words, a silence that was only broken by the wind in my ears and the annoying screech of the tires as we rounded tight curves at a high speed. When we got to the church where the vigil was being held, Dallas pulled the car into a corner parking space in the back of the lot, which was almost full.

As we walked, I adjusted my tie, and he touched my bent elbow lightly with his hand. That was his way of saying he was sorry. Then he squeezed it a little. That was his way of saying he had my back no matter what. I desperately needed someone to have my back, and my irreverent brother was the only option at this point.

The service itself was a blur. It was in an old Protestant church with vaulted ceilings, stone walls, stained glass windows, and an organ that looked like it belonged in an ancient cathedral in Europe. Pamela would have preferred her friends to gather somewhere outside, like at a park, to remember her. She said she never felt closer to God than when she was hiking or running through the woods. This pomp and circumstance was not her.

At the insistence of Alex and Joan, still all the way back at Bingham, Pamela's friends chose to have the vigil at the church. I suspected they probably knew deep down in their hearts that she would have hated it. This was par for the course for Pamela's parents. They were classic overbearing WASPs who wanted to control everything down to where their daughter's vigil would be held, even if they were still hundreds of miles away. It was all about them putting on a good show. After all, they were the grieving parents, and I was nobody in their eyes. My opinion didn't count.

After the vigil, I stood solemnly in line with Pamela's friends, accepting handshakes and awkward hugs from strangers. I made small talk and tried to keep from looking at my watch. Eventually, Dallas came up behind me and tapped me on the shoulder.

"Time to go, brother."

Emily, Pamela's best friend from law school, turned sharply and looked in my direction. Her husband, George, who was between us put a hand on my shoulder and on hers as if he were about to referee a fight.

"You're not coming to the reception at the restaurant?" Emily asked me tersely.

"Emily, I would like to, but I'm exhausted and—"

"He's got Polly this afternoon," Dallas interjected smoothly with the bold lie.

Emily stiffened, but George turned to me with a sad, knowing smile like we were in some sort of conspiracy, like he could understand how someone might want to off their wife. If I were married to Emily, I would want to push her off a steep ledge into a secluded canyon somewhere. I wasn't even married to her, and I still imagined doing it.

"It's okay, Darwin. This is surreal for all of us. Go be with your daughter."

George patted me on the back, and Dallas led me by my elbow out of the receiving line and into the brilliant midday sun in the parking lot.

"I was thinking pretty fast on my feet, wasn't I?" Darwin

said smugly, obviously proud of how he saved me from more time with Pamela's friends with his lie.

"Yeah, but what if they find out Geni isn't letting me see Polly? Then they know I lied. They will make more assumptions about me based on that."

"Bro, don't worry, they've already made assumptions about you. Plus, I'm the liar, not you."

We jumped into the red convertible and sped away from the church. This time, I was thankful for Dallas' intense driving. I wanted to put as much distance between me and Pamela's friends as fast as I possibly could.

21

CELIA DIGS

SOME PEOPLE SAY THE DEFINITION OF INSANITY IS doing the same thing over and over and expecting a different result. And here I was, talking to the same people over and over again at the Bingham Reserve, hoping to learn something new about Pamela's disappearance, something investigators had missed.

My editor had reluctantly given me the green light to stay on the case for a few more days because the story was trending online, bringing lots of new visitors to our website and social media. I knew the official search had been called off at the request of the resort owner but that teams of volunteers were still quietly searching, and that Jack was quietly joining them in his off-duty hours. I wanted to write about the search being called off, but I also didn't want to call attention to Jack's search, so I was sitting on it for now.

I still believed there were answers to be found here, it was just about talking to the right people, people I hadn't fully probed before.

As Morris drove me up the mountain after yet another trip into town to talk to the locals, I witnessed the mighty beauty of the summer in full swing: its lush green canopy, majestic trees swaying in the balmy breeze, sunlight filtering through the branches like a prism beneath the cloudless blue sky. It was so breathtaking that it was nearly impossible to believe anything bad could happen in a place as picturesque as this. But that was part of the complexity of the mountain. Once you wandered deep into the forest where the light couldn't penetrate, it was a different place. It was a place where a woman could vanish, disappear without a trace.

Morris dropped me off at my cottage. I thanked him, grabbed my computer bag, and headed inside. As I opened the screen door to the porch and went outside to breathe in the mountain air, I was met with another deceptively spectacular view of the bright green foliage dotting the valley below me, gently rustling in the wind. I sank down into one of the old rocking chairs and thought about how this place was starting to pull me in. Despite the tragedy, I had a strange attachment that was hard to put into words.

"Aren't you ready to come home yet?" Matt asked as we talked over FaceTime. I was gently rocking in a wooden chair on the front porch, watching him trying to put a fitted sheet on our bed without my help. He had propped the phone up on a dresser facing the bed. The corners of the sheet kept popping up each time he thought he had tucked them securely beneath the mattress. I wanted to laugh out loud, but I knew it would only make him more aggravated.

"No, I kind of like it here. It's so peaceful, in a spooky way. It's hard to explain. Maybe we should think about buying a vacation home here."

"I think it's creepy. There's been zero sign of that woman. Don't you think it's a little weird?"

I knew he was right, but I couldn't help myself. There was a magnetic pull that was keeping me at Bingham. And as much as I was frustrated by the lack of answers in Pamela's disappearance, I was equally smitten with the mystery of the place. I suppose it was this curiosity that had always defined me as a journalist. While Matt recognized it, he didn't necessarily understand it or approve of it.

We finally said goodnight, and I mock-kissed him through the screen of the phone.

I closed my eyes and started to doze as the rocking chair swayed softly beneath me, making a creaking sound on the wooden boards below. I was exhausted from the day and needed to get some sleep. Talking to people all day long was emotional work that zapped your energy like nothing else. My first order of business in the morning was going to be to pay a visit to Eddie, the river guide. I recalled our first conversation with him the day he took Matt and me paddle boarding. I suspected that he knew more about this place than anyone else did, and that he, of all people, might have insights that no one had bothered to explore, even the investigators.

I hiked down to the river by myself the next morning and saw Eddie with a scrub brush and a pail of soapy water, washing the brightly colored kayaks that were lined up along the shore in a neat row.

"Hey there."

Eddie looked up knowingly, like he had been expecting me all morning. And then, he turned back to his work, speaking to me with his head down, deep in concentration.

"Hi, Mrs. Finch. What brings you down here? You signed up for an outing today? Kind of rough terrain for you to be walking. I could have picked you up in my truck."

I always marveled how everyone here addressed me so formally, often interchanging Miss and Mrs. but never using my first name. I'm sure it was part of the training the staff received here. Eddie scrubbed feverishly while he talked, his eyes focused intently on the blue kayak in front of him.

"No worries. It was a good, challenging hike. I enjoyed it. And no, I'm not here for an excursion. I'm actually here for work."

The truth was I had been terrified hiking down the narrow, muddy path with its tight switchbacks, but I didn't want him to know that. I wanted him to think that I was tough and that it was no big deal. And while it was scary, it seemed far less dangerous than driving down the road in his old truck.

Eddie kept scrubbing, pausing only for a second to wipe soap out of his eyes with the back of his free hand.

"Is that so. What kind of work do you do?"

"I'm a reporter for a newspaper in Philadelphia. I'm doing a story on that woman, the one who disappeared, Pamela Stevens."

This time, he dropped his rag back into the bucket and stood up to face me, his wet hands on his hips making dark fingerprint marks on his beige work pants. He was wearing the familiar tan shirt with his name on the pocket and construction boots. For just a second, he looked imposing, like he might just grab me by the neck and throttle me. But then the corners of his mouth turned up into a slight smile.

"Is that so? Well, I'll be darned. I didn't know you were a big city writer. Too bad there's no story here. No sign of her. Wish we could have found her. But it's looking pretty hopeless right now. Very sad."

Eddie shook his head and looked down at the ground like he might be imagining Pamela in a bear's den, chewed up into a thousand tiny pieces.

"I know. You were just so helpful that day my husband and I went out with you on the water. I mean, you had a lot of insight into this area and what might have happened. I kind of just wanted to pick your brain."

"Pick away, but I'm not sure there's much up here," Eddie said with a sly smile, rapping himself on the head with a closed fist like he was knocking on an empty skull.

"I mean, you kind of said it that day when we met you. If she wasn't found right away, she probably wouldn't be found. Right?"

Eddie looked away from me across the water like the answer might be in the woods on the other side of the deep blue reservoir.

"True. If she fell, which is probably what happened, even if she was alive when she landed, there's been no sign of her for more than a week, which means she likely didn't make it. Some wild animal probably got to her. Hate to say it, but that's what I think. Not based on anything but a lifetime of experience in these here woods."

I examined this boy-man standing in front of me, thinking about how refreshing it was to talk to someone so straightforward with no agenda but to tell the truth. These mountain people were very different from the usual crowd I interviewed in Philadelphia. I could get used to this type of candor.

"Thanks so much, Eddie. Have you heard anything else about the search or about the case?"

"Nope, not really. Some people around here like to gossip, spin stories in their heads. Some of them say the husband may have had something to do with it. It's possible, of course. But I think the most logical answer is usually the right one. She fell. It's a shame, but it happens. It's a dangerous trail."

And that's when I decided I would have to see for myself. It was time for me to hike Deadman's Pass, to walk in Pamela's footsteps.

Eddie gave me a ride back to the lodge from the reservoir in the battered pickup truck, and the hairpin turns of the narrow service road made the tight switchbacks of the foot path seem like a generous thoroughfare. I was shaky when he finally pulled up to the front of the resort and tipped his hat at me after I slipped him a ten-dollar bill. I didn't tell him what I was about to do because I was pretty sure he would try to talk me out of it, that it was too dangerous for someone like me.

The break from the direct sunlight beneath the shade of the trees only added to the ambiance of the setting. I was listening to Led Zeppelin on my AirPods as I hiked up the trail. "The Rain Song" was the perfect music for the scene in front of me as a gentle breeze nudged the leaves in waves like the subtle movements of a symphony, seemingly in time to the music in my ears.

I carefully placed my feet one at a time as I navigated the rocky path broken up by the occasional twisted tree root. In some areas, the path was all rock. I studied the steep, sheer boulders methodically, looking for footholds and narrow ledges that my fingertips could grab onto. I imagined how slippery the rocks would be after a rain—treacherous. I was breathing heavily, but I liked the feeling of the mountain air in my lungs and the intense stretching of my muscles. Still, there was a foreboding feeling that I couldn't escape. Like the mountain was mocking me for even trying to navigate this difficult trail. *Who are you, city girl? You're no match for me.*

When I got to a plateau, I looked around for a broken limb that I could use as a walking stick and found one off to the side near the path. It fit perfectly in the palm of my hand. I placed it on the ground in between the rocks to steady me as I spread my legs to move as gracefully as possible up the trail without falling. *Don't fall. Don't fall. Don't fall.* I said the mantra over and over in my head as if saying it might keep me from falling.

In between the heavy brush, there were small holes where I could see how the edge of the trail simply dropped off to the gorge below. It was easy to imagine taking one wrong step and slipping over the edge to your death. One minute you were walking along, admiring the natural beauty, and the next minute, you were flying through the air, wind rushing by your head, knowing in seconds that your body might get snagged on a gnarled rock ledge and break into a million pieces. Hopefully, you would pass out and never regain consciousness before you hit the bottom.

I tried to picture what it would be like to know in those last few seconds that you were about to die. I shook my head and tried to get rid of the disturbing image. It was something I had thought about before when I saw the people jumping out of the World Trade Center after the planes hit on 9/11. At the time, I couldn't imagine that it was the best choice to jump from such a height to a certain death in the street. But later, when I reflected on the horror, I realized that they had no choice. It was either that or be burned alive.

As I walked slowly along the trail, taking very careful and deliberate steps, I let the song seep into my thoughts. I breathed deep, thinking about the seasons of emotion, the wonder of devotion. I stopped and leaned against a tree, looking down through a clearing at the jagged rocks below me, jutting out in every direction. No one could survive a fall from here. It wasn't possible. I knew this, yet there was still some sliver of unreasonable hope that made me believe Pamela Stevens might walk out of the woods at any moment and tap me on the shoulder. That's when I heard the rustling in the brush behind me.

I turned down the music and listened again for the sound. There it was. A slight rustling. Was it an animal? A person? My heart started racing. I knew that I had to look, but I was terrified of what I might find. When I turned around, I saw the branches of a bush swaying ever so slightly. I sighed and smiled. It was probably a squirrel or a bird, or some other small woodland creature. But then, the branches started moving more quickly, more violently, like someone or something was about to step out onto the trail and confront me. All the strange feelings I had about this place hit me at once as a panic attack of major proportions welled up inside of me.

    I thrust my AirPods into my pocket and started running back down the trail the way I had come. Even as I sprinted, I watched every step, every rock, every root, thinking about how one misstep could put me over the edge. My breathing was ragged. My heart was pounding. There was a ringing in my ears, but I kept going. I thought of Matt. I thought of the boys, but mostly, I just thought about getting out of the woods alive.

    Had something or someone chased Pamela Stevens? Is that why she fell? I wanted to turn around to see if I was really being pursued or if my paranoia had just gotten the best of me. The trees seemed to be speaking to me, the branches and leaves swaying softly in the breeze as if to say I was crazy for being afraid in a place this lovely. I didn't want to risk slowing down even for a second to look back.

    As the trailhead approached, my footing got more secure, and I pushed myself to cross over it into the field that would take me to the lodge. I ran like I was completing the last few seconds of a marathon. I finally stopped in the grass and leaned over, trying to catch my breath, resting my hands on my bent knees. I felt like I was going to throw up. I had gotten too close to the beast. Only, I didn't know what the beast was. I was starting to think I was in over my head, and maybe it was time to leave this place and let this all go, just like Matt had told me to do.

    Did I see something? There was something, something dark

in the bushes, but was it a bear or a man or a deer? Or was it my mind playing tricks on me? I honestly didn't know. Suddenly, I felt a hand on my shoulder. I jumped and did a pivot turn in the direction of the touch.

"Mrs. Finch, I mean, Celia, I didn't mean to scare you," Wilson, the old man from the barn, said. It took me a second to remember I *had* told him to call me Celia when we first met. It felt comforting to hear my name, even from a stranger.

"It's okay," I replied, putting my hand over my heart as I tried to steady myself.

"Everything okay?"

"Yes, I think so. I'm not sure. I was on the trail, Overlook, or whatever you guys call it, Deadman's Pass, and I thought I saw something in the brush. I know I heard something. It just kind of freaked me out."

I stood wide-eyed, staring at this rugged mountain man who looked like he was amused by me. He held a rake in one hand and his work gloves in the other.

"Well, you probably did. Lots of critters out there in the woods. Especially this time of year. Weather is so nice, cooled down a little this week, they're coming out of hiding and ready to play."

"Yes, you're probably right. Not a big deal. Thanks," I said with an embarrassed, shaky voice, putting my hands on my hips to appear confident when I had no confidence in anything at the moment.

Wilson's assurances did nothing to help me swallow my fear, but now I just wanted to get away from him, to be alone and process the whole ordeal. He was a nice enough man, but he didn't understand what had happened to me or how it made me feel. He was from here and used to this kind of interruption from creatures in the woods. I was a city girl. As much as I enjoyed a good hike, I was not crazy about wildlife. And I still wasn't convinced that the interloper had been an animal.

"You have a good day now," Wilson said, waving as he headed back in the direction of the horse barn.

I walked slowly in the opposite direction toward the lodge, thinking about what my next steps should be. Was I out of moves? Was the story over? I wasn't sure, but then I saw my next move coming out of the lobby onto the porch carrying a cup of coffee. It was Major Jack Sorrells. I made a beeline in his direction.

I knew that the search had officially ended, but I heard through the grapevine that Jack was still hanging around in his off-hours and walking the trails on his own or joining the volunteer searchers. As far apart as our worlds were, Jack and I shared common ground, the desire to find Pamela Stevens.

I had been texting him again since our coffee chat, and I felt strongly that he was starting to warm up to me. At first, he ghosted me, ignoring my texts, but in the last day or so, he had started to respond. Sure, the responses tended to be brief, but I was making inroads with him. Being a good journalist was all about earning the trust of your sources. It happened over time, not overnight. Even though it had only been a few days, I felt like I was slowly earning Jack's trust, that he no longer saw me as the elitist out-of-town reporter who had said something insensitive at the press conference.

As he watched me drag myself across the lawn in his direction, Jack smiled and took a big swig of his coffee.

"Someone suddenly decide to take up exercise?"

"Very funny. I was hiking Overlook, but something spooked me in the woods, and I sprinted out. Scared the heck out of me."

"Interesting. What was it?" He looked at me with a coy smile, in the same way Wilson had looked at me. I was starting to get paranoid that the locals had meetups where they talked about me behind my back.

"What was what?"

"The thing that spooked you?"

"If I knew what it was, I wouldn't be spooked by it, would I?"

Jack gestured for me to sit down on the wooden chair across from him on the stone patio. I was thankful to have a place to rest. I sat down and took a big sip of water from the bottle that I carried on an exercise belt around my waist.

"So, why the sudden desire to hike Overlook?"

"The same reason you do it. I can't let this go. I want to know what happened to Pamela Stevens. You know as well as I do that the more days that pass without anything new, the less likely she will be found alive."

"This seems like a lot of reporter involvement to me. Aren't you supposed to keep your stories at arm's length, not get too emotionally involved?"

Carol Lee. The name whispered in my ear. We both fell silent.

Jack looked off in the distance at the mountain like the answer to Pamela's disappearance might just be floating there above it, suspended in midair amidst the clouds, waiting for one of us to reach out and grab it.

"Is it over? Is it officially a cold case at this point?" I asked, poking the bear.

Jack whipped his head back in my direction. I was successful. He was poked.

"We don't call them cold cases anymore. We call them unsolved cases because there's always a chance they can be solved. It's only been a week."

"Okay, my bad. But is anyone but you still working on it?" I asked this knowing the answer, that of course he was. But I wanted him to say it to me.

"Is this off the record?"

"Sure, if you want it to be."

"I want it to be."

"Then it is."

"Okay, the truth is that no one really gives a hoot about this rich woman who parachuted in for a few days of outdoor luxury. But I don't look at it that way. We have a missing woman, and I don't care who she is or where she's from. She's a human being and deserves justice like anyone else. So does her family. But tell that to the sheriff. He and I don't see eye to eye on this one. He's a good guy, but more practical than me. He runs the sheriff's office like a business. Says we don't have the resources to keep working this one. And he's right."

I could see the redness creeping up Jack's neck into his cheeks. I admired his passion and dedication to the case despite the sheriff's obvious wishes to be done with it. This perseverance made me like Jack even more. Now, I needed him to like me.

"Well, you're still here. That's something."

"It may be something, but it's not enough. I need more people to search properly. And not city girls like you who are going to come screaming out of the woods."

I smiled broadly at his sarcastic comment. Jack was right. I was a city girl, and I did come screaming out of the woods. But I also knew a thing or two about criminal investigations.

"Or you just need a good lead?"

"True, that would help too."

"So, what if you let me write an article about the case? Interview you. It would be a follow-up, basically where the case stands now. You don't have to talk about your continued searches. I don't want to get you into any hot water with the eriff. It might help generate some leads, bring some people f the woodwork who know something, or saw something, 't think it was relevant until now."

oved to the edge of the wooden chair to be closer to

Jack, hoping my closeness would encourage him to trust me enough to go on the record and do an interview with me. Instead, my leaning in was making him even more uncomfortable. He scooted his chair back away from me.

"I'll think about it," Jack said stoically, not giving away his thoughts on the issue.

"Okay, that's fair. I'm not going anywhere. You know how to find me."

"I sure do."

Jack stood up and walked back into the lobby of the lodge, leaving his mostly untouched coffee on the stone ledge in front of his chair. I thought about yelling after him that he had forgotten it, but I decided that it was better to leave our conversation right where it had ended. I wanted him to think about my proposal. I wanted him to realize that he was stronger with me in his corner than he was without me.

22

JACK REGROUPS

Figures I would run into that reporter when I was trying to keep a low profile at the resort. Evelyn knew that I was still hanging around, still trying to make some sense of this case, but since Martin gave me my marching orders and the sheriff told me to knock it off, my investigation had been under the radar for the past few days. While I had Evelyn's blessing, I still had to keep everything very quiet.

Celia Finch had initially rubbed me the wrong way at that press conference, but I'd moved past that, and she was growing on me. After we had coffee together, I decided her heart was in the right place; she just had a lot of Yankee in her that sometimes caused her to come across as brash. I had dealt with plenty of people like that before. Sometimes, you had to give them another chance to show you who they really were before you dismissed them.

The fact that she had gone up to Overlook by herself showed that she had some grit and could be an asset to me if I ⁿy cards right. She clearly wanted us to work together to Stevens. It was tempting, but I had been burned by ⁿre. When I had my fall from grace after the Billy

Barnes case, they staked out my house, my office, even my church. It seemed like every time I got out of my car at the grocery store, there was someone there with a microphone, or a camera, or an iPhone trying to ambush me. These days, it's hard to know who's a real journalist and who's just a social media influencer with a cell phone looking to push your buttons and make you do something stupid on video.

For some strange reason, I was beginning to trust Celia Finch. She seemed like she really did want to get to the bottom of the case. Maybe it wouldn't be such a bad idea to do an interview with her and see if we could shake the bushes a little, motivate someone with information to come forward. Sheriff Lansing wouldn't like it, that's for sure. He would want to know why I was still wasting my time with this dead-end case. But I was getting to the point where I didn't care anymore about what other people thought. I had worked so hard to gain my career back after what happened in the Barnes case, and for what? To be told what to do for the rest of my life in every single situation? I was not about to back off when we had a missing woman who had vanished without a trace in my jurisdiction.

"Why not trust her?" Cindy said as she methodically cut her chicken breast into tiny bites. She read somewhere that it's better to eat small bites and chew them slowly. Then, your stomach knows exactly when you are full, and you won't overeat. It gives your stomach a chance to catch up to your brain. Sure, Cindy had gained about ten pounds over the course of our marriage, but she was beautiful to me. I couldn't understand what she still saw in me when I looked in the mirror and saw the forty pounds I had gained since our wedding day.

"I don't know. I'm just skeptical."

"Right, but that's a bias you have. You were burned by the media after the Billy Barnes case. They were horrible to you. But this is different. She's right, doing a story with her might just be the thing to bring in the *one* tip you need to solve this case. You know as well as I do that all it takes is one good lead."

She took a small piece of chicken on her fork, combined it with rice, and delicately put it into her mouth, chewing slowly while she waited for me to answer.

"You're probably right. But I'm nervous about what the sheriff will think. He was pretty adamant that he wanted me to move on. I don't want him to know that I deliberately ignored his orders."

"You've spent too many years placating too many people. You have to do what you know is right, no matter what the risk is. I support whatever decision you make, no matter the consequences."

This was why I loved Cindy. She always knew how to say the right thing at just the right time. Even when I thought she was disappointed in me, she wasn't. She was always by my side, always my champion. Maybe this was what a successful life was all about: having someone who had your back no matter what.

"You're right. I'll call her tomorrow."

I brushed the bangs out of Cindy's eyes and kissed her tenderly on the cheek. *How did I get so lucky?*

When I met with Celia the next morning, it was chilly. Even summer mornings in the mountains can bring unseasonably cold air with them. It was invigorating, but I wasn't sure she could handle it. We were sitting outside at the lodge on the porch again, and I could see that her lips were turning blue, her teeth were chattering slightly. She was wearing a thin, long-sleeved workout shirt. This city girl didn't know how to dress for the weather here.

"Why don't we move this inside?"

"I thought you'd never ask," she said, grabbing her phone and her notebook and running toward the door.

We found a quiet spot in the corner of the lobby near the grand fireplace. We stopped at the complimentary coffee bar before we took our places in the large, overstuffed armchairs in front of a blazing fire, which seemed strange for a summer morning, yet it was very comfortable.

"So, I am very reluctant to do this, but for some reason, I trust your intentions. My wife does too, by the way."

"Thank your wife for me. I promise I won't let you or her down. What's her name?"

"Cindy. Cindy is her name. She talked me into it."

"Good woman."

"She's the best."

I told her about my frustration when the state police pulled out and how I used volunteers to create search teams after that. I skirted the issue of the sheriff telling me not to put any more resources into the case. Throwing him under the bus would do nothing but harm to the investigation at this point. I told her I was still walking the trails by myself, determined to find a clue, any clue. I told her how this case had gotten under my skin like no other, and that I wouldn't quit until it was solved. It was like uncorking a bottle of champagne; once I started, everything just flowed out of my mouth like a geyser. It was out of my control. When we finished the interview, I took a big gulp of my coffee and stared into the fire, transfixed by the flames and a little afraid of what I had just done. But it was done. There was no going back.

"Jack, you're amazing. Honestly, I've covered a lot of crime stories over the years, and your dedication to this case and passion for finding a resolution is second to none. I really admire you. I'm not just blowing smoke at you. I mean it."

I looked at this woman, this stranger in front of me, saying kind things, and thought of how down I had been about myself for so many years. Even though Cindy had always supported me, and my daughter had too, it was like I couldn't see a way out of my self-deprecation. Celia's praise seemed to buoy me like nothing else had in the last decade. Suddenly, I could see myself as she saw me, as someone worthy of respect. It made me feel lighter than I had in years.

"Thanks. I'm just being honest with you. I don't know any other way to be."

"Well, Pamela Stevens and her family are lucky to have someone like you on their case."

I smiled and looked back at the fire. As I watched the flames devour the logs, I said a silent prayer that Celia's confidence in me would play out just as she hoped—that I would find Pamela one way or another.

23

EVELYN HANGS ON

I KEPT WAITING FOR THE OTHER SHOE TO DROP WITH Martin. Surely, he was going to fire me for insubordination. Each time he passed me in the hallway, he smiled and gave me a small salute. Was he messing with me? Was he just waiting for the right moment to can me? This fear put me on edge, but as the hours passed, I started to think that maybe, just maybe, I had been spared for some reason.

While I was relieved, I was also re-evaluating everything in my life. Why was I working for a man I disrespected so much? Why was I still working in the luxury resort business at all when it didn't truly feed my spirit? The answer was obvious: the money. I had spent so many years clawing and climbing my way up the corporate ladder to pull myself out of poverty that I had never even considered what I wanted to do with my life, what would add meaning to my soul instead of cash to my bank account.

Art had always been a love of mine. While I had hours of unsupervised television time when my mother was working or sleeping, I preferred to take the big box of crayons that one of my kind elementary school teachers had given me and dra elaborate designs on scrap pieces of paper. My mother refused to buy me paper, saying it was too expensive, but my teachers, who recognized my passion and talent, gave me scraps of paper from their classrooms that they would have normally thrown away. They would gather them up in a brown paper bag and hand it to me discreetly before I got onto the school bus to go home.

In my teenage years, I briefly dabbled in painting when a teacher took me under her wing and allowed me to use her studio after school. I was overwhelmed by the choices of paint as I stared at my blank canvas perched on an easel by the window, bathed in perfect afternoon light. My joy was short-lived; as soon as I was old enough for a work permit, my mother made me get a job to help support us. From then on, every afternoon after school, I was behind the counter at the local convenience store selling coffee, candy bars, and condoms. That was the end of my art career.

I recalled my mother's words—*Do you want to be poor forever? Art is not a job. You won't make any money. It's a waste of time.*

But now, I could see a new path. I didn't have to be rich not to be poor; I just had to make a comfortable living. I had already done that. I had saved money. I had invested money, and I had always been frugal. I was in pretty good shape financially. I could do anything I wanted to do. Maybe I would go back to school and become an art teacher. Anything but this.

"Evelyn," Martin said in his shrill tone over the phone. "I feel everything is pretty much under control here. Now that I've those officers off our property, the attention to this mess way. I think I'm ready to head back to Cali and leave hands."

ay he said "Cali" like he was a laid-back surfer

when he was really part of the tech elite. I doubted he had ever had a surfboard beneath his well-groomed feet or ridden a wave into the white sandy shoreline in his life. I paused before I answered. It seemed like a trick, like he was goading me into saying the wrong thing. I also couldn't figure out why we were having this conversation by phone when he was in the office right next door to me.

"I'm glad you're feeling better about it," I replied without conceding anything. I was not about to apologize to this man for doing the right thing.

"Well, it's a good thing I got here when I did. Anyway, I need to get back to the West Coast. Lots of fires to put out. Pardon the pun."

A man who made fun of forest fires was not someone I wanted to work for. Inside, I was thrilled that Martin was finally going to leave me alone. Sure, I would still have to deal with his annoying phone calls, but at least he wouldn't be underfoot. This was a huge weight off my back, and it would give Jack more freedom on the property without Martin's watchful eyes waiting around every corner.

"I understand. I've got things here. You don't need to worry." I told him what he wanted to hear.

"Very good. I'm headed to the airport in a few minutes. Morris is going to take me."

"Excellent," I replied, suddenly realizing I sounded way too excited about him leaving.

He lingered for a moment after this statement, maybe waiting for me to say something friendly, intimate, or more personal. Men had a way of thinking they owned you, of putting you down in little ways that made you genuflect to them subconsciously. It was still the culture we lived in even in the twenty-first century. Martin had always thought he owned me, not just because I worked for him, but because we had slept together on one occasion two-and-a-half years ago.

We'd both had too much to drink. I was lonely and thought it would make me feel better. It didn't. I knew I deserved better than someone like Martin. I deserved someone who truly loved me, someone who treated me with kindness and respect. From that moment on, he thought he had a hold over me. He didn't. I moved past our meaningless encounter almost the minute after it happened. But Martin's arrogance wouldn't allow him to process this truth.

"Okay then, well, keep me posted on everything."

"Will do," I said, hanging up my desk phone before he could have the last word. I heard his tinny voice saying goodbye as I plopped the receiver back into its cradle. Martin was not a good person. I didn't want to work for someone who wasn't good. It was time for me to start writing my next chapter.

Darwin had emailed me and said he was coming back to the resort from DC, that he needed to be here. He had been gone only three days, but based on what I had read in the news, most everyone thought he might be involved in Pamela's disappearance. He couldn't escape these accusations no matter where he was, so he might as well be here. He also told me he was having his mail forwarded to Bingham in the off chance that someone sent him a tip. Secretly, I wondered if there was a small part of him that thought Pamela had run away and might send him a letter—something less traceable than an email or a text.

It wasn't the first time it had crossed my mind, Pamela ⁀ng away. What if Darwin had treated her like Martin ⁀e? Could you blame her for wanting to get away from ⁀ really knew what went on inside someone else's ⁀was possible that beneath her confident exterior there was an emotionally abused woman. It was also possible that Darwin had something to do with his wife's disappearance.

The person who seemed to be targeting Darwin the most was Celia Finch. She implied that he might be involved in all her articles. It was never a direct accusation—more of a subtle dig about him not being completely cleared by investigators yet. She had probably covered a lot of domestic violence situations where a husband was involved in something happening to his wife, but there was not one shred of solid evidence at this point that Darwin was involved in Pamela's disappearance. Until a connection was confirmed, I was going to treat him like the victim he appeared to be. I was pretty good at assessing people, and his grief looked sincere to me.

The problem was that when you mixed grief with anxiety and rage over having people look at you the wrong way, it could get confusing. That's why people thought Darwin seemed suspicious, not because he *was* suspicious, but because he wasn't acting the way everyone expected him to act. At least this was my theory. Celia Finch never asked for my opinion, but I did notice she was becoming rather chummy with Jack Sorrells.

"How are you doing? It's Evelyn," I said to Darwin over the phone after he checked in to his room. "I just wanted to touch base with you. Are your accommodations okay? They will be comped, of course, as we discussed last week."

I had put him in a junior suite in the lodge with a view overlooking the property. It usually rented for $950 a night, but that didn't matter now. With Pamela's disappearance all over the national news, we were not getting very many new bookings. This was exactly what Martin was afraid of. But I was confident that we would be able to turn things around eventually.

There was stunned silence on the other end of the line, and then Darwin finally spoke.

"Evelyn. How kind of you. Thanks so much for asking. I'm okay. Not great, just okay. But I appreciate you welcoming me back. I thought things might be better at home, but they weren't. It was harder being there, around her stuff. It was like she was everywhere I turned. Anyway, this is where I need to be until she's found."

My goal had not been to upset him. I genuinely wanted to see how he was doing. I could hear the grief in his voice. I would let him talk as long as he needed to. It was clear that he didn't have many people in his life whom he could talk to. His train wreck of a brother seemed like he made everything worse.

"I understand there was a vigil for Pamela."

"Yes. Yes, there was. It was very odd. And it's probably just my paranoia, but it felt like everyone was looking at me, accusing me with their silent stares. I still can't wrap my head around the fact that people would think I had something to do with her disappearance. It still doesn't seem real to me."

"What part doesn't seem real? Her disappearance, or their accusations?"

"Both. I just don't know how I got here. I know this is going to sound crazy, but I've had a lot of time to think about everything. I feel like Pamela's energy is still here in the world. When I touch her things, I feel it. It's electric. Like I said, I know it sounds crazy. There's still a part of me that thinks maybe she's alive out there somewhere. If anyone could survive a week in the woods on their own, it's Pamela. You don't know her, but she's fierce."

"I wish I did know her. She sounds like an incredible person. I understand what you're going through. Well, I don't understand exactly. I can't walk in your shoes, but I have lost people I loved before. I know grief. I think you're right though. Her energy is still in the world, no matter what. Even if she is gone, she leaves her energy behind in everything she did and said, in the people whose lives she touched. That's her legacy."

I wasn't sure if I was helping Darwin or making things worse. As soon as the words came out of my mouth, they felt awkward and rambling. It was like I was confirming she was dead, which was not my intention, especially when it was obvious that Darwin still had a glimmer of hope despite the odds that Pamela might still be alive.

"I appreciate what you're trying to say, Evelyn. I do. But what I mean is that her energy is still in the world because *she* is still in the world. I mean for real, not as a metaphor. I really believe she might still be alive, as out there as that sounds."

"Oh," I replied, not knowing how to respond. The poor guy had not come to terms with reality, and who could blame him? It was a very sad and shocking reality.

"Again, thanks for the call, Evelyn. I appreciate your kindness. You've been great through this whole thing. I will see you at some point today. I'm going to take a little time to myself for the moment."

Suddenly, he was gone. I stood there staring at my cell phone, wondering what just happened. Did Darwin really believe his wife was still alive? Or was he just a desperate man holding onto any shred of hope, no matter how unlikely it was? I thought of the wedding ring—Pamela's wedding ring. Deep inside my bones, I believed Pamela Stevens was dead.

24

DARWIN MOURNS

I SAT THERE STARING AT MY PHONE AFTER I HUNG UP with Evelyn, wondering why I had opened up to her the way I did. Once again, I had said far too much. There was no way she didn't think that I was crazy. But at least she seemed to be welcoming me back to the resort with open arms. That was something. She was one of the only people who didn't appear to think I had something to do with Pamela's disappearance.

If she knew about the situation with Victoria, I'm sure she would look at me differently. But that was all behind me now. I knew with total clarity that whole thing was a mistake, and that Pamela was the only woman I ever truly loved. I had just figured this out too late.

I didn't really have anyone I could talk to except for Dallas. And while he had good intentions, he was very likely to share my private thoughts with the world. I pictured him standing around at a bar with a bunch of guys: *You guys aren't going to believe what my brother said. He thinks his wife is still alive even though there's no friggin' way that's possible. Can you believe that? Says he is still sensing her "energy" out there in the world. Poor guy.*

No, unfortunately, Dallas could not be trusted. I didn't

know if Evelyn could be trusted either. I didn't know her that well, but my gut said that she was a good person. I don't think she necessarily believed everything I was saying, but she didn't judge me either. I would have to go with my instinct on this one and hope that Evelyn wouldn't run to that Philadelphia reporter and repeat our entire conversation. I had seen Celia Finch lurking around the lobby when I checked in, and I immediately turned in the other direction so she wouldn't see me. The last thing I needed was her nosing around in my business. She hadn't come out and directly said she thought I was guilty of something in her articles, but the idea was there, hovering over the copy for anyone with half a brain to decipher.

Not unlike the nosy newspaper reporter, Pamela had always been very critical of me. And it wasn't just me who she judged; she was very critical of anyone who crossed her path. It was one of the main things that had made me question our love over the years. Frankly, it was the thing that pushed me toward Victoria. Victoria was so nice, almost benign, but in a refreshing way. There was no drama with her.

Pamela argued with waitresses about the bill, yelled at the drycleaner for not perfectly starching my shirts, and generally pissed people off if she thought they were getting in her way. Her inability to settle was a quality that made her appear strong when I first met her, but it began to annoy me the longer we were together. She often embarrassed me with her bravado.

But now that she was gone, I had nothing but love for her. It was like all the negative things about our relationship were replaced by a sense of surety that I had always longed for with her. I missed her so much that my body physically ached when I thought about her. I couldn't sleep at night. I would wake up in the darkness and reach across the bed expecting her to be there, breathing softly, her back to me, her skin warm to the touch. And when I didn't find her, I panicked. I sat straight up in bed, scanned the room to get my bearings, and then I remembered that Pamela was missing.

I hated that word, "missing." It was in every news report, in every headline, and on the tip of everyone's tongue. It implied that she had just been misplaced, and as soon as we remembered where we had left her, she would be coming home.

I also knew that people used the word in a hopeful sense because "missing" wasn't nearly as bad as "gone" or "dead." But I didn't think she was missing or dead. I didn't think it was an either-or predicament. I had nothing to back my feelings up, just something in my gut that was telling me she was still of this world and hadn't crossed over to the next one yet. It was now up to me to try and figure out what this feeling meant. I decided that being in the place I last saw her, here at Bingham, was the best way to achieve this goal.

Pamela's life insurance payout was an unexpected gift. I had forgotten that we had purchased such a large policy when we first got married. She made more money than I did, so it was only natural that she would have the largest policy—four million dollars.

When I went home for the vigil, Davon told me to start pulling important papers together. It would be some time before the insurance company paid out, but at some point, if Pamela wasn't found, they would have to agree that she was most likely dead, at least that's what Davon told me.

"It's just common sense, Darwin. She disappeared in a very rugged place where it's quite possible she will never be found. Eventually, we will prod the insurance company to agree that she is, in fact, dead. No disrespect. I mean when you're ready, of course," Davon said.

I wanted so badly to talk to him about the case, to share things I couldn't share with Dallas or Evelyn. I knew that even though he was my friend first, he was also my lawyer, so he was bound by confidentiality no matter what I told him. But I was afraid that he might judge me, or even worse, blame me for what happened to Pamela.

I was worried that if I told him about my suspicion that Pamela might have found out about me losing my job due to the Victoria situation and then staged her own disappearance, he would dig in on that theory and not let go.

There was no love lost between Davon and Pamela. She thought he was a bad influence on me—that he wanted to go to bars to pick up women instead of hanging out and doing guy stuff like playing pool or watching a game on TV. This couldn't have been further from the truth. Davon was straight as an arrow. He didn't even drink and was in a serious relationship with a woman he adored. Secretly, I think Davon and Pamela were jealous of one another. They both thought they were smarter and more successful than the other one. Both had dual degrees, and both had their own legal practices with big-ticket clients. But most importantly, both had a piece of my undying admiration, and both wanted to be number one in my world.

Davon showed me on paper how the insurance money would allow me to pay off all our debts. Pamela and I had been investment-rich and cash-poor for years, allowing our consumer debt to balloon out of control. We were beholden to ridiculous and unnecessary interest payments on our debts. I had told Pamela over and over that we should sell some things, cash out a few investments to get back on track, but she constantly reassured me that everything would be okay. And now, it finally would be okay because, as far as the insurance company would eventually be concerned, she was gone. I would be debt-free.

Davon wasn't shedding any tears over her disappearance. He

scoffed when he saw our financial situation, one that he squarely blamed her for creating.

"You've got to be kidding me, dude. You let her make these decisions that could have bankrupted you for no good reason. It's time to get your finances in order. I can help you do that," he scolded.

The townhouse would be paid off, as would the credit card bills, and I would be pretty much free to do whatever I wanted. I could live off our remaining investments and not ever have to work again. It was tempting, but at the same time, the prospect of doing this without Pamela or Polly was depressing. I would choose to keep the towering debt if it meant having them back in my life.

When I was in DC, Geni had not budged on letting me see Polly. To be fair, she was very straightforward about it. I had asked her repeatedly, and her answer stayed the same: "It's not the right time, Darwin. She's a teenage girl. She's too fragile right now. I think we need to wait until this whole thing blows over."

This was another reason I had returned to Bingham. If Pamela wasn't in DC and I couldn't see Polly, what was the point? In fact, what was the point of anything anymore? As I gazed out the window of my room across the lush green lawn to the forest beyond, I thought of how Pamela's death would ironically make my life easier because of the life insurance. But I could not have anticipated that her loss would make me feel so empty inside. As I peered into the woods, I shuddered a little, thinking about the darkness beyond the tree line. There was something a little evil about this place despite its beauty. I had my window open, and when the wind rustled the trees, it sounded like a thousand tiny screams. I wondered if one of them was Pamela's. Had I made a terrible mistake by coming back here?

"Geni, I just really need to see her. We can do it wherever you want. In fact, why don't you fly her here to North Carolina? It's so quiet and serene. We'll get to spend some quality time together," I said over the phone, trying to keep the desperation out of my voice.

"Darwin, you've got to be kidding. That's the last place I want her to be. What if they find Pamela's body? How would you handle that with Polly there? Not an option. I appreciate you wanting to see her. Like I said before, you can always talk to her on the phone, by text, or by email. Nothing's changed with that. I just think this is a very difficult time for all of us, and she needs to be with me where she's safe and out of the spotlight."

"Pardon me, Geni, how is it difficult for you? I'm the one whose wife is missing. And why is Polly not equally as safe with me as she is with you?"

"Well, for starters, her father is the one being implicated in the disappearance of his wife."

"'Implicated'? How do you figure that? Am I in jail? Have I been charged? Arrested? Where are you getting this from?"

"Come on, Darwin. You know what people are saying."

"Not really. I'm trying to ignore things that aren't true. And besides, it doesn't matter what they think. It matters what you and Polly think."

"We don't know what to think."

"Geni, come on. I know we haven't always seen eye to eye on everything, but you know me better than anyone, maybe even better than Pamela does. You know I'm not capable of harming someone. And for you to even entertain the possibility in front of my daughter is appalling. Plus, why in the world would I come back here if I had something to do with it?"

"I didn't start it. It's the girls at school. They're the ones putting ideas in her head. I've been defending you the best I can."

I was quiet for a while, realizing that even the people who knew me the best, who knew me the longest, who loved me, like my daughter, were doubting me. This was not good. I had to get control of the situation and not let vicious gossip destroy my reputation.

"Okay, well, I'm not going to continue to argue with you about this. I would just appreciate a little support. I've lost my wife. People are looking at me like I'm a monster, and I'm not able to see the daughter I love more than anything else in the whole entire world."

"Well, if you love her so much, you'll give her some time and space to deal with this."

She was right. I would back off. I was starting to think that maybe the best thing for Polly was not to have me in her life at all.

25

EDDIE'S FIND

It was my favorite time of year to be on the trails. Even though it was still summer, the air was cool in the morning and easy to breathe in. It was not like the humid air in other parts of the state. The leaves were so green they sparkled when the sunlight hit them, and they rustled gently like a thousand tiny claps when a breeze slipped through. Very few people ventured up the mountain in the early morning, not at a fancy place like Bingham. Rich people liked to sleep in and then slowly sip their coffee on the veranda before venturing out.

When I had some downtime, I liked to take my mutt, Cleo, for a little hike when no one was around—just me, my dog, and nature. This was the way life was supposed to be. Even though I technically worked in the hospitality industry, I wasn't a big fan of people.

I chose the Overlook Trail because it was the most challenging. I liked that the edge was so close, just one misstep away. Sometimes, I played little games with myself, seeing how close I could walk to the edge of the trail without falling into the gorge below to my death. After a rainstorm, for example, one slippery rock, one buried, muddy tree root could be the difference between living and dying. The idea of it thrilled me. I had always been like this, a risk taker who wasn't afraid of death.

Of course, I'd been hiking these trails my whole life, and I knew how to be safe, unlike the tourists who breezed in for a day or two in their fancy hiking gear like they were through-hiking the Appalachian Trail. They looked the part, but they didn't have a clue. One missed trail marker and they were lost in the wilderness and calling 9-1-1 on their cell phones for help. This meant we had to race up the mountain in our rugged-terrain vehicles and rescue them. It happened at least once a week.

Sometimes, I worried about Cleo because she would dart off the edge of the trail chasing a bird or a squirrel, but then she would always pop her head back up to show me that she was okay. My daddy always told me you can't control a bird dog in the wild, you've just got to let them go and hope for the best. We lost a lot of family dogs when I was growing up because they would run out in front of a car on a country road or dive into a pond that was too deep, but Daddy said they just weren't strong enough to survive, and when you found a dog that wasn't weak, he or she would stick around for a long time. I had had Cleo going on four years now. She seemed to be sticking around.

When we rounded a bend on the trail and Cleo disappeared, I didn't think anything of it at first. Then I called her, and she didn't respond. I could feel fear welling up in my throat. I ran up the trail calling for her frantically. I was glad Daddy wasn't here to see me. He wouldn't have approved of a man acting so upset about a lost dog. He would have accused me of acting like a girl, which in his mind was the worst thing any man could do.

"Cleo? Cleo! Where are you, girl? Come on now. Don't play games with me, where are you, girl?"

I heard her whimpering and ran in the direction of the pitiful sound. When I looked over the edge, I saw that she had slipped onto a craggy ledge just below the trail. After the ledge, there was nothing but a freefall into the gorge a mile or so below. I lay down on my stomach and reached out with both arms to grab her. I could see that she had cut her hind leg on the rock when she fell. She was scared but dragged her leg and slowly shuffled to me until I was close enough to reach out to her.

"It's okay, girl. I'll get you fixed up."

I put her in my lap and pulled out a small first aid kit from my backpack. I washed the cut on her leg with an antiseptic wipe as she whined and struggled a little, and then I put a bandage around the cut to stop the bleeding. I filled a collapsible dog bowl that I always carried with water from my bottle. She sipped it and then lay down under a tree to rest from her ordeal. I could feel my heartbeat starting to return to normal now that she was okay. Despite what Daddy had told me about dogs, Cleo was my world, and if anything happened to her, I couldn't imagine going on. I was soft that way.

I looked back over the edge, thinking about how lucky I was that Cleo had landed on the ledge instead of falling into the gorge. Even though I was a risk taker, I was also a little afraid of heights. It was a secret I hid from most people, especially from Daddy.

When I peered over the edge ever so carefully, I saw an odd item on the rock. There was something black and muddy with little bottles sticking out of it. Next to it was what looked like a cracked cell phone. I lay down on the trail again on my stomach, just like I did when I rescued Cleo. I grabbed a nearby stick and used it to pull the items closer to me. Once they were within my reach, I shimmied a little closer to the edge and extended my arms as far as I could and grabbed them.

I sat there on the trail studying what appeared to be a runner's belt. It was covered in mud and badly weathered from being out in the rain. The plastic bottles were still partially filled with a blue liquid, probably some fancy sports drink those tourists liked to drink. The cell phone screen was smashed, with a thousand tiny spiderweb-like cracks spreading out in every direction.

I didn't have to study them for too long. I knew immediately who they belonged to. They belonged to Pamela Stevens. Her name was written right there in faded Sharpie on the canvas belt. She was the missing hiker everyone had been looking for. I slid the items into my backpack. I was so thankful that I just happened to come this way today and that Cleo just happened to fall off the trail onto that very same rock. It was almost like it was meant to be.

I recalled the first day the woman went missing. I had just returned to the lodge from the reservoir. I heard rumblings that she had fallen from the vicinity of the Big Rock. When I got back, I got Morris to give me the keys to the van, and I headed down the mountain. I told him I needed to go to the agricultural supply store and get a few things for the barn—something that Wilson had asked me to do last week, and I had forgotten about. Morris just shrugged and tossed me the keys. My hands were shaking, but I tried to act cool in front of him and just nodded a thank you in his direction.

I had decided I was going to be the hero of this story. As soon as I got to the bottom of the steep mountain road, I pulled the van off the pavement onto a gravel trail that led to the base of the gorge. I made sure I pulled in far enough so that anyone passing by would not see the van. I quickly hiked in, and with the help of the GPS on my phone, I found the approximate spot beneath Overlook Trail where the woman would have landed. I started directly below the trail and moved out in concentric circles, using a machete to cut through the thick brush. There was no sign of her, and I was running out of time. I had to get the van back up the mountain to Morris so he wouldn't get suspicious, and I had to get back to work before anyone noticed I was missing. I decided that I would have to come back later and look for her.

Just as I was turning to leave, I saw a glint of something shiny in the brush. I reached down and picked it up. It was a diamond ring, the biggest diamond ring I had ever seen. *It must be hers,* I thought. On instinct, I grabbed it and put it in my pocket. It had probably slipped off her finger when she fell. This meant she had to be nearby. But I couldn't risk being gone too long. I felt the weight of the ring in my pocket against my leg as I walked. I headed back to the van, marking the spot with a pin on my phone for future reference.

As soon as I got back to the lodge and parked the van near the front door, there was a lot of commotion. The initial mild concern about there being a missing guest had turned frantic. A few employees were standing around a game table with a large map spread out on top of it. Wilson was tracing something on the map with his finger while he talked and the others listened. I passed Evelyn in the hallway. She had an anxious look on her pinched face, and she turned and grabbed my arm.

"Eddie, I need your help. I need everybody's help. You've probably heard. We have a missing hiker. She's been gone for several hours. Her husband alerted us, so we're searching for her ourselves right now. I really don't want to have to call the sheriff's office if we can help it. We have to find her. I know you know this mountain like the back of your hand," Evelyn said in a rush of words just above a whisper.

"I can help, for sure. Do you know what trail she was on?" I asked, trying to keep my voice neutral and without emotion.

"She was on Overlook."

"I'm on it, boss. Why don't you have a group walk the trail, and I'll go to the bottom of the mountain, to the gorge beneath the trail. I hate to say it, but if she fell, that's where she would have ended up."

"You're exactly right. I knew you were the person I needed to talk to. Let's keep this theory between us right now, okay? I don't want to alarm her husband unnecessarily. Take the van. I'll tell Morris."

I couldn't believe my luck. I was now being assigned to do the very thing that I was doing quietly earlier. Evelyn squeezed my arm to thank me and nodded for me to go. Suddenly, I felt important; Evelyn knew I was the person for this job. She had always been so good to me and had given me lots of opportunities to try many different roles at the resort. Even though I didn't have a college degree and had barely finished high school, she always made me feel like I was smart enough to work here. She looked like one of the fancy people, the way she dressed and talked, but I knew that was all an act. To get along with them, she had to look like them and act like them, but I suspected that she was more like me than she was like them. The way Evelyn had taken a shine to me made me think we were most likely from similar backgrounds. She just hid it better than I did.

I went back to the same gravel road and parked the van again. This time, I was determined to find the woman. I headed back into the underbrush with my machete. I wondered if I found her mortally wounded, like a deer, wouldn't it be the humane thing to put her down?

By the time I got back to the lodge, it was getting dark, and there were deputies from the local sheriff's office everywhere. They had set up a command post in front of the building with large lights and tables with maps spread out across them. I took a deep breath when I got out of the van. I hated to disappoint

Evelyn, and more importantly, I hated to disappoint myself. I had tried my best. Evelyn came running up to me, wearing jeans and wrapped tightly in a black shawl like a cocooned caterpillar. I had never seen her so casually dressed, or so hysterical.

"Eddie, please tell me you found her."

"I didn't, Miss Evelyn. I'm so sorry. I tried. I really did. I did circles beneath that trail around the gorge. I whacked the underbrush with my machete, looking for any sign of her. But it's getting dark, it's impossible to see anything right now. We'll have to try again tomorrow when it gets light."

"You're the best, Eddie. They're bringing in dogs, drones, helicopters, and a team that can rappel down the rock face into the gorge. I couldn't stall anymore. I had to call the sheriff's office. We need their resources."

"That makes sense. You did the right thing," I said, feeling disappointed that I had not found her, and now, someone else would likely be the hero and not me. But I also felt pride at how well this important woman was treating me. I felt so confident that I gave her shoulder a little squeeze like the one she had given me earlier. I could feel my chest puffing out.

"I know it's late. You probably need to go home."

"If you want, I can just stay here tonight and help with the search again at first light."

That's when Evelyn did something very much out of character. She hugged me and held on tight for several seconds. I finally counted to three in my head and gently pulled away from her embrace. It felt especially good to be hugged by her, but it also felt good to be hugged by anyone.

"I don't know how to thank you, Eddie. Just go see Simone at the front desk. Tell her we spoke. She'll give you a key to a room."

I walked into the lobby and headed right for Simone, trying not to let my face give away what I was feeling. There were so many emotions swelling up inside me like a tidal wave.

"Can you believe this, Eddie? A missing hiker?" Simone said in a whisper, as if all the officers milling around the lobby didn't already know what was going on.

"No, ma'am, I can't. I'm going to stay tonight so I can help with the search at dawn. Miss Evelyn said to come get a room key from you," I said, trying to sound casual.

Simone looked back at her computer screen, obviously trying to figure out which rooms were vacant, but she kept talking to me as she worked.

"I mean, this is bad, Eddie, *really* bad. The negative publicity could ruin us. We've got to find that poor woman before a bear or a rattler finds her."

Or a man, I thought to myself. Simone handed me the key, and I grabbed a small disposable toiletry set that they kept at the front desk for people who forgot theirs. There was no drug store or grocery store within thirty miles of the resort, so if you forgot something, you were most likely out of luck. Bingham thought of everything to make sure their guests were comfortable. That's what made them a luxury resort, all the little touches. They thought of things the visitors didn't even know they needed until they needed them like makeup wipes and organic honey for your tea.

When I got to my room, I immediately went to the bathroom, stripped off my work clothes, and jumped into a scalding hot shower. I used the soap to rub my skin raw. Sweat and grime had built up on me from my hours plodding through the brush at the bottom of the mountain. I called housekeeping and asked them to deliver a work shirt and work pants to my room that I could wear in the morning. We all wore a uniform and had the option to have it laundered at the resort or bring it home and wash it ourselves. I got so dirty when I worked that I had one for every day of the week. Mama usually washed them for me.

As I lay beneath the down comforter, two pillows propping up my head, scrolling through the hundreds of television channels, I imagined what it would be like to live in this kind of luxury day in and day out. How could you be upset if you slept in a comfortable bed like this every single night and could choose from so many television channels? I took a sip of the complimentary mineral water on the bedside table beside me. This was the life. And it occurred to me with a sudden irony that this was the life that Pamela Stevens had lost.

26

DARWIN TAKES A VACATION

When Simone handed me my forwarded mail at the front desk on my first day back at the resort, there was a postcard on top of the stack. It looked like one of those scams you get from time to time. It said that I had won a free vacation to a Caribbean island, one that I had never heard of before called Barbuda. The advertisement said that all I had to do was call the number on the card, make my reservation, and everything would be paid for as long as I agreed to sit through a two-hour presentation about buying a timeshare when I got there. It seemed too good to be true but, at the same time, exactly what I needed.

Since returning to Bingham, I realized the same number of eyes were judging me that had been judging me in DC. I needed to get away from all the people accusing me of unspeakable acts with their sideways glances. I also needed to get away from my custody battle with Geni that was going nowhere. But mostly, I needed to get away from everything that reminded me of Pamela.

Coming back here was a big mistake. Now, everywhere I looked at Bingham I saw her. I saw her casually walking across the lawn to the trail and giving me a backhanded wave. I saw her sitting at the bar, drinking a glass of champagne and throwing her head back in raucous laughter when she was a bit drunk. I saw her sitting with a book on the front patio by the firepit, drinking a mug of hot cocoa in the cool morning air, with a scarf wrapped multiple times around her neck. I had to get away from everything. She had been unusually calm and happy here, not her intense self. It made me sad to think about this. Going to a place I had never heard of, a place like Barbuda, seemed like the perfect way to escape all things Pamela.

The only thing that wasn't included in the all-expense paid trip was my airfare. I could make a flight reservation online, but this destination seemed to be very remote and tricky to get to. It appeared that I would have to take two flights and a boat. I needed help to work out the logistics. Pamela had a relationship with a travel agency in the northeast that had always lined up her business travel. Occasionally, we used them to plan our fabulous vacations—yet another expense that we should not have added to our debt column. But now, with the insurance money that Davon promised would be coming in, flying to an exotic island didn't seem like splurging anymore.

I called the 1-800 number on the card and got a friendly sounding young woman on the other end of the line who once again explained that everything would be covered if I agreed to attend the timeshare meeting.

"You're going to love Barbuda. It's the best. Very secluded and quiet. It's a great place to relax and get away from everything," the young woman said excitedly like she was still trying to sell me on it, even though I had already told her that I was in.

"It sounds great. It's exactly what I need right now."

After I hung up, I called the travel agency and asked for Ramona. Ramona worked in Philadelphia, but her clients were all over the country. With so much work happening remotely these days, many people had given up their brick-and-mortar offices for the freedom and flexibility of working from home. Ramona was one of those people. I had never met her, but Pamela swore by her.

"Ramona, Darwin Stevens here. Pamela Stevens' husband."

There was a deafening silence on the other end of the line. And then, Ramona finally spoke.

"Darwin, how are you? I mean, I know things haven't been good recently. I was so sorry to hear about Pamela. I really enjoyed working with her over the years. She's a tough cookie. I'm praying for you and your family, praying for a miracle."

I hated that word "miracle." I never knew how to respond to a statement about miracles. I didn't believe in them, never had. I certainly wasn't going to start now in my darkest hour. But I had to be polite. Ramona meant well.

"Thanks. I'm okay. It's been pretty rough, surrounded by all the things that remind me of her. She always spoke very highly of you too, by the way. I appreciate all the help you've given her in the past and given us with our vacations. That's why I'm calling. I really need to get away from all this chaos, to be alone with my grief, I guess."

"Gosh, I get it. This must be so tough. Again, I'm so sorry. Where are you thinking about going, or do you know? Do you need some suggestions?"

Maybe this was a bad idea. I stopped for a minute and thought about what this must look like to her. It would look like I was running away. Yet, I was running away. I had to stop worrying about what other people thought if I wanted to get on with my life. This was part of my plan, to get on with life, whatever that looked like. Right now it looked like a trip to Barbuda.

"I'm trying to get to Barbuda. Can you help me with that? I know it's kind of challenging to travel there."

"Barbuda. Wow, that's off the grid," she said with surprise in her voice.

"I know. But I hear it's very beautiful and relaxing, and not very crowded. I just need to regroup and figure out what my life is going to look like without Pamela, and I think this may the perfect place to do it. I got this postcard about a free trip, and I don't know, it just seems like a sign or something. It's one of those freebie deals if you agree to go to a timeshare meeting. Hope it's not a scam. I know it sounds crazy. Anyway, I'm in North Carolina, so I guess I can fly out of Charlotte if that works. I know Barbuda is difficult to get to."

"Of course. It is kind of a hard place to get to, but I can make it happen. Do you have the dates you wish to travel?"

"Date."

"Excuse me?"

"As soon as possible. Just a departure date. I only want to purchase a one-way ticket for now. I want to leave everything open-ended. You know, in case I decide to stay for a while."

I could hear Ramona tapping furiously on her keyboard. She was either looking for flights or emailing the police that I was trying to leave the country. I didn't care. I had passed caring hours ago. I wanted out. I was not in custody. I was not an official suspect. No one had told me that I needed to stay in the country. I was free to do as I pleased. And what I wanted to do was to get away from everything and everyone, especially from this dark place that seemed to be closing in on me with every passing second. What had once seemed so beautiful to me was now tainted by the loss of Pamela. Even in the daylight, with the bright sunlight shimmering beneath perfectly blue skies, there was a darkness that hung over this place. I feared that if I stayed, it would get me just like it had gotten Pamela.

27

CELIA TAKES FLIGHT

When I got the call from my old college friend, Ramona, she was breathless with excitement. I think part of her always wanted to be a news reporter, but her parents encouraged her to do something more practical and flexible, so, she opened her own travel agency. In her spare time, she watched and read every true crime story that she could get her hands on. Even though she wasn't a journalist, her instincts were good when it came to following the thread of a mystery.

"You know that guy you've been writing about, the one whose wife went missing in North Carolina? Guess where he's going?"

"I have no idea, but I'm pretty sure you're going to tell me."

"Barbuda!"

"Ba-what? Where in the heck is that?"

"It's this super remote little island in the Caribbean. Beautiful, but not much there. It takes two planes and a boat to get there."

"How in the world do you know this? Not about Barbuda, but about Darwin going there?"

"Weirdly, his wife, Pamela, was a longtime client of mine.

She used me for her business travel and occasionally for their vacations."

"Okay, so Darwin is going on vacation. I'm sure he wants to get away from all the chaos surrounding his wife's disappearance. I heard he went home to DC for a vigil or something like that for his wife and it was brutal. Everyone is looking at him sideways, as you can imagine. But still, going on a tropical vacation when your wife is missing is a little much."

"Well, apparently, he must be back in North Carolina because he's flying out of Charlotte. I don't think he's going on vacation."

"What do you mean?"

"He bought a one-way ticket."

"Interesting."

"I thought so too. I immediately thought of you. Maybe he's taking the life insurance money and running? Maybe he has another woman stashed in Barbuda? Maybe he's trying to get away from the investigators?"

"I guess anything is possible. But he's not charged, as far as I know, so he's free to do whatever he wants. Plus, life insurance doesn't pay out that quickly. That could take months."

"But don't you want to know why he's going?"

"I do, but we can't just accuse the guy of fleeing the country because he's involved in his wife's disappearance. I've got to have proof. It *is* weird that he's apparently just gotten back here to Bingham and now he's leaving again so soon. I've been all over this property and I haven't seen him yet. He's probably trying to stay away from me. He probably thinks I think he's guilty of something. I haven't reported that, but I wouldn't be surprised if he thinks I'm implying it in my articles."

The wheels in my head were spinning. I had always thought Darwin's behavior was suspicious despite his ironclad alibi. His weird speech at the press conference made me even more convinced that he was hiding something. Now, it looked like I might be right. I knew my editor wouldn't clear me to go on a wild goose chase to Barbuda. But I did have a treasure chest of unused vacation days.

"I think you have to go there and see for yourself what he's up to. At least that's what I would do if it were my story. That's why I've already taken the liberty of finding you a moderately priced hotel and flights. I was pretty sure when I told you about this you wouldn't want to miss the opportunity to follow this up. Am I right?"

"You know me too well!"

I wondered if there was a kind of travel agent code of ethics, a confidentiality agreement where they weren't supposed to share their clients' travel plans. If there was such a thing, Ramona didn't care that she was violating it for what she believed was a greater good.

I knew that Matt would think I was crazy if I told him I was going to Barbuda to follow Darwin Stevens. Things had finally settled down at home, and he was no longer accusing me of being obsessed with the case. I had stopped talking about it incessantly over the phone and tried to ask more questions about the boys when we spoke. I promised them I would be home very soon.

But I also hoped he would understand that this was something I needed to do to bring this case to full closure. I toyed briefly with the idea of telling Jack about it but decided I needed to get my ducks in a row first. I needed to follow the tip and see where it led me. If I was right, if Darwin was trying to escape the country and start a new life with another woman, then I would bring Jack in. As a reporter, it wasn't my job to tell investigators anything, but as a human being, and as a woman, I wanted to do the right thing by Pamela Stevens.

"Ramona. What am I going to do with you? What are you getting me into?" I said with a chuckle, amazed that she always seemed to find a way to live vicariously through my job, which she perceived as much more exciting than hers. I thought her job was much more exciting than mine because she got to travel around the world at a major discount.

"I'm just steering the ship in the right direction. Okay, you should have an email with all your travel details. You leave in four hours. I charged it to your card on file."

"I guess I should thank you, but this also feels a little like you're playing junior detective again. I'm afraid you've streamed one too many true crime documentaries."

"Fair. But unlike other women who stay up late watching them with a bottle of wine, taking notes on how to kill their husbands, I know an actual investigative journalist who can fulfill my dreams while I stay right here in my spare bedroom running my business. I stay safe and get to watch you catch the bad guy."

"Wow, that sounds like quite a deal for me. I'll keep you posted."

"You better. You owe me for this one. Don't forget it."

When I hung up with Ramona, I sent my editor a note telling her that I had a family emergency and needed a few personal days. I also sent Matt a text telling him I was leaving North Carolina for a few days to cover a story and that I might not have great cell service. I didn't want to lie to him—it really was a work trip, just not paid for or sanctioned by my company.

Part of me was a little disappointed to think that this might be the oldest story in the book, that Darwin Stevens may have gotten rid of his wife so that he could take the life insurance money and run away to live happily ever after in paradise with his girlfriend. I imagined she was younger than Pamela, probably more beautiful and surely a gold digger. I had to stop this narrative from spinning out of control in my head. I honestly had no idea if there was life insurance or a girlfriend. I was getting ahead of myself.

As I pictured this scenario, it didn't ring true in my head. Darwin, even with his strange behavior, didn't strike me as a stupid man who would off his wife and start a new life with a mistress. Still nothing else was making sense. What could this trip mean? This one-way ticket? Could he just be wanting to get out of town? It was possible. There was no way to know for sure unless I traveled there myself and witnessed what he was doing. The best-case scenario was that he was simply trying to escape his profound grief and the accusatory glances by getting as far away as he could, to a remote part of the Earth where no one knew who he was. A big part of me hoped this was the case. I hoped my trip to Barbuda would be fruitless and that I would find nothing but a sad man who missed his wife.

The other part of me knew that people were complicated and that Darwin's reasons for leaving the country could be multifaceted. He could very well have played some role in his wife's disappearance.

I googled Barbuda, trying to figure out what I needed to pack for this last-minute trip just north of the equator. Predictably, the weather forecast showed that it was going to be hot—very hot. I didn't have many wardrobe choices because I had packed for a long weekend in the mountains with chilly mornings and cool nights. I would have to buy some clothes in the airport.

I was going into the trip with an open mind, but if I saw Darwin Stevens in Barbuda with another woman, it was game on. He would become the prime suspect in his wife's disappearance. That's when I would bring Jack Sorrells into the equation.

28

CELIA UNDERCOVER

In her email, Ramona had included a map of the tiny island and tips about where to eat and how to get around. She recommended renting a bike or a golf cart the first day as cars were not permitted on the island. She had thought of every small detail. Ramona would have made a good investigator.

At first, I worried about Darwin spotting me, but then I realized he was trying to distance himself from the case. He wouldn't be paying attention to a tourist in a T-shirt and jean shorts with a baseball hat on and no makeup quietly reading a book at a café table in the town square. He had too many other things to worry about. Plus, he would never suspect that a reporter would follow him all the way from North Carolina.

I started with coffee in the morning and then got lunch and a Diet Coke. As early evening fell, I ordered a small dinner and a glass of wine. If anybody cared about me commandeering a table from dawn to dusk at the local café, no one said anything about it. After all, I was a paying customer, and people here on the island seemed pretty laid back.

I tried hard to focus on my book, but every few seconds I would look up to watch someone whiz by on a bike or a person walking with a bag of groceries. So far, no one even remotely looked like Darwin. I was starting to wonder if he was even here. But Ramona had been so sure about his plans. I had to trust her. At this point, I didn't have much of a choice. I was here.

I knew what Darwin looked like after studying him at the resort, but I also kept a few photos of him on my phone that I had screenshotted from Facebook, just in case I needed to jog my memory. All the white men who went by were either too old or too young to be him. What if he was holed up in a bungalow with his mistress somewhere and never intended to go out in public? This was a distinct possibility, and one I hadn't thoroughly worked through.

I was getting very burned despite my hat and frequent applications of sunblock. When I looked in the bathroom mirror at the café, I could see that my chest where the V-neck of my T-shirt exposed my skin was starting to look lobster-red. Even as the sun was going down, it felt one hundred times stronger than it did in North Carolina. My Yankee skin was not adapting well to the Caribbean climate.

The next morning, day two of my stakeout, I wore a caftan that covered more of my body and a large, wide-brimmed straw hat. Every time I looked up from my book to assess a passer-by, I would lose my place and be forced to start the paragraph over again. This made for some very tedious reading. I was beginning to lose patience with my mission when, suddenly, I saw him. Darwin was riding a beat-up, blue beach bike with bent, rusty handlebars, and he was carrying a small black knapsack on his back. Luckily, I had propped my rented bike against a concrete wall nearby. I threw a five-dollar bill on the table to cover my drink and grabbed my bike. I knotted the caftan tightly at my waist so that it wouldn't get caught in the spokes of the wheels. My goal was to keep up with Darwin without getting too close. I still didn't think he would recognize me in my tourist get-up, but I didn't want to take any chances. We had exchanged a few pointed glances at Bingham, and I figured, all that time, he may have been studying me while I was studying him.

I tried to look casual as I pedaled down the rutted gravel road, hoping not to skid on the tiny rocks and fall. This would no doubt draw his attention. I rode bikes a lot in our neighborhood in Pennsylvania with the boys, but most of the time I was focused on them not killing each other, not on my own safety. And, I was always wearing a helmet and workout gear, not a caftan, a straw hat, and flip-flops. My outfit might protect me from the sun, but it would do nothing to protect me in the event of a crash.

Darwin looked carefree on his bike as he zigzagged back and forth down the lane, taking his fingers off the handlebars every few moments and gliding like a little boy. He looked so much different than he had at the resort. When he turned his head to the side, I caught a glimpse of his face. The drawn, anxious look I had seen on him at Bingham was replaced with something much more serene and peaceful. And there was only one reason I could think of that he could be happy right now, so soon after Pamela's disappearance—another woman.

Eventually, Darwin turned down a driveway. I followed but waited until he was almost at the house before I turned in quickly, stashing my bike in some brush and hiding behind a tree. From my vantage point, I could only see Darwin's back as he walked up to the front door. The door swung open, and a woman embraced him tightly in a bear hug. His frame completely obscured her, but I could see her thin arms and delicate hands clutching his back. Then she led him inside, and the door closed.

That was it. This was all I needed to see. Darwin Stevens had most likely killed his wife, taken her money, and then escaped to this island to be with his girlfriend. I leaned against the tree, waiting for the cloak of darkness so that I could retreat. I didn't want to risk them seeing me as I rolled out of the driveway.

I knew exactly what I needed to do next. I was going to call Jack and give him a heads-up about what was going on in Barbuda. While it wasn't my job to solve crimes, and in fact, many would argue that it was the opposite of my job, I couldn't help but want to get the information into the right hands. I could tell that Jack had never recovered from his perceived career-suicide a decade ago, and he needed a big win to get himself back in everyone's good graces. For some reason, I had a soft spot for the guy and wanted to help him catch this jerk—if Darwin did in fact do something to his wife.

"Jack, it's Celia Finch," I said quietly into my cell phone after I was safely back at my hotel. I didn't think anyone could hear me through the walls, but I wanted to be careful, just in case.

"Celia, to what do I owe this honor?"

"Well, you're not going to believe what I'm into right now."

"No, Celia, I'm sure I won't. Please don't make me guess. I don't have that kind of time or energy."

"So, I discovered through a source that Darwin Stevens had bought a one-way plane ticket from Charlotte to this tiny, remote island in the Caribbean called Barbuda."

"Bar-boo-huh?"

"Never mind, that's not important right now. What's important is that I followed him here."

"You did what?"

"I know it sounds kind of crazy. I mean, it is crazy, but it panned out. I'm onto something."

"It sounds like stalking or obstruction of justice, which is a crime either way. That's what it sounds like you're into."

"Okay, just stop for a minute and listen to me. I suspected that he was escaping, taking his wife's money, and coming here to meet a mistress, and that's why I followed him. It was just a hunch, but guess what?"

"I'm sure you're going to tell me."

"I was right. He's here with a woman. I saw him with my own eyes, hugging her and going into a house. I think he may have killed Pamela."

There was silence on the other end of the line. This was probably the first time anyone had said this potential outcome out loud, and obviously, Jack needed time to process it.

"Anything is possible. But having a girlfriend doesn't prove Darwin killed his wife. Plenty of men have women on the side, and they never lay a hand on their wives. Cheating does not make someone a killer."

"I get that. But it makes it more likely that he did something to Pamela. It gives him one more reason. You need to come here and see for yourself, and then you can judge whether I'm right or not, whether Pamela's disappearance was really a domestic violence murder."

Again, there was silence on the other end of the line. And then Jack spoke.

"How did you get this tip?"

"That's not important right now. Plus, you know I'm not revealing a confidential source. What's important is that you get your butt down here and check out this situation for yourself."

"Okay, well, how in the heck am I supposed to get to this Bar-buddha place anyway?"

"I will text you my travel agent's contact information. She'll line up the whole thing. She's a good friend. She'll be discreet."

"Okay," Jack said reluctantly.

"And Jack, one more thing."

"What is it?"

"Get here as fast as you can."

29

JACK GOES FULL CIRCLE

I KNEW THERE WAS NO WAY SHERIFF LANSING WAS going to okay this crazy mission. He would tell me the department didn't have the resources to fund a pipe dream like this when we had a serious fentanyl problem in our county that was leading to almost weekly overdoses and deaths. He would tell me to be patient and wait until Darwin returned to the country. But what if he didn't return? He had allegedly bought a one-way plane ticket according to Celia. That didn't sound like a guy who was coming back anytime soon. That sounded like a guy who was running away from something.

I told work I needed a few mental health days after the stress of the search for Pamela, which had led nowhere. After what I had been through a decade prior with the Billy Barnes case, no one questioned my need to take a little mental health time. I told Cindy the truth. I couldn't lie to her. I knew she would be afraid for me, thinking I was going down another dark rabbit hole I wouldn't be able to pull myself out of. I had to convince her that this time things would be different. I had my eyes wide open and knew exactly what I was doing. If I was wrong about Darwin Stevens, I would back off; no harm done.

"You're going to need more than an affair to prove he wanted his wife out of the way. Plus, he has an alibi, so did he hire someone to do it?" Cindy rattled off her questions with her hands on her hips, her body language a grand visual display of her disapproval.

Sometimes, Cindy drove me nuts with her super-sleuthing. Granted, sometimes she was right on the money and saw things that I didn't. But other times, she was parroting verbiage directly from a true crime documentary or from one of those mystery novels that she loved to read, which had zero to do with solving actual, real-life crimes.

"I agree. Plenty of men cheat on their wives and don't kill them. In fact, most men who cheat don't kill their wives. But this is a little different. We don't know if this is an accident or a homicide. I've got to figure that out first. Leaving the country so soon after your wife's disappearance, possibly getting a big life insurance payout, and potentially rendezvousing with your girlfriend on a remote island do not exactly paint the picture of innocence."

"I agree, but I don't know why you can't just tell the sheriff the truth instead of using your precious vacation time to go and do this."

"Because he won't approve it. And this is something I need to do. If this woman was killed by her husband and I let him get away with it, I'll never forgive myself."

Cindy got quiet. I could tell by the look on her face exactly what she was thinking—that this was really about letting Rosa down, that I had never forgiven myself for that, and now, I was hoping to solve this case as a substitute. Maybe in the beginning I had thought about assuaging my guilt over letting Rosa down, but now, I just wanted to find Pamela for her family and friends. It wasn't about Rosa anymore.

"Okay. But promise me you'll be careful. Don't do anything rash. Just get the information and then come back and run it up the flagpole through the proper channels. Don't try to be a hero. You don't have jurisdiction there. Do they even have an extradition agreement with the US?"

I put my hands up in the air and shrugged. I had no idea. And she was right; my badge was no good in Barbuda.

With that, she pulled me in for a tight hug. She struggled to get her tiny arms around my big frame. I could feel her heart beating a hundred miles an hour against my chest. It was in moments like these that I realized I had everything I needed right here in front of me. Sometimes, I was just too full of my own self-pity to recognize it.

As I sat on the tarmac looking out the window of the airplane, watching the valets unload luggage from the carts and onto the plane, I thought about how strange life was that a country boy like me was on the way to a small exclusive island to meet a big-city reporter and possibly solve a murder case. Never in my wildest dreams did I know what adventures lay ahead of me when I got into law enforcement. I got into it for the right reasons—to help people. But somewhere along the way, I had lost *my* way. I had lost sight of what was truly important. For the past few years, I had just been going through the motions, trying to stay beneath the radar while I climbed back up the law enforcement ladder in the wake of the Rosa tragedy. I was so focused on getting to that next rung that I didn't take any risks because I was afraid to be knocked back down again. Now, I realized that being successful without integrity meant nothing.

As the plane began to take off and I could hear the wheels retract, I put my head back and closed my eyes. I didn't fully comprehend just how exhausted I was. Within seconds, I was asleep, dreaming about a mysterious Caribbean paradise called Barbuda.

I was jet-lagged and bleary-eyed when we landed in Miami, having had a fitful two hours of sleep in the small coach seat. While I was honestly too big to fly coach comfortably, I was too cheap to fly any other way. Cindy and I had a nice life, but we were not financially secure enough to upgrade our seats to first class when we flew.

After a puddle jumper to the Bahamas from Miami, I awkwardly rolled my bag onto the shuttle that would take us to the ferry. I had no idea what to pack because I didn't know exactly what our surveillance would involve—so I took too much. On one hand, I wanted to blend in, so I brought tourist clothes. On the other hand, we might be in the bushes at night, so I brought black shirts and camouflage pants.

I sat down on a cushioned bench on the ferry with a perfect view of the teal blue water with bright green layers interspersed. I could almost see straight to the sandy bottom. I had never seen water so clear before. The water off the coast of North Carolina tended to be murky and full of silt, which gave it a slightly brown tinge. Seeing the bottom there was usually out of the question.

As the ferry pulled away from the dock, I eased into the gentle sway of the boat making its way through the waves. I felt like if I leaned my head back, I could fall asleep again. But I resisted the urge. Of all the inane rabbit holes I had gone down to solve a case, this was most likely the biggest one ever. But here I was, on my way to a place I had never heard of and couldn't even pronounce. I was chuckling about this, giddy from lack of sleep, when my phone rang.

"Are you close?" Celia asked, sounding flustered.

"Closer than I've been all day. I'm on the ferry. You should have told me this was an odyssey."

I silently congratulated myself on using such a big word with a journalist, although I doubted she would notice. She seemed very distracted by what was happening on the other end of the call.

"Well, get here as fast as you can. He's in the house with the mystery woman. I will pick you up at the dock on a golf cart, and we'll go right there."

"Okay, I'm doing my best. I can't exactly jump in the water and swim there."

Then I heard silence on the other end of the line. Celia didn't even get a chance to hear my joke. She had hung up on me midsentence. Clearly, she was getting down to business and had no time or patience for my sarcasm. I looked across the water at the small island that was starting to come into focus. The sun was beginning to set, but my suspicion that I might be in over my head again was just clocking in for the night shift.

30

EVELYN UNCOVERING

WHEN HIS SHIFT ENDED, MORRIS BROUGHT ME Eddie's dirty backpack that he carried with him everywhere. He said he had found it in the back of the van after he took Eddie down the mountain to the employee parking lot. Eddie had obviously forgotten it. Morris brought it to me for safekeeping, asking me to lock it in the office and give it to Eddie the next morning because he was going to be off and wouldn't be able to do it.

"No problem," I said to Morris with the weariness that accompanied another long day of putting out a thousand little fires.

"I didn't look in it. But there could be a wallet, keys, maybe a phone. I don't want him to freak out about it. That's why I thought it was best to give it to you."

"I get it. It will be safe here."

I took the grungy backpack. At first, I considered emptying it and washing it before placing it in my office, but then I decided to just hold it at arm's length. But as I put it down, I felt that there was an extra weight to it that seemed abnormal for the types of things someone might need in a typical workday. I had always been curious about Eddie and his mountain-man ways and wondered what prized possessions he carried around with him in his nasty, fraying bag all the time.

I had given him a shot, even though he barely had a high school degree and was very rough around the edges. He had exceeded all my expectations as an employee. He was always on time, polite to the guests, and worked hard at any task I gave him. He was willing to learn and was a quick study. But I did wonder what his life was like outside of work. He never talked about his family or his home life. Based on the way he looked and acted around me, I suspected that he came from a working-class background, not unlike mine, and probably had faced a lot of hardship. I could tell by the way he looked at me that he thought I was one of the fancy people. He treated me delicately, with caution, like a porcelain doll that might break if he touched me the wrong way.

I decided it wouldn't hurt to peek inside Eddie's bag. I could always say that I was looking for his cell phone. If I didn't find one, I could call him and tell him I had his bag.

I closed my office door and unzipped the bag slowly, turning my head every few seconds to see if someone might catch me snooping. I knew that I was alone, but the voice in my head was still telling me to watch out—*Don't do it, Evelyn. It's someone's private property. It's not right.*

I thrust my hand into the bag, fished out a few items, and laid them on my desk. There was a balled-up sweatshirt, a plastic deodorant stick, a comb, and a cell phone. I inspected the phone a little closer and realized that it was caked in dry mud, and the screen was shattered. It was clearly broken, obviously not the one he used on a regular basis. I dug into the bag again and pulled out a runner's belt with several empty water bottles attached to it. The belt was also caked in dry mud like the phone. I turned the belt over and over and thought about how this was an odd item for someone like Eddie to own. He didn't strike me as a runner, but maybe he used it for hiking. Although it seemed a little too highfalutin for someone like Eddie, who usually carried what appeared to be an old-timey plaid thermos.

I turned on the overhead light so that I could inspect the belt more closely. I turned it inside out and saw something written in black Sharpie on the material. It was faded and hard to read, so I took it over to my desk lamp and put it in the direct light. I had to catch my breath when I finally recognized the big block letters: "PAMELA STEVENS." This had to belong to Pamela Stevens. There was no other plausible explanation. Why in the world did Eddie have it in his backpack? I quickly grabbed my phone and took a picture of it. Then I shoved everything back into the backpack, zipped it up, and set it on a shelf behind my desk.

I stood there staring at the bag like it was radioactive. My mind was going in a million different directions. Eddie must have found these items, but why did he keep them from me? Why did he keep them from investigators? Maybe he was getting ready to turn them over to the sheriff's office and just hadn't done it yet? Nothing I rationalized made any sense.

And then, a chilling thought came over me. What if Eddie knew what had happened to Pamela? What if he was covering up for someone—someone like Darwin? Suddenly, things started to come into focus. Maybe Darwin had paid Eddie to help him get rid of the evidence. A little money to someone like Eddie would seem like a lot. A shiver went down my spine as I thought about this. I shuddered and reached for the blanket on my couch to wrap around my shoulders.

I decided I would need to tell Jack what I had discovered and figure out a way to keep the backpack from Eddie until Jack could get here and examine it. If I took the items out of the backpack and gave it back to Eddie, he would surely notice right away that they were missing. I couldn't risk that. I had to be smart about this. *Think, Evelyn, think,* the voice in my head kept saying over and over. There was a good possibility Eddie didn't even know the backpack was here, that he couldn't recall where he left it, or maybe he thought it had been locked in the van overnight.

Whatever I decided to do, I knew that I had to do it fast.

31

CELIA AND JACK

I COULDN'T HELP BUT CHUCKLE A LITTLE WHEN I thought about what strange bedfellows journalism created. Here I was in the middle of the night, sitting in a rented golf cart in the bushes with a good old boy cop from North Carolina on an isolated Caribbean island. You couldn't make this up. This is exactly what I loved about my job: the sheer unpredictability of the situations I found myself in. Getting bored was never something I worried about.

Jack had a camera with a long lens pointed at the front door of the home—the door I had seen Darwin go into a few hours earlier, the door where he had hugged the mystery woman the previous evening. There was no guarantee he or his lover would be making an appearance anytime soon, but we had to wait. At least, this was Jack's plan.

"Patience, my dear. This is what a stakeout is all about. Remember, this was your idea. I took two planes and a boat to get here so that I could sit in these bushes with your impatient self and watch the front door of a love nest with my telephoto lens."

"Patience has never been my strong suit."

"That doesn't shock me."

"Well, if you're a true hustler in my industry, you have to push to get what you want. Basically the opposite of being patient."

"True, but a good investigator knows that, in our business, everything is about timing. Crimes don't get solved just because we want them to. They get solved because we have the patience to wait people out until they do something stupid, like we believe our friend Darwin Stevens is about to do."

I was quiet for a moment as I took a big sip of Diet Coke. I was trying my best to stay awake, but the more I drank, the more I needed to go to the bathroom.

"So, quick personal question."

"Shoot."

"Where do you go to the bathroom on stakeouts?"

"Usually, in an empty bottle."

"For real?"

"Yep. Would you prefer that we wet our pants?"

"I don't know. It just seems kind of gross."

"Shush," Jack said, putting a hand over my mouth.

I was annoyed with him for trying to silence me, and I was about to slap his hand away when I realized the door had opened and Darwin was coming out with a woman. They were smiling and holding hands. He led her down the stairway from the porch. They seemed so happy, like they were floating on an invisible rainbow as they skipped down the stairs. The string of lights that lit the path down the driveway gave the whole scene a dreamy quality, like fireflies were encircling their heads.

I recognized the woman right away. Her tall, strong physique, her wavy brown shoulder-length hair, her angular face, a face that some people might call handsome. I had studied what felt like dozens of photos of her online. She wore a long blue flowing sundress with small white flowers on it. Her body was tan and toned. Her hair was streaked with fine blonde tinges from the sun. They were both wearing flip-flops. They talked in hushed tones as they walked right by us, headed for the beach access across the street.

Jack was busy taking photos. Neither of us said a word. When they disappeared onto the beach path through the dunes into the darkness, he laid his camera down in his lap and looked at me, bewildered. I imagined I, too, had a bewildered look on my face. I could feel it in the way my mouth drooped, and my eyes were open way too wide. But I couldn't help myself. This was something we never anticipated or expected.

"I do believe we just saw a ghost," Jack said slowly in a monotone voice. "Because I'm pretty sure that was Pamela Stevens on her husband's arm."

Neither of us spoke or moved for a solid minute.

"What does it mean? What do we do now?" I asked Jack with sincerity.

Jack looked at me like I had just asked him to explain quantum physics.

"I have no earthly idea. I guess whatever this is, whatever this was, he was in on it with her from the beginning. That's the only explanation I can come up with. This means the resources, time, and manpower we put into the search, it was all for nothing. He made a fool of us. They both did."

"Is it a crime?"

"To pretend to be missing? To collude with someone? To take life insurance money fraudulently? It sure is. There's a whole list of crimes here. Obstruction of justice, conspiracy, fraud."

"So, what do we do? Do you arrest them and take them back?"

"I don't have any jurisdiction here. I have to think about this for a minute."

We sat there much longer than one minute. I looked in the direction of the path, willing Darwin and Pamela to come back so I could get a better look at them. I wanted to see their faces. I could tell by their body language when they passed us on their way to the beach that they were smitten with each other. For some reason, this gave me more comfort than catching Darwin with another woman, even though I knew it now appeared they had committed a long list of crimes.

"Okay, Sherlock, times up. What's the plan?"

I could barely see Jack in the passenger seat of the golf cart. He was just a dark silhouette, his large frame hunched over as he considered our next move.

"I got no idea. I already told you."

32

EDDIE PANICS

I realized as soon as I got into my truck that I didn't have my backpack. Of course, I immediately panicked. I had kept it close for the past few days, knowing that Pamela's things were in it. I pictured them like hot lava, burning a hole in the synthetic material and revealing themselves to Morris. I hurriedly called Morris, who didn't answer.

I grabbed some chew from my center console and stuck a big wad in my mouth. I didn't need to panic. There was no reason for Morris or anyone else to open the backpack. He would probably just hold onto it and give it to me tomorrow. But why wasn't he answering his friggin' phone?

I decided he must be with one of the guests. Maybe he would answer my text, but I had to play it cool. I had to act like it was not a big deal. After all, I had my phone and my car keys. I could wait until tomorrow to get the backpack.

I watched my screen nervously. Finally, I saw the three little dots radiating, showing me that Morris was reading my text. It seemed like an eternity before he finally responded.

"I gave it to Evelyn," his text read.

I stared at the five words. To anyone who had nothing to hide, these words meant nothing at all. It was just an inconvenience. I'd get the bag tomorrow. But what if Evelyn decided to look inside? She might be curious to see what I carried around in my old dirty backpack all day long. I shook the thought out of my head. I couldn't wait until tomorrow morning. I wouldn't be able to sleep thinking about the possibility of Evelyn finding Pamela's things in my bag. It would open a whole new set of questions that I wasn't prepared to answer.

I decided I would have to drive my old truck back up the mountain and pay Evelyn a visit. I would have to tell her that something important was inside the bag that I couldn't live without for one single night, so I had to come back to get it. What that thing was, I had no idea. I would improvise.

I put my old truck in drive and headed up the mountain, praying the transmission wouldn't crap out on me during the steep climb up the winding road. I couldn't help but notice how the trees at night, with their spindly branches, seemed to be looming over the road like they might just snatch my truck right up. I shook the thought from my head. This was my place. Nothing could hurt me here, right? But as my headlights illuminated the tree line, I started to question every shadow around every curve. In one turn, I thought I saw eyes—yellow, glowing eyes staring right at me—most likely the eyes of an animal, but maybe not.

I tried not to think about what would happen if Evelyn looked inside the backpack. There would be serious consequences. She would want to know why I had Pamela's things, why I had not turned them in right away when I found them. But I was trying to keep a positive attitude as my old truck hemmed and hawed, lurching up the mountain. I liked Evelyn. She had been good to me. Better than any manager that I had ever had. But I had to protect myself at all costs. That's what Daddy would've told me to do, to buck up and act like a man.

When Daddy first went to prison, I didn't understand that he was going to be gone for a good long time. Me and my mama and my sister would go visit him on Saturdays. We would sit on the hard, green, scratched bucket chairs, get soda and cookies from the vending machine, and fidget while Mama and Daddy held hands under the table and talked in hushed tones that we couldn't hear all that well.

All around us, families similar to ours visited with one another. Some of the inmates in their orange jumpsuits held their small children on their laps. Some of the couples kissed across the table until a guard came over and told them to stop. "No physical contact," they would bark.

For a long time, this seemed like a normal life to me because I didn't know anything else. Then I started talking to the other kids at school whose fathers came home at night after work. It was only then that I discovered my life was not normal. I didn't even really know why my dad was in prison until he told me when I was seventeen.

"Son, I killed a man in a bar fight. I stuck a pool cue into his chest, pushed it clean through. Broke it in half. He bled out right there on the floor in the tavern. I was blackout drunk. Don't even remember what we were fighting about. Then I had to pay for my crime. It wasn't worth it."

That's when I found the scrapbook my mother had made with clippings from the newspaper about the case, and I became obsessed with my father's story. I was digging in the cabinet beneath the television set, looking for a deck of cards to take to a poker game with my buddies. Behind the rolls of wrapping paper, beneath an old stack of magazines, there it was. It was a large brown scrapbook simply labeled "Case" in my mother's handwriting. I scoured every single article, memorizing details and faces from the black-and-white newspaper photographs. I secretly vowed that if I ever saw the lead detective, the prosecutor, the judge, or any member of the jury in person that I would get revenge on them in Daddy's honor. But it was just a silly vow from a troubled teenager, not something I ever really intended to act upon.

Eventually, Daddy got out on parole, and after a short stint on house arrest, he was free to go back to a somewhat normal life. He had been convicted of manslaughter instead of murder since it was unclear who started the fight. His sentence was just sixty-four months, a little over five years. Once he got out, not a day passed that he didn't tell me I needed to avoid prison at all costs.

"You can't get a job with a felony record, son. Just look at me, working for pennies. And I don't even want to tell you what happens on the inside. It's ugly stuff, kid. Ugly. Don't ever put yourself in that position. If you find your foot on the wrong side of the law, at least don't get caught."

Daddy's words echoed in my head as I wound my way up the mountain to the lodge. I had already crossed the line. I had a dead woman's belongings in my backpack. I decided I would remain hopeful that Evelyn had resisted any urge to violate my privacy, so I wouldn't have to do anything I might regret.

In the days that had followed her disappearance, Pamela's ring felt like an anvil in my pocket. I didn't want to get caught with it, but I also didn't want to lose it. At night, I lay in bed trying to figure out what to do with it. Some nights, I would pull it out from beneath my mattress and look at it by the light of the moon peeking through the cracks in my venetian blinds. The ring shone so brightly beneath the reflection of the moon that I imagined anyone outside my window might see it twinkling.

I knew it was expensive. I considered going to a pawn shop in another town and selling it. Surely it would bring me enough money to get to Mexico. But it also seemed like a pretty sure way to get in trouble, selling the ring of a missing woman.

Finally, I decided it was best to get rid of it somewhere else so nobody would know I had been carrying it around all this time. If they found out, they would want to know why, and I didn't really have a good answer.

So, I dumped the ring in the brush on a little trail that led down the side of the lodge to a stream. It was an easy trail that a lot of people hiked, especially staff members on their breaks. I thought it had a better shot of being found there by someone else, and then nobody would accuse me of finding it under Big Rock and not turning it in.

Frankly, I had no idea what I was doing. I was just making things up as I went along.

When I walked into the lodge that night looking for my backpack, it was quiet, as I had expected it would be. Most of the employees had gone home for the evening. Only a skeleton crew remained on the overnight shift in case guests had any pressing needs that couldn't wait until morning.

As I walked down the hallway, I could see that Evelyn's door was slightly ajar. A thin shaft of light bathed the narrow corridor in front of her office. At first, it was quiet. Then I heard her talking. But it didn't sound like she was talking to a person. She was speaking in a hurried, stilted tone like she was leaving someone an urgent message. I crept closer, keeping in the shadows so that I could eavesdrop on her without her seeing me. Part of me didn't want to hear what she was saying because I knew my future was now in her hands.

33

JACK COMES UNDONE

I HAD RARELY BEEN SPEECHLESS IN ALL MY YEARS AS an investigator. Nothing surprised me. Or at least that's what I thought. I had seen it all. I had seen a woman killed and cut up with a chainsaw and shoved into a cooler. I'd seen the remains of a dead man who'd been thrown into a pen with wild boars who tore his body to shreds. I had seen a pedophile who kept a little girl chained in a box in his basement for a year. I had investigated a murder where a man wrapped his wife in plastic, dug out the floor of his basement, and then poured a new concrete floor over the top of her body. Murders in a mountain community were rare, but when they did happen, they were almost always bizarre.

I was rarely outsmarted. Billy Barnes was the only person that I could recall who had ever gotten away with a serious crime on my watch. And that one was due to my poor judgment. I prided myself on knowing people, on paying attention to details that other people didn't notice and figuring out what people were capable of. Darwin had given me some negative vibes, sure. He was clearly insecure and had possibly been emasculated by his wife at times, but he didn't seem like the type of person to engage in grand-scale fraud. I had obviously underestimated him. My radar had been way off.

Celia and I drove in silence as we headed back to the little downtown and our hotel. I suddenly remembered the ring that Evelyn had shown me—Pamela's ring. I never mentioned it to Darwin because he was still in my sights, but I asked her parents to give me a photo of it, telling them it would help us identify Pamela if we found her. Why had she dumped it? The only explanation was that she wanted to make it look like something bad had happened to her, that maybe she had been abducted or attacked by an animal and that the ring was left behind. This detail surely meant that Pamela Stevens had carefully planned and staged her own disappearance, in my opinion.

My only satisfaction was that Celia was as surprised as I was. Given that she was a highly educated woman working for a big-city newspaper, it gave me some comfort in knowing that we had both missed all the signs that Darwin and Pamela might be in cahoots. The problem now was, what was my obligation? I could easily walk away from this and pretend I was never here. After all, wouldn't revealing Darwin and Pamela's scam make me look stupid, like I had been searching in vain for a woman who had outsmarted all of us? The problem was that Celia had witnessed this debacle, and I didn't think there was any amount of persuasion that would keep her quiet. The story was too good. Suddenly, she broke the silence.

"What now?"

"I've got to think about this. I say we go back to North Carolina and really think this thing through. To arrest them, I need a judge to sign off on a warrant, and then Barbuda will have to agree to extradite them to the US, which is highly questionable. A lot of countries have extradition agreements with the US, but I'm not sure about Barbuda. It may be a sovereign place where people come because they know they won't be extradited. Pamela is a lawyer, after all. She would know things like that."

"That all makes sense. But maybe I should do a pre-emptive strike—write a story about what we saw, scare them into turning themselves in."

"Or scare them into running even further away. I really think we need to take this one step at a time."

"I get that, but I'm the one who invited you here. I brought this to you. It's my scoop. My story to tell."

"It is, and it will be. We just have to be smart about it."

The humid breeze rushed by us as I steered the golf cart down the rutted road into town. The moon was full, illuminating the water to the right of us with little dangling specks of light that made it seem magical. It made me think about Cindy and how much I would have liked to have shared this beautiful place with her instead of a smart-alecky reporter who thought she knew more than I did.

As we pulled into town, I took my phone out of my pocket and saw that I had three missed calls from Evelyn and one voicemail. I decided I would listen to the message when I got back to the room, in case it was something new that I didn't want to share with Celia.

"Anything important?"

"No, I think we just got back into cell range, so some of my messages are just now popping into my phone."

She smiled knowingly and patted me on the back.

"Good night, Jack. I'll see you in a few short hours for the ferry ride. I promise to sit on this at least for tonight. But let's talk about it on the way home. I can't hold the story forever."

"Agreed," I said, relieved that I still had some time to negotiate with her about holding the information. Maybe she wasn't as bad as I thought she was. I had always just viewed the media as a big, angry pack of hungry wolves. I now realized that it was possible for each individual journalist to have his or her own redeeming qualities, just like cops. I just never took the time to get to know them, until now.

My room was boiling hot. I opened the balcony door to let the ocean breeze waft in. It wasn't much of a change, as the air coming in from the outside was equally humid. I sat down at the little green desk and turned on the tiny lamp that was shaped like a palm tree to examine my phone again. What could be so important that Evelyn had called me three times in a row and then finally left me a message? I had an out-of-office message on my voicemail, but I guess she must have been desperate to reach me. I put my speakerphone on and hit the little arrow to play her message. Her elegant voice filled the room.

"Jack, so sorry to bother you while you're on vacation. Something has come up, and I really need to speak with you. I found some items that I think belong to Pamela Stevens. I found them in an employee's backpack. Anyway, I'm wondering if he might have had something to do with her disappearance. Please call me when you get this."

When the message ended, I stared at my phone, speechless for the second time in one day. Was this employee in cahoots with Pamela? Did he help her get out of the resort? Out of the country? None of this made sense. I was convinced now more than ever that I needed to get back to North Carolina and put the pieces of this strange case together before I made another move. This was not something that could be rushed, no matter what Celia's deadline was.

The next morning, I played it cool when I saw Celia. I was not ready to bring her in on Evelyn's suspicions. Not yet. While it would be great to bounce this off her and see what she made of it, I didn't want to risk her using it in her story. I was still gun-shy when it came to reporters. She needed to prove to me that I could trust her before I would be willing to share more information with her. That she had called me here to Barbuda was a good start.

With the time difference, I hadn't been able to return Evelyn's call, but I figured I would be back soon enough, and she and I could have a face-to-face meeting about what she had discovered as soon as I returned to Bingham.

My mind was racing with possibilities. Maybe Pamela had left some things behind to make it appear that she had been the victim of foul play, like the discarded ring? Maybe this other person was working with her and Darwin? There were so many options. I needed a big whiteboard and a dry-erase marker to write everything out. I was a visual thinker, and I needed to see all the possible tangents laid out like a roadmap before I could unravel what had really happened.

"Hear anything from home?" Celia asked, catching me off guard as we slowly made our way through the choppy blue surf in the growing dawn light to the mainland.

"Nothing important."

We sat in silence again. I was itching to tell Celia about Evelyn's call, but everything inside of me was telling me not to do it under any circumstances. That's when I felt another vibration on my phone. I looked down and saw that it was a text message from overnight. It must have gotten stuck in the international cell phone vortex and was just now coming through. It was a series of photographs of a cracked, muddy cell phone and a weathered running belt with water bottles attached to it. One of the photos was zoomed in on the faded words written in Sharpie on the inside of the belt: "PAMELA STEVENS."

Celia was looking at me sideways. She could tell by watching my face that something was going on. I cupped my hands around the phone so that she couldn't see the photographs.

"Got a secret you're trying to hide from me?" she asked coyly.

"No, just law enforcement stuff. Plus, I'm struggling to see this tiny screen in the sunlight."

I knew that I didn't sound convincing, but I didn't care. I was trying to catch my breath. There was one line of text under the photos: "These were in Eddie's backpack."

I froze as soon as I saw her words. Eddie was one of the employees who helped us with the search. He was the river guide, a local kid. He was very knowledgeable about the mountain and gave us lots of good insight as we searched. Was it possible that Darwin had paid him to make it look like Pamela had disappeared? Maybe he had dumped the ring? What was he planning to do with Pamela's stuff?

I had no answers, but I knew one thing for sure. I had to get back to North Carolina and speak with Evelyn as soon as possible.

34

EDDIE LISTENS

I GOT BOLD AND STEPPED A LITTLE CLOSER TO Evelyn's office so that I could hear what she was saying. She was distracted, so I was hoping she wouldn't hear me creeping around the corner even as the hardwood floors in the hallway groaned a little with each of my steps. I missed the first part of her message, but it was obvious to me she was leaving a message for that investigator who had been hanging around here all week.

"Something has come up and I really need to speak with you. I found some items that I think belong to Pamela Stevens. I found them in an employee's backpack. Anyway, I'm wondering if he might have had something to do with her disappearance. Please call me when you get this."

Good girl, Evelyn. You didn't give him my name. I had gotten there just in time.

I knew that if the investigator called back that Evelyn would give him my name. I was, unfortunately, backed into a corner; I didn't feel like I had any choices. If something happened to Evelyn, the investigator would suspect the employee who had these items was responsible. But by that time, I would have burned them in my backyard. There were plenty of sketchy people who worked at Bingham. I would surely not be at the top of the list. There was the little issue of Morris knowing Evelyn had my bag in his office, but I would tell him I picked it up from her as soon as he told me about it. There was no way to prove she was looking in *my* bag and not some other employee's.

I braced myself for what I was about to do. I went back to the lobby and grabbed a large iron poker from the massive stone fireplace. I was shaking even though I had decided that this was the right course of action. I would rush into her office before she knew what was happening. I would make sure it was fast and painless. I was fond of Evelyn. I didn't want to see her suffer. Unfortunately, at this point, I had no other choice but to kill her.

35

CELIA, SURREAL

I WATCHED JACK CUP HIS HANDS AROUND THE PHONE. There was something he wasn't telling me, and I desperately wanted to know what it was. But I also knew that I had been pushing boundaries with him. His first priority as an investigator was to solve the case, not to give me a scoop. Even though my tip from Ramona had put us in this position, I still had to honor the fact that he owed it to himself, to his department, and to the community to handle this situation professionally.

Still, my brain was spinning with possibilities. The sun had risen in front of us as we neared the mainland, casting orange and yellow hues across the sky like a watercolor painting bleeding into the clouds. I thought about Matt and the kids for a moment, how much they would have enjoyed this beautiful place, but instead, I was sitting next to this big, burly detective who basically tolerated my company. He certainly didn't like me.

"So, it's going to take all day to get home. Beautiful place, but sure is hard to get to."

I thought making small talk might get Jack to open up. If I could just get him to trust me, then he might share more information about what was really going on. I wasn't going to immediately hop on my computer and write about it; I just wanted to be kept in the loop.

"Yep, it's a big pain. And I really need to get back," he said anxiously.

He stressed the word "need," which only added more credence to my suspicion that something was going on back at Bingham that he wasn't telling me about.

"So, are you going to come clean with Sheriff Lansing about what we discovered?"

"I don't know yet. There may be some complicating factors that I need to work through first."

As soon as he said this, I could tell he regretted it. But the door was now open, and I intended to walk right through it. I couldn't wait any longer to figure out what was going on.

"What kind of 'complicating factors'?"

"Off the record?"

My pulse quickened. I had succeeded. He was going to tell me what was happening. I wouldn't be able to use it right now, but at least I would know the truth.

"Off the record. Sure. You can trust me."

"Well, there's a possibility that someone else may be involved, may have helped Pamela Stevens disappear. I need to nail it down before we go accusing people so I can make sure we get everyone who was part of this. That's the only way to achieve real justice."

What he was telling me made sense. Of course they hadn't pulled this off on their own. But who was he talking about? One of their friends, family members, or someone at the resort? I didn't have time to ponder it. The ferry whistle blew as the boat pulled up to the dock. We were homeward bound.

36

EVELYN GOES DOWN

After I left Jack the message, I paced around my office trying to decide what to do next. Should I have left Eddie's name on his voicemail? I didn't want to accuse someone without more investigation. But at the same time, what if Eddie did have something to do with Pamela's disappearance? Shouldn't someone know about it? My conscience was wrestling with my loyalty to Eddie. I decided to go with my conscience. I wouldn't specifically accuse him, but I would put Jack on notice so that he knew what he was dealing with.

I decided that since Jack wasn't answering my phone calls, maybe he would see a text. I could understand him not answering his phone on vacation, but a text was much more in your face. He wouldn't be able to ignore it, or at least that's what I hoped.

I quickly pulled the photos I had taken of the broken phone and Pamela's running belt into a text message. I decided to add one line of copy—not an accusation per se, just the facts: "These were in Eddie's backpack."

Just as I hit send, I felt the most excruciating pain in my head. I knew immediately in my last seconds of consciousness that I had been hit in the skull with something very heavy and sharp and that I was going down. As I slumped to the ground, I also realized who had come for me to keep me from talking. But it was too late. Jack knew what was going on now. My life had finally amounted to something. I was at peace knowing that I had made a difference in the case. I would finally be the person who did the right thing, even though I would be dead.

37

EDDIE ESCAPES

I saw Evelyn crumpled on the ground, blood pooling around her wounded head. I stared at her for a moment, not believing what I was seeing. I felt like I was in a movie—that none of it was real. I was still having a hard time understanding that I was capable of taking a life, especially the life of someone I had admired.

I snapped out of it and grabbed the cell phone still clutched in her small hand. I had to pry her fingers open to get it out. It was locked, but I imagined the passcode was the same passcode we used for just about everything at Bingham—Martin's birthdate. It was a little secret Wilson had filled me in on years ago that everything from the combination lock at the boathouse, to the computer at the check-in desk, to the alarm at the lodge used the same code, 12-26-80.

I typed it in and held my breath. The phone immediately sprang to life. Evelyn had a photo of the mountain at sunset as her background picture. It looked like it was taken from the back patio of the lodge. It made me sad to think she would never see this beautiful image in person again. But it also made me sad that she had orchestrated her own death by giving in to her curiosity and violating my privacy.

I quickly looked at her call log and realized that her last call to Jack had been the one where I heard her leaving a message a few minutes ago. She had made three previous calls to him, but they were just a few seconds long. He had never picked up the phone, and it was more than likely that she had left him only the one message that I heard.

Just to be safe, I popped into her text messages. *No.* She had sent him a series of photos of the stuff in my backpack. But that wasn't the worst thing. As I scrolled down, I could see that she had given him my name in the text: "These were in Eddie's backpack."

The words swirled around in my head in Evelyn's voice as if her dead body was saying them directly to me. I was trapped. There was no way out now. My only option was to escape. I knew the mountain and the woods better than anyone. It was time for me to disappear just like Pamela had.

38

DUTY CALLS, JACK

As we waited for our connecting flight in Miami, I knew that things were going to move very fast once I got back to Bingham. First, I needed to speak with Evelyn to find out about these items she found in Eddie's backpack that might be connected to Pamela's disappearance. Eventually, I would have to speak with Eddie as well, if he was willing, but I had to take everything one step at a time and be very careful not to reveal what I had witnessed in Barbuda. I didn't want to give anything away. I wanted to see if I could trip Eddie into revealing that he had been in a conspiracy with Pamela and Darwin to help her disappear.

Celia was looking at me sideways again, like she could literally see the wheels turning in my head and smoke coming out of my ears. I knew that it was only a matter of time before she prodded me to spill everything.

"It might help if you talked to me about it, used me as a sounding board—off the record, of course. I'm pretty good at figuring out complicated stuff. That's what I do for a living," she said with her now-familiar playful sarcasm.

I picked at my stale soft pretzel and took a swig of my flat

Mountain Dew that I had bought at a kiosk near the gate. Celia, on the other hand, was eating a power bar and drinking water. This was why she had such a healthy physique, and I was sporting a dad bod.

"I hear you, and I appreciate the offer. But you're not an investigator. You're just a journalist. It's not the same thing, even though you seem to think that it is."

"True, but what we do does overlap. We talk to people, gather evidence, and try to piece things together. You might be surprised at how good I am at solving puzzles."

She smiled and took a child-sized bite of her power bar. It looked like cardboard covered in birdseed. I much preferred my stale pretzel with mustard to her dinner.

I looked around and realized no one was within earshot. I needed to get what I knew off my chest and figure out what it all meant. I had to trust someone. It might as well be the person sitting next to me.

"You know Evelyn, the manager of the resort?"

"Yes, I know Evelyn."

"Well, she found some items she thinks belong to Pamela Stevens in an employee's backpack. A broken cell phone and a running belt with her name on it."

I opened the message on my phone from Evelyn and turned the screen in Celia's direction, scrolling through the pictures as she watched. She looked at the screen and then up at me with wide eyes. I handed it to her so she could inspect the photos even closer.

"So, what does it mean?"

"That's what I'm trying to figure out. Evelyn told me in a voicemail that she thinks this employee, Eddie, may have had something to do with Pamela's disappearance. So, that makes no sense unless Eddie was hired by Pamela and Darwin to make it look like something had happened to her. Maybe he was going to plant her stuff somewhere. Maybe they were paying him.

"And there is one other thing. A couple of days ago, Evelyn found a diamond ring that I confirmed belonged to Pamela. It was on a small trail leading down the side of the lodge. A lot of employees apparently go there on their breaks. It's nowhere near Overlook. So, that seems a little too staged to me, like someone was trying to make it look like something bad had happened to Pamela when we now know for sure it didn't. So, my best guess is that this Eddie kid must have been working with them, that it was some kind of conspiracy that would allow them to disappear together for whatever reason."

"But why dump her belongings now, more than a week later? It seems to me that should have happened right away if that was the plan, to end it for good, to make it clear that she was most likely dead instead of dragging it out."

"I agree, that's why I'm so confused by this new wrinkle."

"You have a call," Celia said, handing me back my phone.

I looked down and realized it was one of the investigators on my team, Barry. It had to be important for him to be calling me on my day off. I sincerely hoped that Evelyn had not jumped the gun and taken the items she found to the sheriff's office instead of waiting for me to handle it.

"Jack Sorrells," I said, trying to sound official like I didn't know who was calling.

"Jack, it's Barry. We got a big mess here at Bingham. I know you're on vacation for a few days, but we really need you back here right away if there's any way possible."

Barry, my lieutenant, did not usually sound frantic. His voice was shaking. It took a lot to get him riled. Something must be very wrong.

"Barry, what is it? What's going on?"

"We've had a murder."

"A what?"

"A murder at the resort. The manager, Evelyn. She's dead. Someone hit her over the head with a fire poker, crushed her skull. There's so much blood. Vicious. Seriously, I've never seen anything like it. Makes me sick to my stomach. She seemed like such a nice lady."

Barry's voice trailed off. We didn't have many murders in our part of North Carolina. And Barry was young. He had moved up the chain of command in the department fast. I couldn't remember if he had ever been called to an actual murder scene. I knew it had to be brutal for him. And Evelyn, poor Evelyn. She was a good lady. She didn't deserve to die in such a horrific manner.

"Barry, listen to me very closely. I think I know who may be behind this."

"How do you know, Major?"

"I just do. There's an employee there named Eddie. He's a local. He's a mountain man, a survivalist, probably knows his way around a shotgun too. He's no doubt very dangerous if he did this, and he's out there somewhere. I need everyone on this. I'll be there in a few hours. I need you to handle things for me until then."

"Yes, sir," Barry replied, his voice sounding even more shaky.

"And Barry?"

"Yes, Major?"

"Please be careful. I don't know what else this guy is capable of, but I wouldn't put anything past him."

Celia stared at me as I ended the call.

"Who's dead?" she asked me in a panicked voice.

"Evelyn. Evelyn's dead," I told her without emotion. I was so shocked that I felt numb. It was like someone else was saying the words and I was hovering above myself watching the scene unfold.

"Oh my God, oh my God," Celia cried, her hands going to her mouth.

"Listen to me, we've got to keep it together. My priority now is to catch this maniac. I need to focus. Promise me you won't breathe a word of what we discovered in Barbuda, not until I have time to figure everything out."

"I promise," she said, nodding her head vigorously in assent.

At this point, I actually believed her.

By the time we got to the resort, the parking lot was a command center again, just like it had been in the beginning of the search for Pamela. There were large lights on rolling platforms poised over folding tables with maps. Deputies and other volunteers huddled around the tables getting their assignments. This time, instead of looking for a missing woman, we were looking for a killer. I still couldn't wrap my head around the fact that Eddie felt like he needed to get rid of Evelyn just because he was caught in a conspiracy with Pamela and Darwin. If he had turned state's evidence and testified against them, he would have likely gotten probation. Killing Evelyn tanked any chance of a deal.

I walked into the huddle and put my hand on Barry's shoulder. He had risen to the occasion just like I expected him to do. I was proud of him. Maybe I wasn't such a bad leader after all. I did have a knack for spotting people with potential.

"Wow, Major, it sure is good to see you."

Barry looked so relieved, I thought he might hug me.

"Okay, let's get down to business. Where are we with the search? What have we covered, and what still needs to be covered? I assume all roads going out of the area have checkpoints?"

"Yes, sir. Roadblocks at every entrance and exit to the resort. We also have deputies at the county line in every direction. We've put out an APB to the surrounding towns on his vehicle. It's an old pickup truck, very recognizable if you get right up on it, but also one of dozens like it in this area. I think he's still in the woods. That would be my guess. We blocked everything so quickly. Unless he got a ride out, he's still here."

"I agree. Good work, Lieutenant."

I squeezed Barry's shoulder, and I could tell he appreciated my praise. I wanted to search every inch of the mountain tonight, but it would be impossible in the dark.

"Do we have the state police helicopter at our disposal? Has anyone called them?"

"They're on their way, sir. Should be landing in the field any minute. Would you like to go up with them?"

"Yes, I would. Radio them and let them know I'll be joining them. But first, I need you to take me to the crime scene. Take me to Evelyn."

Seeing the dead body of a stranger was a lot easier than seeing the dead body of someone you knew. Even though I hadn't known Evelyn for very long, she wasn't a stranger. I felt like I had gotten to know her well enough during the investigation that it made my heart physically hurt when I saw her body.

The crime scene investigators were still working around her, gathering evidence, but I could see her small head matted with blood. There was a pool of sticky blood on the floor and a massive spatter of dried blood on the wall. Her body was twisted unnaturally, her arms stretched out like a "T" and her legs curled underneath her like a child in the fetal position. One of her black heels was kicked off, lying near her body, and the other remained on. One of her hands was in a tight ball, and the other was open, revealing long nails polished the color of pearls. I said a silent prayer to God in my head, hoping that she hadn't suffered. I wasn't sure if she had any next of kin, but Barry was already working to locate family members before we released her name publicly. You never wanted anyone to find out about the murder of a loved one by reading a story online or watching the news.

"Anything unusual? Anything jumping out at you?" I asked the two crime scene techs who were dressed in scrubs and wearing blue booties over their shoes and purple latex gloves. I stood back so as not to contaminate anything.

"Nothing yet, Major. Just one single blow to the head, blunt force trauma. Appears to be this fire poker we found near the body. My guess is that it came from the fireplace in the lobby. It's not usually something someone brings to a murder. Looks like a weapon of opportunity."

"Find anything on her? In her pockets? Hands?"

"Nope."

"What about a cell phone?"

"Negative."

"That's strange. I don't think I ever saw her without it. It was always glued to her hand."

"We'll keep searching. It could be somewhere in the office. But it's not anywhere in plain sight."

Just then, Barry rushed into the room.

"Major, your chariot awaits," he said, gesturing to the front lawn outside Evelyn's window where I could see the bright lights of the state police helicopter and its furiously turning blades.

The tall ornamental grass at the edge of the building under the spotlights was waving and whipping around from the wind the helicopter was kicking up. It was like an eerie scene from a science fiction movie. Something in my gut was telling me not to go, but I ignored the feeling.

"Thanks, Barry. Fingers crossed we can spot him from the air."

"Fingers crossed, boss. Fingers crossed."

From the air at night, the forest appeared black and dense. To say we were looking for a needle in a haystack was a dramatic understatement. But the flood lights mounted on the bottom of the helicopter did illuminate stretches of woods in a way that even sunlight was unable to do. The inky night was suddenly cut by an onslaught of light. The treetops swayed with their disapproval as we disrupted the natural world below us.

My eyes were weary from a long day of traveling home from Barbuda, but I knew that I had to stay focused. Regardless of what had happened in the Pamela Stevens case, Evelyn was dead, and I had to find the person who was responsible. While there was definitely a connection between Evelyn's death and Pamela's disappearance, it wasn't important for me to figure that all out now. What was important was finding the most likely suspect in Evelyn's murder, which, based on her messages to me, was Eddie. He was a dangerous man who definitely felt trapped right now. I knew what happened when dangerous people were cornered: more violence.

The pilot told me that the helicopter was equipped with infrared technology, which meant he could send out a wavelength and scour the area we were flying over and look for the heat that mammals emit from their bodies. Of course, it was likely the beam might pick up a bear or a deer instead of a human, but it was a starting point. It was all we had.

"Thanks so much for doing this, Jeb."

"My pleasure. Just glad it all worked out, that we were available. Been on the other side of the state for a few days, looking for a little boy lost in the flooding along the Neuse River. Super sad. Literally swallowed his mother's car. She survived, but we haven't been able to locate the kid. They finally called off the air search. Unfortunately, he's likely to wash up eventually," Jeb said.

"Sad story."

"They all are. We don't usually fly for happy reasons. Sorry that we had to pull out on your missing woman search last week. Corporal's orders. They don't let us burn too much fuel these days. Too expensive. We don't have the budget for it, or at least that's what they tell us."

"No worries. I know it wasn't your fault. It was frustrating, but I don't blame you or anyone else. It's just the way it is these days. None of us has enough resources to do our jobs."

As my eyes scoured the landscape below us through the viewfinder of the cameras mounted on the bottom of the helicopter, I squinted. I imagined what it would be like to do this every single day, trying to spot the needle in the dark forest. Occasionally, Jeb might be the conduit for a happy ending—finding a lost child, rescuing an injured person—but I was pretty sure those triumphs were few and far between. I assumed that Jeb presided over many more sad endings than happy ones.

That's when I saw it, an almost imperceptible movement at the base of a tree in a small clearing in the gorge.

"Jeb, can you circle back over that little clearing again? I thought I saw some movement there, near the base of that big tree."

"Sure thing, I can also zoom the camera in and turn on the infrared feature to see if it picks up anything."

Jeb flew as low as he could without putting us in danger of hitting the tops of the trees. He banked steeply to the left and circled back around, this time giving me an even better view of the tree and the small clearing. It was blurry when the camera zoomed in, but there was a figure there moving slightly.

"There's something there."

"Yep, you're right. The infrared is picking it up. Hard to say if it's a person or a bear, but bears generally don't like the light or the sound of the copter. They hide from us. So, there's a good chance it's a person."

"What do you think we should do?"

"I can land in the parking lot at the base of the mountain, and we can radio the SRT and get them to meet us there. You can't go in alone."

I knew he was right, that I needed the special response team as backup to approach Eddie safely. But part of me just wanted to go in on my own. I wanted to talk to him, to figure out exactly what was going on. I didn't want this to be suicide by cop. I pictured Eddie as a trapped animal who might just throw himself in front of a hail of gunfire to avoid the certainty of going to prison. If Eddie died, I would never know what the connection was between him and Pamela.

"Okay, that seems reasonable. Let's do it."

I listened as Jeb called the SRT on the radio and told them to head down the mountain to the parking lot to meet us. He told them we would wait for them to arrive.

We landed in the empty parking lot. As soon as Jeb turned off the helicopter rotors, I took off my headphones and unbuckled my seatbelt. I had a plan.

"Hey, Jeb, I'm sure it's going to be a few minutes before the team gets here. I need to run into the woods for a quick second," I said, trying to think of any excuse to slip away.

"I hear you, buddy. I may do the same thing. The coffee is going right through me," he said, smiling and holding up his travel mug in my direction as proof.

"Cool, let's meet back here in a few. I need to brief the team before we go in," I said, feeling guilty about misleading Jeb. In my head, I told myself the end would justify the means if I could just get Eddie to turn himself in without an exchange of gunfire.

"Sounds good."

Jeb was a good guy who was doing his job professionally. Still, I had to get to Eddie first, by myself. I had to get him alone and see what he knew. It was risky, but it was the best chance I had to unravel this whole mess. There was no chance of getting the answers I was looking for if I approached Eddie with a team of armed cops in military gear, and he was shot.

The woods seemed much darker now without the glow of the helicopter's flood lights, but I had noted the latitude and longitude on my phone when we zeroed in on the location from the air. I was now using my GPS to direct me. Luckily, it wasn't too far from the parking lot. I walked gingerly over rocks and underbrush, trying not to make too much noise as I approached. Although there was no way Eddie didn't see and hear the helicopter landing, which meant he would be on guard.

As I got close to the clearing, I could see a large tree that was hollowed out at the bottom. The opening was dark, like a cave—big enough for a person or maybe even a bear to fit inside. I wasn't sure which one seemed scarier, a bear or a man with a gun. I took a deep breath and shined my flashlight into the hole.

"Eddie, if you're in there, I need you to come out with your hands up, very slowly. It's Major Jack Sorrells. You know me. I'm not going to hurt you, but I can't promise you others won't. So, if you listen to my commands and do exactly what I say, I can keep you safe."

I listened closely. There was a rustling beneath the silence coming from the tree. It could easily be an animal. I might have gotten the SRT team down here for a wounded bear or deer that had sought refuge inside the tree. But then I heard something else. It was a throat clearing, a human throat clearing. There was no doubt in my mind that the sound came from a person and not from an animal. I hit the record button on the officer-issued body camera attached to my chest. It was too dark to see anything, but at least there would be audio of what happened next.

"Eddie, you don't have a lot of options right now. At this moment, there is a SWAT team ready to swoop in here and make a big ruckus. I don't want that. I'm pretty sure you don't want that either. Let's do this calmly. I can help you if you cooperate with me."

There it was again, the throat clearing. I knew Eddie was inside the tree now. I just had to find the right words to draw him out.

"Eddie, I know about everything. About Evelyn. About Pamela. It's going to be a lot easier if you just come out here and tell me the truth."

I didn't know anything about Pamela's connection to Eddie, but I thought just saying these words out loud might prompt some response from him. This is what I had come here for, and I was working against the clock trying to get him to talk to me before the SRT got anxious and came into the woods.

"It was an accident," a meek voice said in the darkness.

I inched a little bit closer, keeping my right hand on my gun, which was still in the holster but unstrapped and ready to be pulled.

"What was an accident, Eddie?"

"I pushed her. It was a crazy impulse. She fell. I didn't mean for it to happen. I didn't mean for her to die. She was someone from my past, from my family's past. Someone who hurt us. Someone who hurt *me*, and I just couldn't control myself when I saw her."

"Pushed who?" I asked, moving three steps closer, pulling my gun out of my holster, gripping it with two hands, and pointing it directly at the dark opening of the tree.

"That lady. Mrs. Stevens. On the trail. I did it. I'm responsible. I killed her. But I promise you, I didn't plan it. It just kind of happened."

"Okay, I understand."

I didn't really understand, but it didn't matter. He confessed to killing Pamela. He honestly thought she was dead; the fact that she was still alive was clearly something he was not privy to. So, there was no conspiracy.

"And then, I didn't have a choice."

"A choice about what, Eddie?"

I knew he was about to confess to killing Evelyn. I looked at my watch and realized I had been gone seventeen minutes. If I didn't wrap this up soon, the SRT would be barreling into the woods to save me, guns drawn.

"About Evelyn. I had nothing against her. She was nice to me. I really liked her. She gave me a lot of opportunities."

"So, why? Why did you do it, Eddie? Why did you hurt her?"

I was now ten feet from the tree. In the moonlight, I could see Eddie's construction boots peeking out at the edge of the opening. He was sitting down. I still had no idea if he was armed. I kept my pistol pointed into the darkness just above his shoes.

"I had to because she was going to tell you about what I did to that woman, the woman on the trail. She called you. I heard her. I was trying to stop her from giving you my name. I didn't know she had already sent you a text with my name until after it was all over."

"I get it. You were scared. You did something out of fear, something impulsive. You've told the truth now. Don't you feel better? You don't have to hide anymore, Eddie. What I need you to do is get up real slow and walk toward me with your hands up in the air where I can see them."

I kept one hand on the gun positioned on the tree and reached behind me with my other hand to grab my cuffs off my belt. Slowly, Eddie emerged from the tree with his hands in the air, just like I had asked him to do. He was still wearing his work uniform with his name on it. But now, it was splattered with Evelyn's blood. He walked slowly in my direction, just as I had instructed. He looked like he was about to cry and with good reason. He just confessed to a law enforcement officer that he killed two people, and his confession was recorded by my body camera.

"I need you to kneel down real slow and put your hands on top of your head, Eddie. Take it easy now."

Eddie looked more like a boy than a man or like a cornered, scared animal that was walking into a trap. He did as I said, and I was able to put the handcuffs on him behind his back and then pull him to a standing position. I re-holstered my handgun and patted him down from top to bottom to make sure he had no weapons on him. Then, I got ready to lead him out of the woods.

"Freeze," a voice screamed over a megaphone.

Suddenly, we were blinded by floodlights coming in every direction from the trees around us. We were surrounded by the SRT.

"Stand down," I yelled back. "Suspect is in custody without incident. He's cooperating. He's cuffed and clear of weapons."

39

EDDIE REVEALED

THE DAY I SAW PAMELA RUNNING THE TRAIL IN HER expensive sports gear with her shiny, pink sneakers, oblivious to the nature around her that was being drowned out by her AirPods, something welled up inside me. It was more than anger. It was rage. It had taken me a little while, but I had finally figured out where I knew her from. She had been a young assistant district attorney just starting out in her career when she prosecuted my dad for manslaughter all those years ago. She was responsible for sending him to prison, for taking him away from my family. I was young when it happened, but later I read every article that my mother had neatly clipped from the newspaper and, for some unknown reason, meticulously glued into a scrapbook, which she had hidden in a cabinet beneath our television in the den. Pamela Stevens was older now, but her distinct features were unmistakable. She was the reason for everything bad that had happened in my life.

When she first walked into the lodge with her husband, Darwin, I was standing in the lobby talking to Simone and Morris. Something inside my head clicked. *It's her.* That night, I went home and pulled out the dusty scrapbook, which now lived beneath my bed. Mama was in the den with the television blaring, watching a game show and smoking a cigarette. As usual, Daddy was asleep in his armchair, an empty beer bottle clutched in his hand next to him. I sat on the bed and turned the pages carefully as if the scrapbook was so delicate that it might disintegrate in my lap. I turned to the photos from the trial, and there she was, the unflappable Pamela Stevens. There was no doubt in my mind that the guest at the lodge was the same woman.

I had always hoped that someday I would run into the woman who put my father behind bars, and now that day was here, and she was literally running right at me.

The trail is narrow in some spots, and it was clear one of us was going to have to give way to let the other person pass. I knew that she would expect me to the be the one to give. She would expect me to step into the brush and allow her a wide berth so that her athletic stride wouldn't be broken. That's how the visitors at Bingham always acted—like we were invisible, like they were too good for us. I couldn't do it this time. I pictured my father being led out of the courtroom in handcuffs and her with a smug look on her eager face. I stood my ground and waited for the standoff. I would force her to see me. She wouldn't remember me, but I didn't care. I wanted to be the last face she saw on Earth.

As she got closer, she still didn't seem to see me. All the rage that had been lying dormant inside me for so many years just suddenly bubbled to the surface. Pamela Stevens stood for every single person who had ever passed by me without seeing me. She stood for all the heartache that my family had endured because of my dad's long absence.

We were not rich before Daddy went to prison, but we were certainly poor after he left us, struggling just to survive. My mother did the best she could to provide, but it was tough. She worked as a maid, a nanny, and a night janitor at the high school. But the loss of Daddy's income wasn't the worst part. The worst part was the way people looked at us at the grocery store, like we were trash, and the way the kids bullied me at school, making fun of me for having a daddy in prison. They would punch me in the gut on the playground or in the boys' bathroom. The teachers looked the other way, like they, too, knew our family was trash.

I didn't have a solid plan for what I was going to do to Pamela Stevens, but as she approached, I quickly came up with one. When she got within arm's length of me, I just reached out and pushed her. It wasn't a hard push, but it was enough to send her over the edge. Our eyes locked just before she fell. I could tell that she was confused—*Why did this stranger just attack me?* Only I knew the answer. She would fall to her death with that question fixed in her mind as the air rushed by her face and she gulped for breath in the last seconds of her life.

Part of me wished that I could have explained it to her before she fell. I wished I could tell her about the rage inside of me, how every time I thought of how my life had turned out, how my father's absence had shaped me, how it had forced my mother to work three jobs to support us, the rage grew inside me like a tumor. I was good at hiding it, but it was always there, eating away at me from the inside. I transferred the rage to anyone who failed to see me. Every time someone used a rude or arrogant tone with me, the tumor grew. Every time I did something nice for a guest and got no "thank you" and no tip, the tumor grew. And that day on the trail with Pamela, it had become so big inside of me that I felt like I might explode if I didn't let some of the rage out, and she was the one who deserved the rage the most. Everything was her fault. Everything bad in my life could be traced back to her.

It happened so fast that she didn't even have time to scream. I rushed to the edge of the trail and looked around, but the brush was way too thick for me to see anything. I had to assume she was dead at the bottom of the gorge, or at the very least, seriously injured and would eventually die from her injuries before she was found.

When she fell, I felt nothing—not satisfaction, not relief, not remorse, not even fear. But a few minutes later, as I continued down the trail, I panicked. I knew that if, by some miracle, she lived, she would tell the story of how I pushed her off the trail. I would lose everything because of one mistake. I had to get down to the bottom of the gorge fast and see where she landed before anyone else found her. If she was dead, I would leave her there. If she was alive but injured—which didn't seem very likely—I would have to finish what I had started.

If someone else found her before I did, I was screwed. I would go to prison, lose my job, and devastate my parents. Daddy had stood by me through a lot of bad behavior in high school because he knew his leaving had hurt me real bad. But he would not stand by me this time. Especially if he found out who she was and why I did it. He would tell me it was not my score to settle. He would tell me he had broken the law and deserved the punishment he got, that he had done his time, and that we all needed to move on.

I could hear him now in my head: *Son, I paid my debt to society. I did my time like a man. That's ancient history. Why would you screw up your life to get revenge on a woman who was just doing her job?*

40

CELIA UNWRITTEN

I FLEW BACK TO NORTH CAROLINA WITH JACK INSTEAD of heading straight home to Pennsylvania because I wanted to finish what I started. Especially with the new wrinkle of Evelyn's murder, the story was unfolding by the minute, and I needed to be there right in the thick of it.

When we got to the resort, Jack was immediately pressed into service. He jumped into the state police helicopter and headed out into the dark mountain night for the improbable search from the air. I didn't even get a chance to talk to him about what was going on. Everything was happening so fast.

I knew the helicopter had infrared technology, but I also knew that the forest was thick enough to easily hide a single person on the ground at night—especially a person who did not want to be found. People who knew how to survive in the wilderness also knew how to make themselves scarce.

My head was still swirling with all the possibilities. Why did Eddie feel the need to kill Evelyn? What had she learned about Pamela's disappearance? That Eddie was working with Darwin and Pamela? Surely, that would be an obstruction of justice charge that Eddie could have easily gotten pled down to something lesser if he agreed to cooperate with authorities and testify against them. Yet, Eddie had taken the drastic step of eliminating a potential witness. This motive wasn't adding up to me. Jack and I clearly had something wrong about our theory.

I sat in the lobby drinking stale coffee and writing a first draft of the story on my laptop, which included the stakeout and the sighting of Pamela and Darwin looking like young lovebirds in Barbuda. There was a frenzy of activity in the parking lot in front of the lodge where the sheriff's deputies and state police were headquartering their search for Eddie. Officers came in and out of the lobby, talking in hushed tones, using the restroom, grabbing coffee, and generally looking bored.

"Why in the heck are we doing this at night?" one young officer said to another. He was wearing a bulletproof vest with the letters "SRT" on it, fatigues, and combat boots. He was casually carrying a long rifle through the lobby like it was an umbrella.

"Seriously, man, you didn't see that crime scene. Blood everywhere. He bludgeoned that woman to death. You can't wait on something like that. You've gotta roll. There's no telling what could happen if a civilian finds him first and he feels cornered. We're dealing with a monster."

I pretended not to listen, all the while taking frantic notes about their conversation on my laptop. This was information I would need to get confirmed by Jack later. I had tried to get close to Evelyn's office where the crime scene techs were collecting evidence, but they had put the yellow tape at both ends of the hallway that bordered her office, and no one was getting in.

I considered lying down on one of the overstuffed couches in the lobby and taking a little nap. The all-day trip from Barbuda had worn me out. I didn't want to go back to my cottage and risk missing something.

One by one, employees who had heard about Evelyn's death

came rushing to the lodge. They were standing in small circles consoling one another, hugging, and leaning their heads on each other's shoulders. Most of the women, including Nelly from the stables, were crying. The men hung their heads low and talked quietly. They all looked so different out of uniform, just regular people living regular lives away from this place that took so much of their daily energy. They were in jeans, sweatpants, sweaters, flannel shirts, and most were in sneakers or flip-flops.

The investigators were pulling the employees one by one away from their safe huddles to interview them about Eddie. They would take them to a corner of the lobby and sit across from them in large comfortable armchairs near the fire. I couldn't hear what they were saying from where I sat, but I could tell from the body language of the employees that they appeared somewhat defensive, probably incredulous that one of their own could be responsible for such a horrible crime.

I closed my laptop and leaned back into the soft cushions of the couch. I planned to only shut my eyes for a few minutes so that I could re-group, and then maybe I would get more coffee and get a second wind. There was a good chance the search tonight would come up empty. Eddie might still be on the mountain, but there was just as much of a chance that he was long gone, that he had gotten a ride and was hundreds of miles away from here by now. I knew Jack had no choice but to search the mountain, but it seemed futile in the dark.

As soon as I closed my eyes, the commotion started.

"They got something," one of the young SRT officers I had seen earlier yelled. Their radios were blaring with static and numerical codes I couldn't decipher.

I sat up straight and scanned the room. All the officers immediately stopped what they were doing, put down their coffee cups, and ran out of the lodge. Despite my grogginess, I grabbed my laptop and followed them. I got outside just in time to see them piling into a police van. Once everyone was loaded, they sped off down the hill.

Immediately, I knew that Eddie must have been found, and I was pretty sure that Jack was the one who found him. I wondered if he found him dead or alive. With what Eddie was facing, it would not be out of the question for him to take his own life.

I sat down on the stone steps and listened to the calm in the wake of the mass exodus. There were still a few officers left, milling around, talking in low voices, but there was an energy now to what they were saying, an excitement in the possibility of having cornered their prey.

I knew it was going to be awhile and that it made no sense for me to sit here on the cold stone steps waiting for Jack to return and tell me what was going on. It could be hours before he came back. He would tell me everything eventually. That's what we had agreed on. I trusted him. No one else was going to get an inside track on this story. Plus, we had the shared secret of knowing that Pamela was still alive to work through.

I was turning to go back to the couch in the lobby when I heard a nearby officer's radio go off. This time, there was no static. The voice was clear and loud.

"This is pilot to base, pilot to base. Be advised, despite instructions to wait, Major Sorrells went into the woods alone and has not returned. It's been a quarter hour. I think we're going to need to go in and get him out."

My heart sank. *Jack, what have you done now?*

I fell fast asleep on the couch. I couldn't help myself. As much as I tried to stay awake, the jet lag had crept up on me. When I awoke, sunlight was peeking in through the windows. I sat up, pushing away a blanket that some kind person must have laid over me. I looked out the window to see the sun rising with its pink and orange hues over the mountain like something out of a travel brochure. I glanced around the lobby to see empty paper coffee cups and empty water bottles strewn about. A single employee was walking around with a trash bag collecting the debris that looked like it was left over from a fraternity party, minus the beer cans.

"Hey, I mean, hello. Can you tell me what the latest is? What happened last night?"

I realized as soon as I focused my eyes that the woman with the trash bag was Nelly. She turned to me with sorrow on her face, sorrow that I knew was probably coming from many different places—sorrow about Evelyn's death, sorrow about Eddie's involvement.

"Well, hey there, sleeping beauty. Wasn't sure if you were going to rejoin us," Nelly said, avoiding eye contact as she continued picking up trash.

"I was trying to stay awake, but I failed. Did they find him?"

I pulled my hair back out of my face and fastened it into a messy bun on top of my head with an elastic band from my wrist.

"Eddie? They sure did."

Her voice was monotone. She wasn't giving away what she thought about this development.

"Is everyone okay? Is he okay? Is Jack—I mean, Major Sorrells—okay? Did anyone get hurt?"

Nelly stopped what she was doing now and slumped into the armchair across from me, laying down her trash bag on the floor next to her feet. She looked like a balloon deflating as she sunk into the comfortable chair. It was as if my question had given her permission to stop for a minute and process her physical and emotional fatigue.

"He's okay. No one got hurt. Apparently, that investigator is some kind of hero. Talked Eddie out of running away and kept the SWAT guys from taking a shot at him. Thought for sure it was going to end in bloodshed. Never thought Eddie would give himself up."

I could feel my heart swell with relief and pride for Jack, knowing that he was finally getting his due after all these years of uncertainty. He had accomplished something difficult and admirable, talking a killer into giving himself up without anyone getting hurt.

"That's good. Good that no one was hurt."

"I still don't believe that boy could have killed Evelyn. I mean, we all had our moments with Evelyn. She was a pretty strict boss. But you always knew where you stood with her, and you always knew she cared—really cared. That's why she was tough on us. She took a particular liking to Eddie, gave him more and more responsibility. Eddie was grateful. I just don't think he has it in him to do anything like this."

Nelly shook her head as she said all of this and then looked down at her hands, which lay limply in her lap.

I wanted to be careful about how much I said, but I was also appreciating getting Nelly's insight into the situation, so I prompted her to keep going.

"So, what happened? Where is everyone now?"

"I suppose getting some sleep. He's been booked into the local jail. He'll be in court for his first appearance at two o'clock this afternoon. He's being held without bond, of course. Two murders and all."

I tried not to look shocked at her mention of the word "two."

"Two?" I said, trying to sound casual and curious, not like a reporter.

"Yep. Evelyn and that hiker woman, Pamela Stevens. They haven't announced it officially yet, but my sister is a clerk at the courthouse. Tells me they woke up a judge at three this morning and had him sign arrest warrants for two murders. It don't make no sense to none of us, but that's what's going on. According to the warrant, he confessed to killing both women to Major Sorrells. And he got it all recorded on his body camera. Eddie told him that he pushed that woman off the trail, and she fell into the gorge. Then he told him he had to kill Evelyn because she was onto him. That's what I mean by that officer being a hero. He got a confession and kept Eddie safe while he was being arrested."

Confessed? This made no sense. How could he confess to murdering a woman who was still alive? Why would he do that?

"Nelly, I need to take a shower. Can you get me into a room? I don't want to bother anyone to take me to my cottage. Right now, I just need to shower and change. I've been in these clothes for more than twenty-four hours."

"No problem. Follow me."

Nelly struggled to pull herself out of the chair and waved me across the lobby to a nearby hallway with a big ring of keys in her hand. I needed to get to Jack as soon as possible and figure out what in the world was going on.

Jack's cell phone was going straight to voicemail. I texted him a few times and got nothing. I decided I would go and plant myself in front of his office until he was ready to talk to me. I knew there was going to be a press conference, and I wanted to be there for Eddie's first court appearance, but not before Jack and I hammered out our unfinished business.

Morris and Simone were in the lobby talking when I emerged from my shower and quick change of clothes. Both were red-eyed and puffy-faced like they had been up crying all night long. I asked Simone to stow my rolling luggage behind her desk, and I would get it later.

"I'm so sorry for what has happened," I said, touching Simone's arm. She reached in and hugged me. I was surprised by her display of affection, obviously prompted by her intense grief, but I hugged her back.

"She just didn't deserve this, you know? I mean, she was tough, but the good kind of tough. She made you better, and she cared. She *really* cared," Simone said into my shoulder between muffled sobs. Clearly, they had all been talking about Evelyn, sharing a similar script.

Morris stood next to her uncomfortably, looking down at his feet.

"That's why we're here today," Simone said, pulling away from me and straightening her suit jacket with her silver Bingham nameplate pinned to the lapel. "She would want us to go on. To run the place professionally. Martin is on his way, but he called me this morning and asked me to keep everything going. Says that's what Evelyn would have wanted."

Morris bristled at the mention of Martin, like putting Martin and Evelyn in the same sentence was blasphemous. But Simone didn't seem to notice.

"Morris, can you drive Mrs. Finch into town and drop her off?" Simone asked Morris as he continued to avoid eye contact with both of us. Then she turned to me. "We'll take your luggage to your cottage. You can stay for as many nights as you like. Most of our guests have already left. It's a lot for people to process. I get it. But the show must go on. Just call us when you need to be picked up. I will send Morris back to get you."

Simone gave me a forced smile and straightened her jacket again, turning back to her duties at the front desk. Morris and I headed to the parking lot.

"I'm sorry, Morris. I know Eddie is your friend. This must be hard."

"Not really, just coworkers. I'm not worried about what's

going to happen to him. He deserves whatever he gets. It's just that, what happened to Evelyn, it's all my fault."

He looked up at me now with tears in his eyes.

"How so?"

"I'm the one who found Eddie's stupid backpack in the van and gave it to Evelyn to hold for him. I never looked inside, but she must have. And whatever she found must have incriminated him in that lady's disappearance. It's all my fault. I put her in harm's way."

He looked down again and hung his head low. His body was now racked with sobs. He wrung his hands. I stood awkwardly, not knowing exactly what to do, but then I began patting him on his back like I did with my boys when one of them had a crying fit. I moved my hand in a circle. I didn't want to invade his personal space, but this felt like the right thing to do.

"Morris, you are *not* responsible for anything that happened. You couldn't have known what was in that backpack or what Eddie was capable of. You need to stop beating yourself up about it. These are circumstances beyond your control. You did nothing wrong."

Quietly, Morris finally looked up, wiped the tears from his eyes with his hands, and we walked silently together to the van. Not only did I need a ride down the mountain, I also needed some answers from Jack. As I climbed into the van, my phone vibrated.

"Tell no one what we know. Meet me at my office in 45."

In the daylight, the forest seemed to be encroaching on the roadway, inching closer to the van as we made the hairpin turns like it might swallow us whole. I was reminded that the living, breathing ecosystem had secrets that humans would never truly understand. Even though Eddie was in custody, things were still not right here. The forest wasn't happy.

I sat in the small concrete building in a worn, fraying blue chair that looked like it came out of my grandmother's basement. There were old yellowing posters taped to the walls with curling edges that talked about wearing a seatbelt, the importance of bike helmets, and not leaving valuables in sight in your car.

The receptionist took my name warily and said, "Major Sorrells will be with you in a few minutes." I quietly suspected that he was not in the building yet, and she just said this to make me complacent. But it was fine. He had been up all night long, and I didn't begrudge him getting a few hours of sleep. I waited patiently, scrolling through emails on my phone and wondering how anyone ended up in a little town like this unless they were born here. And if they were born here, why didn't they leave?

I was starting to get restless when Jack finally appeared in the doorway next to the receptionist's desk and ushered me in. I got up and followed him down a long, depressing concrete block hallway, painted a light blue that showed every scuff and scrape of every person who had brushed up against it over the years.

We walked into an office overcrowded with file boxes piled haphazardly everywhere. There were so many boxes that they almost obscured the only window in the room, which looked up at the majestic mountain range. Jack moved some files off a faded green armchair in front of his desk and gestured for me to sit down. His desk was also messy, piled high with paperwork, surrounded by a few family photos and coffee mugs about being a dad or a cop that he had collected over the years. He eased back into a worn leather office chair. A dead fern sat on the bookshelf behind him, right above his head. The wall was decorated with various framed diplomas and commendations and photographs of him being honored or shaking hands with mildly famous people who must have stayed at the Bingham Reserve. The pictures were askew, like whoever hung them up had been in a big hurry. I decided to go ahead and break the ice.

"Congratulations on solving the case," I said, which seemed to take Jack off guard.

"Thanks. I appreciate it. I'm glad we got him without anyone getting hurt," he said, followed by a big sigh. "I was a little worried last night when they dispatched the SRT. I had a bad premonition that the whole thing might end in a shootout. That was the last thing I wanted."

"I bet."

"And so, I'm sure you've heard by now that he confessed to two murders."

"I did, which is confusing to me because we know that Pamela Stevens isn't dead. So, why would he confess to that?"

"I talked to him about it, and he really believes he killed Pamela."

"Why?"

"Because he says he pushed her off the edge of the trail, and no one could survive a fall like that."

"But she did. So, you don't think he was in on it with them? That he was covering up for the fact that she was really running away?"

"I don't. He's not that smart. He's convinced that he killed her. It wasn't planned. He says it was a spur-of-the-moment decision. Somehow, she miraculously survived. I think her poor husband also thought she was dead. I don't think he was in cahoots with her either. Somehow, she reconnected with him, and now he knows she's okay. Why she went all the way to Barbuda, we'll probably never know."

"So, what now?"

"Not sure. It's all pretty confusing. The state police are not going to back down on these charges after his confession was recorded on my body cam. If I come out now and say, 'Oh, by the way, Pamela Stevens is alive,' I'm going to look like an ass. He's going down no matter what, whether it's one murder or two murders. A life sentence is a life sentence."

"So, basically what you're saying is that, either way, justice is served."

"Pretty much, yes."

"But what about Pamela getting away with it, wasting all the time and money and resources your department put into the search?"

"It's only an issue if someone finds out about it."

"What if she resurfaces at some point?"

"We assumed she was dead. It was the logical conclusion to come to after Eddie confessed to killing her. End of story. No one knows what we know. Even Pamela and Darwin don't know we saw them."

"So, we just let her get away with it?"

"I think it does more harm than good to try and straighten it out at this point. I mean, what are they guilty of anyway? Sure, we wasted some time and money on the search. That's true. But they seemed pretty happy together in their little island paradise. I say let's leave it alone."

"And now you're a hero for solving not just one but two murders. You finally get your happy ending."

"Point well taken."

"So, what are you asking me to do? Are you asking me not to print the truth?"

"No, I'm just asking you not to print the whole truth. I'm asking you to omit what we saw in Barbuda. Erase it from your mind. You can write about everything else the way it unfolded. Evelyn's murder, the search for Eddie, his capture, his confession. I told you I would give you the inside track on the details, and I plan to keep good on that promise."

No one had ever asked me to deep-six something so

important in a high-profile story. I sat there and thought about it for a moment. I looked at Jack's family photo with his wife and teenage daughter. They were wearing matching flannel shirts and sitting in a pumpkin patch on a gorgeous fall day with brightly colored leaves adorning the trees all around them. And then there was his wedding photo with his wife: he wore a black suit, and she had on a very traditional, voluminous, white, frilly lace dress. They were cheek to cheek in front of a brick church, looking young and hopeful. There was also a photo of Jack holding his daughter as a baby. He beamed down at her with the kind of unending love that only a parent can have for a child. And finally, there was Jack being sworn in as a young deputy. He was ruddy-faced and lean, shining as he held up his hand with a group of other officers in line to take the sacred oath of office.

It suddenly occurred to me that by sparing Pamela from guilt, I was protecting Jack from having to explain something that would ultimately make him look bad again. He had just achieved the hero status he probably deserved many times over in the past decade, and the only thing that stood between him and it was me.

"Okay, I'll do it."

"You will?" Jack held the edge of his desk and leaned across it in my direction, like he wanted to kiss me.

"Yes, but we will *never* speak about this again. Do you understand? I don't really know why I'm agreeing to this, but I am a person of my word. On my honor, I will keep this between us. It's against my better judgment, but for some reason, I like you, Jack Sorrells. I do believe you're one of the good guys. If I was missing, I would want you to be on my case."

"And I would be on it, in a second."

"I know you would."

"You've changed my opinion about reporters. That some of them might actually be a human first and a journalist second.

The reality is we'll never know the truth about what happened and why. Can you live with that?"

"It will be hard. I won't deny it. But I will do my best. I don't necessarily need to know everything, despite what my husband thinks."

I turned in the final version of my article to my editor that night. It was very factual and straightforward. I described Evelyn's brutal murder and how just before she was killed, she fingered Eddie in connection with Pamela Stevens' disappearance.

From Jack's generous interview, I described in great detail how he located Eddie from the helicopter and how, once he was on the ground, he was able to coax Eddie out of the tree trunk and convince him to tell the truth and turn himself in.

Eddie had confessed to murdering Pamela and Evelyn and had been charged accordingly, and was now in jail without bond awaiting trial. I also remarked on how Pamela's body had never been found.

It was all true; there was not one falsehood in the article, only omission. I left out the part about Jack and me seeing Pamela alive in Barbuda. But in recent days, I had started to doubt myself, to rewrite the story in my head as part of my plausible deniability. Maybe Darwin was with a woman who just looked like his wife beneath the darkness of the Caribbean night as we hid behind the trees with an obstructed view of his driveway. Plenty of men had a type. It was possible.

Still, in the beginning, right after I wrote the article, I would wake up in the middle of the night picturing them together and realize what I had seen was not fiction. Pamela was alive and well and living her best life on a remote island with her husband. Did it affect me? No? Did it harm me or my life in some way? No? Did it bother me? The truth was that it didn't. She had somehow gotten away with the impossible. I was honestly more curious and a little envious. Who wouldn't want to redefine their life if they had the chance to start over? Isn't it something we all think about doing from time to time? And the irony was that she found her new life with her old partner. There was something so serendipitous about Pamela and Darwin being together again. I guess, deep down, I was a romantic who wanted to believe that her disappearance had brought them closer together because they both suddenly realized what they had to lose.

Now, I finally sleep well at night. I've reconciled my decision with my conscience. I even silently wish Pamela the best on occasion when I go back to Bingham for a getaway with my family or just Matt. We're even considering buying some property there and putting a little cabin on it. That's how much we love it. When I'm there, I don't feel guilty about how things ended or for the secret Jack and I are still keeping. I feel gratitude for finding this sacred place that gives me a feeling of solemnity and peace like no other place I've ever been. The darkness of the forest is still there with all the secrets it holds, but I've learned to respect it instead of fear it.

Jack is now the sheriff. His boss retired, and he was elected last year. We are still in touch, bonded by our shared secret forever. The experience taught me that life is gray. The lines between right and wrong can be blurry. Some people might call this situational ethics, but I just call it reality. I don't think anyone who has lived a full life can honestly say they've never ventured into blurry territory. One thing is crystal clear to me. Eddie is behind bars, and that's exactly where he belongs.

41

PAMELA

AT FIRST, WHEN I AWOKE ON THE ROCKY LEDGE, I thought I was dead. The dark sky above me was so clear and full of twinkling stars, I was sure I must be in heaven. You don't see stars like that in the city. Then, as I tried to focus my eyes, the feeling started to come back into my limbs. I realized that I was injured but alive. I wiggled my toes and my fingertips. Everything hurt. There was pain shooting from my right lower back into my hip and all the way down my leg to my toes.

I lifted my arms and then wrapped them tightly around me, feeling patches of dried blood in various spots on my skin. Yes, I was alive. I tried to remember what had happened. And then it came back to me. A boy, a young man, a man in a work uniform with a dog, had pushed me off the trail for no reason. It was so strange, but I remembered it clearly. I was jogging, listening to a podcast, when I saw him. I thought he would move over to let me pass, but he didn't. When I got closer, he reached out and shoved me off the trail. I must have fallen onto this craggy ledge and hit my head, and now here I was, in the dark, alone and injured.

The thing I remembered the most was his eyes. Our gazes

only locked for a split second, but I could see a darkness that came from somewhere deep inside of him. It was like witnessing pure evil in a person's soul through his eyes.

I sat up too quickly, and my head spun around. I realized that I probably had a concussion. Gingerly, I felt the back of my head where a large knot had started to form. I searched around in the dark for my cell phone and my water bottles, moving slowly and methodically because I knew from studying this trail on the map that at the edge of this rock was a steep drop straight down into the gorge.

It was too dark for me to see anything on the ledge, plus I didn't want to risk falling off the edge. I sat there aching, trying to figure out what to do next. That crazy young man had wanted me dead, so I was in danger out here if he was still around. I had to get away—out of the area, back to the inn, or to a road where I could flag down a car.

My phone was probably smashed into a million pieces at the bottom of the gorge. If I had it, I would call Darwin. He would send the cavalry to find me right away, to rescue me. Despite all our hard times, I knew that Darwin loved me and would be very worried right now. So, why had no one come for me? Did no one realize I was missing?

I stood up on the ledge, hugging the steep wall of the mountainside. My entire body was shaking. I raised my arms and felt for the edge of the trail. I would have to pull myself up. One wrong move and I would be plunging into the gorge below. But I had no choice. What if the maniac who had pushed me returned to finish the job? If he wanted me dead, he would surely be upset that I had survived. He could be hiding behind a tree on the trail, just waiting for me to return from the ledge. There was no choice but to try and get out of here.

I took a few deep breaths and then summoned all my strength as I put each hiking boot on a rocky foothold to bring me back up to the trail. Then, with one swift movement, I tugged my entire body up onto the crooked, muddy path. Flat on my stomach, I shimmied like a snake across the stony earth, pulling my feet over the edge at last and then collapsing with my face in the dirt. Every part of my body was in pain, but miraculously, nothing seemed to be broken.

It was going to be very hard to navigate the dark woods at night without a light, but I stood up and started slowly back down the way I had come. I figured I was about halfway into the trail, so I could go either way, but better to go the way I already knew than risk traversing an unknown part of the trail ahead.

I stepped cautiously, feeling for half-buried roots and jagged rocks that might trip me up. Occasionally, I stopped and leaned against a tree, swallowing my own spit. I was parched, dehydrated, in desperate need of water. I had lost my running belt with my water bottles attached to it in the fall. I fished in my pocket and remembered that I had some gummy bears in a zippered compartment in the back of my pants—they were designed for runners with special electrolytes to keep your energy up. I grabbed two and popped them into my mouth.

Suddenly, I heard a rustling in the bushes. I stood very still. It could be the boy, or it could be a bear. Both were terrible options. I crouched low next to the tree and hugged my knees. I could go off the trail, but then I might never find my way out. Yet, if I wanted to avoid the person trying to kill me, it seemed like the best option.

The other option was for me to wait until it was light to walk out. By then, people would surely be looking for me. That's when it occurred to me that I had a choice. It was a choice that very few people ever got in their lifetimes.

I had read an article on the anniversary of 9/11 where a man inside Tower 2 had gotten out but then decided to disappear. He was in financial trouble, in a bad marriage, and his kids were too young to miss him. He was worth more to them dead than alive. He had disappeared to an island where he made a simple life for himself as a fisherman. His ruse was only discovered when someone vacationing on the small island had recognized him from their neighborhood growing up. They snapped a picture and put it on Facebook, saying, "Doesn't this look like our classmate Bart who died in the Twin Towers?"

Eventually, there were so many comments that one of the friends who happened to be a New York City police officer took the information to his investigators. They tracked Bart down, who now went by George. He was arrested and charged with life insurance fraud.

Bart had a good idea, I thought as I tugged my way through the dark woods, stopping periodically to listen for animals rustling in the bushes around me. Bart didn't execute his idea well. But I was smarter than Bart, and I felt like I had the potential to disappear for real.

Darwin and I had gotten swept up in the rat race—working too much, spending too much. We had been living way beyond our means and racking up debt. It had put a strain on our marriage. If I disappeared, Darwin, like Bart's wife, would get the life insurance money, and he would be able to pay off all our debt. Maybe this would make things right between us again.

Somehow, I would need to get out of the woods without being seen and get enough money to get out of the country. I had a friend from college, an artist, who had gone to a retreat on a small island a few years after she graduated. I remembered her saying it was the most beautiful place on Earth, and that it was so quiet you could hear yourself think. This was exactly what I needed. This was exactly what Darwin and I needed. A fresh start. I just had to find a place like that, a place where I could think.

But for it to work, I couldn't bring him into the loop at first. He had to be the grieving husband. Darwin wasn't a good liar. For this to be convincing, I had to keep him out of it. We would reunite later. I would make it happen. I would figure it out.

Finally, after an hour of carefully stepping over treacherous rocks and shimmying through dense brush, I stepped out of the woods onto a road. I saw headlights and put up my hand. The car rolled to a slow stop, and I could hear the passenger side window roll down. I peeked my head inside.

"Need a ride?"

"I sure do," I said, pulling open the door and sliding into the passenger seat to begin my new life.

EPILOGUE: CELIA

When I told Matt that I thought we should move to the mountains, at first, he looked at me like I had lost my mind. But the more we talked about it, the more the idea took root for both of us. This case had taught us that life was short, that we only had one shot at raising our kids, and that the outdoors was the perfect place for our little balls of restless energy that didn't fit well within the walls of a city brownstone.

We started scouring the internet for cabins in the foothills of the Bingham Reserve in a little town called Laurel. We had both felt so at home there, so relaxed, so much more of ourselves than we did in the hustle and bustle of the city.

The newspaper said I could work remotely. Matt would still have to travel some, but there was an Amtrak train from Laurel twice a day that went right to the Charlotte airport. We decided we could make it work.

It would be an adventure, one that we would be on together, just like Darwin and Pamela. For better or worse.

I was sitting on the back porch of our new home, looking up at the mountain, trees all around with their warm fall hues—yellow, red, and orange leaves. I swayed in the rocking chair with a steaming hot cup of coffee next to me on a small table. The former owners had left the porch furniture behind to our delight.

I had dropped the boys off at their new school in town, a sweet combined elementary and middle school where the teachers hugged the kids and knew them all by name. Matt was on a business trip to Chicago and scheduled to return the following day.

My heart burst with joy each day as I wound down the gravel path and saw my new home nestled amongst the trees, a tire swing in the side yard, mountain bikes perched on the front porch, and two kayaks leaned against the side of the house.

It was nuts, but in a weird way, Pamela Stevens, wherever she was now, had led us to this new, authentic life. For this, I was grateful.

I rocked slowly, halfway through reading a book I had just started the day before. I'd become a voracious reader since moving here. I was on a first-name basis with the librarians at the library in Laurel. It was quiet, except for the light breeze rustling through the leaves. And then my phone rang.

"Celia Finch."

"Hi, are you the reporter who covered the woman's disappearance at Bingham over the summer?"

It was a man. I couldn't place his accent.

"Many journalists covered that story, but yes, I did do a lot of work on it. What can I help you with?"

"Well, I've got something to tell you. I've been thinking

about it for a long time. I wasn't sure who to tell. I don't want anyone to think I'm losing my mind."

I gripped the cell phone tightly, feeling the old familiar pit in my stomach when I knew something was about to blow my world up.

"I think I saw her. I picked up a woman that night in my car. I think it was her. She's not dead."

The End

ACKNOWLEDGMENTS

I would like to thank my publisher, Teri Rider of Torchflame Books, for enthusiastically inheriting me from my previous publisher and generously supporting my newest mystery novel. I'd also like to thank our publicist, Jori Hanna, for her guidance and creative ideas for promoting this project. And finally, I'd like to thank editor Chelsea Robinson for meticulously editing this manuscript without changing my voice or the meaning of the story. You all made *Whispers on the Mountain* and me better!

ABOUT THE AUTHOR

Amanda Lamb is a veteran television crime reporter who recently retired from T.V. news after more than three decades in the trenches. She is also a podcaster who hosted, wrote, and co-produced three true crime podcasts including *The Killing Month August 1978, What Remains,* and *Follow the Truth. Follow the Truth* was honored with the regional Edward R. Murrow Award for excellence in journalism. Amanda has written and published a mystery series with Light Messages Publishing and Torchflame Books featuring a television reporter seeking truth and justice. The titles include *Dead Last, Lies That Bind* and *No Wake Zone*.

Amanda is also the author of three true crime books based on murder cases she covered as a television reporter, four memoirs, and two children's books.

Amanda owns **Stage Might Communications**, a consulting and content creation company. She is the host of *AGELESS: Opening Doors with Amanda Lamb* which features women over fifty talking about personal and professional transformation.

Amanda is originally from the Philadelphia area and holds an undergraduate degree from Duke University and a graduate degree in journalism from Northwestern University. She is the married mother of two strong young women and one enthusiastic poodle named Dolly Parton.

To learn more about Amanda and her work go to her website, alambauthor.com.

ALSO BY AMANDA LAMB

Dead Last

Maddie Arnette traded in her hard-news crime reporting hat for a simpler and gentler life after her husband died tragically leaving her the single mother of twins. When Suzanne Parker falls to the pavement in front of Maddie during the Oak City Marathon in her small North Carolina city, Maddie assumes it's an accident. But then Suzanne whispers words that make Maddie's skin go cold and sends her crime-fighting antenna into high gear—my husband is trying to kill me. Maddie is soon swept back into full-time crime reporting in an effort to keep Suzanne safe.

Lies that Bind

Maddie Arnette has built her whole life around the narrative that her father murdered her mother. When a woman in the grocery store claims that Maddie's father did not kill her mother, the revelation forces the journalist toward a reckoning. She barely has time to absorb this earth-shattering news when she is called to report on what appears to be a suicide. Tilly Dawson is found shot to death on her driveway, a gun by her side. Before long, the tough television reporter finds herself delving once more into a dark world of violence, secrets and intrigue.

No Wake Zone

After a near brush with death, Maddie Arnette heads to the charming coastal town of Cape Mayson, North Carolina to heal. She temporarily trades in her microphone for a paddleboard. But when she finds a dead man floating in the water, her sabbatical turns into a quest for the truth. Maddie must continue to confront the ghosts of her past as she seeks justice for two men: one in a watery grave and one behind bars.

Find these books and more at torchflamebooks.com.

THANK YOU!

Thank you for reading! If you enjoyed this book, please leave a review on Amazon, Goodreads, BookBub, The Story Graph, or anywhere else you like to track your recent reads. Alternatively, you could post online or tell a friend about it. This helps our authors more than you may know.

- The Team at Torchflame Books